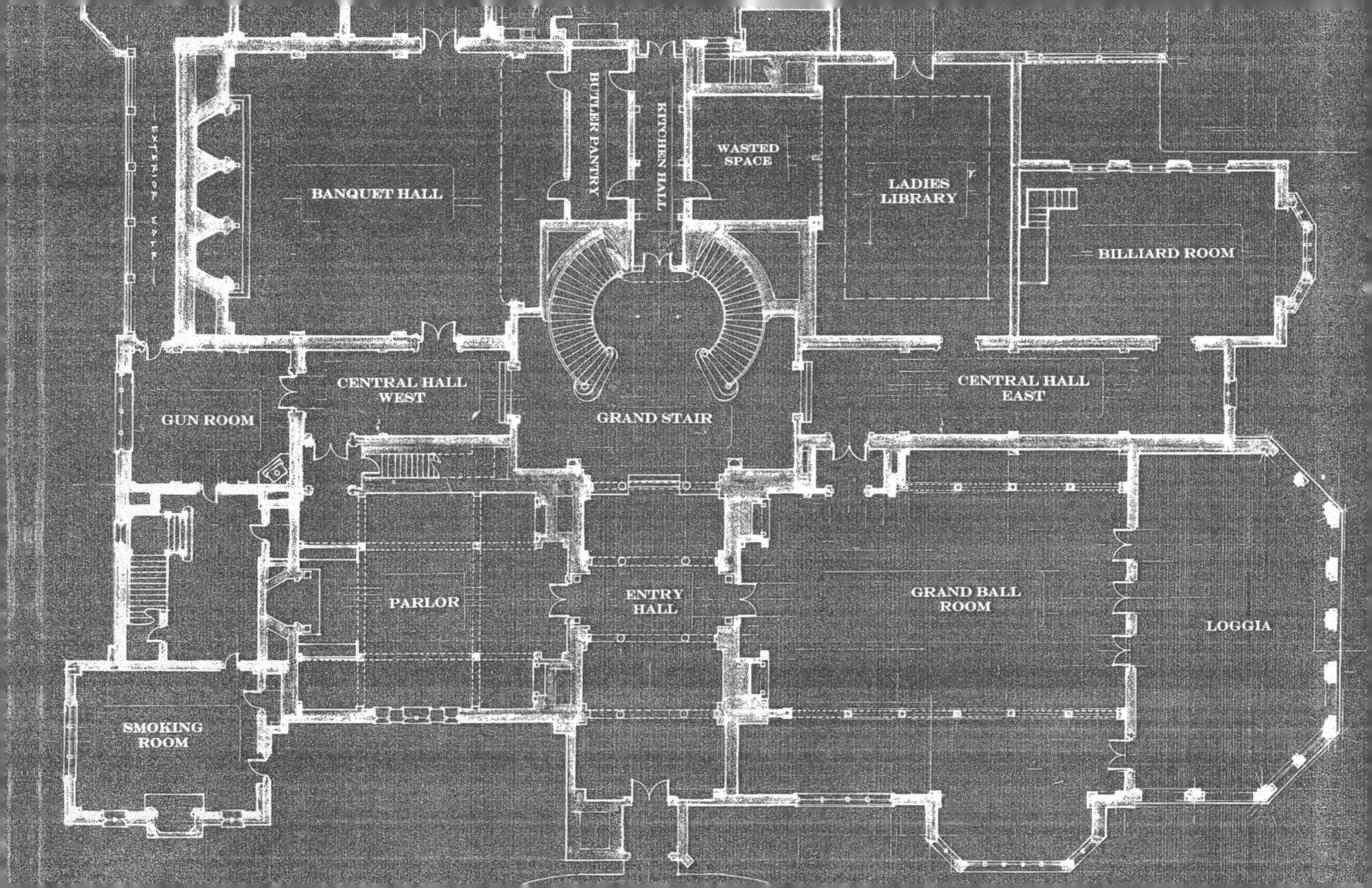
BANQUET HALL
BUTLER PANTRY
KITCHEN HALL
WASTED SPACE
LADIES LIBRARY
BILLIARD ROOM
EXTERIOR WALK
CENTRAL HALL WEST
GUN ROOM
GRAND STAIR
CENTRAL HALL EAST
PARLOR
ENTRY HALL
GRAND BALL ROOM
LOGGIA
SMOKING ROOM

THE DIARY OF ELLEN RIMBAUER

THE DIARY OF ELLEN RIMBAUER

My Life at Rose Red

EDITED BY
JOYCE REARDON, PH.D.

HYPERION
NEW YORK

ISBN: 0-7868-6801-5

Designed by Casey Hampton

FIRST EDITION

10 9 8 7 6 5 4 3

Joyce Reardon
Department of Paranormal Phenomena
Beaumont University
Seattle, WA

Dear Reader:

In the summer of 1998, at an estate sale in Everett, Washington, I purchased a locked diary covered in dust, writings I believed to be those of Ellen Rimbauer. Beaumont University's Public Archive Department examined the paper, the ink and the binding and determined the diary to be authentic. It was then photocopied at my request.

Ellen Rimbauer's diary became the subject of my master's thesis and has haunted me ever since. (Excuse the pun!) John and Ellen Rimbauer were among the elite of Seattle's turn-of-the-century high society. They built an enormous private residence at the top of Spring Street that became known as Rose Red, a structure that has been the source of much controversy. In a forty-one-year period at least twenty-six individuals either lost their lives or disappeared within its walls.

Ellen Rimbauer's diary, excerpts of which I offer here, set me on a personal course of discovery that has led to the launching of an expedition. Shortly I will lead a team of experts in psychic phenomena through the doors of Rose Red, the Rimbauer Estate, in an effort to awaken this sleeping giant of psychic power and to solve some of the mysteries my mentor, Max Burnstheim, was unable to solve before he went missing in Rose Red in 1970. (I never met Dr. Burnstheim, but I consider his writings the most progressive in the field of psychic phenomena.)

Many thanks to my publishers, Beaumont University Press. I hope the publication will widen the public's perception and acceptance of psychic phenomena, and firmly anchor a fascinating historical period in the growth and expansion of the Pacific Northwest. I have taken great pains to edit this document to a readable size, deleting the repetitive sections and omitting those I found offensive. For the extremely curious, or the voyeuristically minded among you, a portion of those edits can be found archived on the World Wide Web at www.beaumontuniversity.net. Photos of the house can be viewed on the Web site as well.

Good reading. In the name of science I will pursue the truth of Rose Red, wherever it may lead me.

Sincerely,
Joyce Reardon, P.P.A., M.D., Ph.D.

The following are excerpts taken from Ellen Rimbauer's diary, dated 1907–1928. Any and all editing has been done at my discretion. Some effort has been made to protect the integrity of Mrs. Rimbauer and her descendants, though never at the cost of content. What follows are the words of Ellen Rimbauer, in her own hand, with as few editorial comments as possible.

—Joyce Reardon, November 2000

THE DIARY OF ELLEN RIMBAUER

17 APRIL 1907—SEATTLE

Dear Diary:

I find it a somewhat daunting task to endeavor to place my thoughts here inside your trusted pages, I scarcely know if I am up to the task, but as my head is filled with lurid thoughts, and my heart with romance and possibility, I find I must confide in someone, and so it is to your pages I now turn. I have lived these nineteen years in full premonition of that time when a man would come into my heart, into my life, and thrill me with love, passion and romance. That time has now come. I swoon just thinking of John Rimbauer, and some of my thoughts are not at all becoming of the lady I am expected to be.

My physical desire does at times possess me. Am I influenced by my reading of popular novels, as my mother is wont to say, or am I sinful, as my father has implied (no, not with words, but by branding me with his raised eyebrows and scolding brow)?

I must admit here too to the simultaneous impression that danger lurks within an arm's reach. Death. Dread. Destruction. Born of guilt, I wonder, for the unladylike fantasies to which I succumb when alone in the dark? (Or is the source of these images something, some force entirely exterior of myself, as I am prone to believe?) Does another world exist? For it seems to me it must: a force apart from human experience. A power, all of its own, and not one familiar with the God to whom I pray. Something darker, external, other-worldly. Something altogether unknown. It lurks in the shadows. I feel its presence.

I would be lying here if I did not admit to a certain thrill this looming sense of the future, of the unknown, affords me, both the unknown of what John Rimbauer's touch might bring to my life, as well as this sense of a larger, darker force at play.

John Rimbauer is a partner in a large oil company, Omicron

Oil, along with a Mr. Douglas Posey, an affable, quiet gentleman whose company I've had the good fortune to keep, along with that of his wife, Phillis. Oil, I'm told, holds great promise as a fuel for lighting homes, and perhaps someday even heating them. John says that oil water heaters for the home are all the rage in the East. Kerosene is being used in motorcars. I hope someday to perhaps take the train with John back to Detroit, where he does business with the Rockefellers. Oh, but my head spins with such fancy: dinner with John D., himself! A banker's daughter from Seattle, Washington! And yet . . . I sense the world is about to unfold at my fingertips. John is the key to that world. I feel certain we are to be engaged within the month. Dare I say that with such honesty? Only here in your pages, Dear Diary!

John has ordered the construction of a grand house. Grander than any house in all the state, perhaps in all the land. He tells me of it often, as if it is to play a significant role in my life as well, which I now feel (nearly) certain it will. (I am blushing as I write this!) He has offered me a motorcar ride to the construction site, and I have accepted. Within the week we shall ride together to what may prove to be the site of our future happiness together. (One hopes for happiness. This dread I feel—will it too play a role? I can only hope and pray that this sense of impending doom will be overcome by the light and love my future husband and I shall share.)

11 MAY 1907—SEATTLE

With trembling hand, I find myself reluctant to record in your pages the horrible events of this day. Several weeks have passed since my last entry, weeks given to one delay after another brought on by John's business affairs (or so I'm told), my own infirmity (a woman's monthly "ritual of roses" as my mother refers to it) and John's apparent inability to arrange a convenient time for the two of us to visit the construction site. At last that time was set, for to-day, this very day, and I awaited John's arrival on the front steps of my family home with what can only be described as a beating breast. Such anticipation!

Much to my disappointment (and to my mother's, too, all things confessed) an offer of betrothal has not been received. Certainly not by me, nor has John approached my father (my mother has informed me in the strictest of confidences) with any discussion of dowry. My, but the weeks have crawled by slowly. Twice, I've been told by trusted friends that John's motorcar, or one just like it, was spotted late, late at night on the high road between the city's loading wharfs and the Hill where John currently makes his residence. I am confident that these excursions can be easily explained by the importing of barrels of oil to those wharfs—as this happens at all hours, night and day. But of course a tiny part of the woman in me fears another truth altogether, as that part of town is known for its debaucheries. Who is this man I hope to marry? I scarcely know!

My fears have found their way into my prayers, and I find myself in sin, making silent requests to the powers that surround us to punish John Rimbauer if any transgressions be known. Just last week, as I made such a "dark prayer" at the side of my bed, an enormous wind—quite like nothing I've ever seen—took wing and delivered not only a branch but an entire tree to my window, shattering glass and throwing debris as it was ripped from its roots. Oddly, no other tree in our yard was affected, nor did any neighbor report any such wind. I attribute that reckoning to the very substantial power of prayer, though my mother calls such reasoning foolish, despite her being a woman of Christ. Dear Diary, let me tell you this: if that tree had anything whatsoever to do with my prayer, it had nothing to do with Christ. On that evening, neither Christ, nor God, were in my prayers. Oh faint of heart, dare not read on. For it was to Him I prayed. The other Him. The other side. For if transgressions have been made, then John Rimbauer has already switched his allegiance, whether aware of it or not. It is to His Power that I pray.

I have taken a moment to lock the door. (I am staying these nights in my sister's room while repairs continue to my own.) Increasingly, I feel as if someone is reading over my shoulder as I write. John? My mother? I know not. But it is a disturbing notion, and one that requires of me certain precautions to which I have now dedicated myself. I not only lock the binding of this diary, but I secure it safely in a locked drawer as well, the small keys kept around my neck, and hidden down my dress, on a silver necklace once worn by my great-grandmother Gilchrist. Certain small oddities, events unexplained, continue to perplex me and drive me to these precautions. (Just yesterday my hairbrush switched sides of the sink, all of its own, as I ran water on my face. I swear it's true! I lifted my head to find the brush available to the left hand, when only moments before it had been held in my right!) Some furniture has been found out of place. One of my dresser drawers stuck yesterday (the one bearing love letters from John) and would not come open, even under the efforts of Pilchert, our butler. To-day, I'm told Pilchert will remove the back of the dresser in an effort to reach the drawer's contents. If taken individually, not one of these small events would matter to me. But collectively? Are they to be ignored? I find myself both terrified and thrilled—so perhaps I am to blame, not only for my sinful prayers to the other Power but for my innate curiosity and fascination with the other-worldly quality of these apparently disconnected events. The Devil's due, do you suppose?

But wait! To the events of this day!

John Rimbauer picked me up this morning at 10 A.M. in an automobile made by Olds. It is one of only a few such vehicles in all the city. The buggy was quite loud, and the experience altogether exhilarating, though bumpy and somewhat terrifying at times. John drove—I believe quite well, though who am I to know? West on Spring Street to the site of the construction that preoccupies him. The trip consumed some fifteen minutes—the house is to be built atop a hill that overlooks the city. Twice I was nearly thrown out the side (or so I imagined! John assured me I was safe all along.).

John Rimbauer, ruggedly handsome, is a pragmatic man (which possibly accounts for his success in the oil business), extremely sure of himself and even given to moments of conceit. He remains calm in the face of adversity, whether a four-horse team blocking the road or a storm on the high seas. (John is extremely well traveled, having visited Asia, the Americas and Europe.) I find his strength both comforting and disarming, in that John is often an unpredictable mixture of tolerance and intolerance. I have never been on the receiving end of his ill temper, but woe to those who are. Of course I don't wish to be, nor will I tolerate such ferocity directed at me or our children. (Just the thought of children floods me with a keen, passionate warmth, the likes of which I've only read about in my novels. Perhaps Mother is right!) I should like to relate here my recollection of an exchange we had on the trip over.

"John, dear," I said, "do you suppose I should have offended my mother by my refusal of a chaperone?"

"You're a grown woman of nineteen, El." (I *love* this nickname for me he has chosen!) "Your mother was married and with her second child by the time she was your age. I doubt very much you could do anything to shock her."

"You don't know her as I do," I said.

"I am twice your age. I should imagine that concerns your parents. Especially as to my intentions." He lowered his eyes to me, running them down the full length of my dress to where I felt faint. He understands full well this power he has over me, uses it playfully, but on this occasion—and there have been others, truth be told—it was not so much playful as provocative, and he made no effort to disguise or conceal his lust. I felt certain of it at the time. And what was I to do? I giggled, all nerves, of course. Blushed no doubt. I felt the heat in my cheeks. But I kept my chin high and my eyes on the muddy road ahead.

"And what *are* your intentions?" I asked, suppressing a smile.

"To ravish you, of course. To pluck your innocence from the vine of youth and leave you for the next man to marry."

"And my father will come after you with axe and rope."

"And you? Will you refuse me?"

"Your so-called ravishing, of course. Until we are married."

"Engaged or married?"

"We've had other . . . fun, John Rimbauer." Certainly I must have blushed again for I felt it in my face. We had touched. We had kissed. His strong hands knew the shape of my bosom (though never skin to skin!). Once, while dancing, he had pressed himself to me and I had known of his arousal. But he had yet to know of mine. Mother's cautions of "a lady's behavior" fall flat on my ears. She lived in another time. All the girls talk of touching their men—of pleasing them, if for no other reason in an effort to quell their desires and protect their own virginity, that most sacred of marriage rites. John's age perhaps has accounted for no such need on my part. He is experienced. I treasure his worldliness, and believe it affords me much opportunity.

"And more to come," he said. "I trust we both will find . . . ," he searched for his words, "great *reward* in marriage."

"John!" I blurted out, like some sniveling twelve-year-old. "*Marriage?*"

"Patience, my dear. Never push me. Never challenge my decisions. If you hold to these two virtues, we will never have a single quarrel, you and I. I am lord and master of my house. I have worked long and hard to earn not only a small fortune but the right to stake out my own territory, and that territory includes opinion. You understand that, don't you, dearest?"

"Yes, John."

"No reservations."

"None."

"Because I am well aware of suffrage, and have no quarrel with a person's striving for individual freedoms. More power to them. But not in my home, you understand? You will find I can be a most generous, most loving partner, my dear. But just ask Mr. Posey what happens when my partners betray my trust or break agreements. I am offering you many things in sharing a life with me. Freedom is not necessarily one of them."

"John Rimbauer, are you proposing marriage to me?" This, I fear, is all I was thinking. All that I heard. Only now as I write down my recollection of events, only now as I recall those words of his clearly, do I feel their full import.

"Patience, my dear. Patience." A smug smile. I felt for sure I knew what this day held in store. As it turned out, I couldn't have been more wrong. Neither John, nor I, could have possibly foreseen events as they were about to unfold.

The property John purchased to hold his mansion, his grand statement of achievement and success, is nothing short of spectacular. It is crowned with a tall forest of cedar and pine, and workers have cleared nearly six of the forty acres to hold the house—if something so large can be called that! (I could not believe the plans John showed me!) Though well out of the city, the house sits at the muddy end of Spring Street. From this location, one can see the entire city below. Spectacular! Just west of the property is a tract that I'm told runs all the way to Canada, and south as far as Mexico. How my imagination runs wild with the thought: one road spanning the entire country. Just think! The redwood forests. San Francisco. Los Angeles, where they are now making films. (Not quite two years ago, when a traveling projectionist brought it to town, I saw *Le Voyage dans la Lune* [*A Trip to the Moon*], adapted from the novel by Jules Verne—I loved this book! The film was fifteen minutes long, the longest ever made at the time, and was shown at Father's bank, of all places, because it had the largest white wall that could be found.) I adore motion pictures, simply love actors and actresses and hope that John and I will include them as our guests when we make our home together—but I'm getting ahead of myself! The property is accessed from the west. John parked the Olds quite some distance from the construction—a gigantic hole in the ground is all!—and, bless his heart, had had workers lay a string of redwood planks, wide enough to walk upon, so I might avoid the mud and ooze. Horse-drawn wagons came and went, burdened and brimming with materials ordered by the foreman, Williamson, a big, Irish-looking man with florid cheeks, a broad mustache and a surly disposition. He did not appreciate a woman being on the premises, I can tell you that. (He made several insinuations upon my arrival, that is until dear John led him aside by the elbow and had words with him, after which he ignored me with full contempt though was loath to outwardly reveal his disapproval of me. I can only wonder now if this brief altercation with my beloved, an altercation that resulted from my attendance there, had something to do with the events that would soon transpire. Oh, Good Lord, pray let it not be so! Nay, do not curse me with the burden of lost life!)

I am forced to wonder now about my musings put forth in my first entry to these pages. Was what happened to-day at the grand house the sense of foreboding danger that I felt so strongly? The end of it, or just the beginning? The manifestation of some dark power greater than can be imagined? Am I a part of this darkness, or separate from it? Controlled by it, or instead by my prayers? The pen trembles under my grasp as I search for these answers. Am I, in fact, already possessed? Dare I think that? Dare I write it? Dare I keep it to myself, for fear of spoiling the arrangements already under way between my beloved and me? But oh, there I go again. Back to the day, and the tragedy that befell us.

The cavernous hole cut into the earth on that forested slope so far from the warmth of my family home forewarns of a structure, in scope and size, that challenges even one's imagination. I admit fully that I had never visited any construction site prior to my journey this day, and that perhaps because of this lacking I write with what borders on ignorance, but I am no stranger to architecture. I promise you that. Furthermore, I now intend to immerse myself in the study of this science, along with that of construction, so as to appreciate fully the efforts being undertaken on our behalf. The sheer enormity of it! (I can only hope this does not match my future husband's ego or conceit, for if so, I am in for a formidable challenge in the years that lie ahead!) To my eye, it rivals in size the university building that occupies the hill to the south overlooking the city, that building that newcomers nearly always mistakenly attribute to be the statehouse. I believe John's house—our house!—will dwarf this structure by such proportion as to render it insignificant, will so dominate that clearing where it will stand that it may be seen for miles. Miles! I tell you! A landmark for generations to come. Why, the hole in the ground, the foundation, is a marvel of excavation. I watched as four-mule teams carved and cut the thick wet soil with blades, followed by workers busy with shovels to fill wagons. Wagon after wagon, hour after hour, and barely a dent in the giant cavity. The scale of this project defies description. I can only say that nothing like it has ever been built. Perhaps even, that nothing ever will be.

The event of the day, to which I wish to address myself, however, was one of horrific consequences, something no person, certainly not a woman such as myself, should ever have to endure. But first to our arrival.

As we studied the magnificent goings-on, the laborers with their shovels, the teamsters with their wagons, the supervisors working their crews with disciplined patience (for the hand laborers are almost entirely Chinese or Negro and need much supervision), I was struck by the militarylike organization of it all. An easy analogy given the sharp tongue of Williamson.

This man Williamson was given to large bones and a massive head; he had a commanding presence. Shouting and gesticulating, he seemed to possess a language of hand signals known to all who worked for him, but especially those supervisors immediately his junior. He lorded from the porch of a rough-hewn shanty, calling names and then waving his arms like a frantic bird, directing deliveries, the removal of mud and dirt and the efforts of the teams. Perhaps John's attendance contributed to this man's nerves, fixing him in an agitated state. Having not met Williamson previously, on this I cannot comment. However, I must tell you, Dear Diary, that on no terms would I have wished to be employed by Mr. Williamson on this day. His bilious, perfunctory tone carried clear across the construction site, often heard echoing right back at us, as if from the mouth of God. (Not an insignificant reference, given the events to follow.) Enough!

John and I made our way to the edge of the giant pit and were witness to the first of the stones being laid for the grand home's foundation. This, as it turned out, was the cause of our delay these many weeks. John had wanted us to witness a momentous occasion, not simply a hole being dug into the earth (although I must confess here that the hole alone would have surely impressed me as well). And there below us, a group of ten or more Chinese ran—not walked—to and from a large pile of stone, inspecting every angle before running—not walking—that stone to a cutter who smacked it with a hammer and chisel that rained stone chips in small showers all around him. From there the stone was whisked to one of several Scottish-looking gentlemen (it was difficult to discern ancestry, given our perspective) who examined the rock, nodded his approval and, applying mortar, positioned it in place. Stone by stone, the first of many of the grand home's walls began to grow, as the Scots worked as a team. (I am told seven thousand stones will be used in the foundation alone!) I found myself mesmerized by the sight. John, as I recall, had several conversations, but I scarcely heard his words. What beauty. It seemed almost alive to me, not as if it were being built, but instead, growing all of its own. The thrill of witnessing this is hard to explain here in these pages. I found it consumed me, awakened a heat in me, not unlike what John Rimbauer is capable of with simply a touch or a whisper. Dare I say I was moved by this? The pleasing fluidity. The sweating Chinamen, some bare-chested, flexing and glistening as they bore their burden. I could not take my eyes off of this activity. Not until, that is, Williamson's voice arose like an ill wind, cursing a string of profanities that forced such a blush on my part my face must have looked like a ripened cherry.

A large, overstocked wagon belonging to John stood in front of the foreman's shack, the driver equally as big as Mr. Williamson, and equally verbose. It was clear, even from a great distance, that Mr. Williamson did not approve of the quality of the items being delivered. I cannot tell you exactly how I discerned this, distracted, even repulsed as I was by the language involved, but the conversation between them went something like this:

"This is not what we ordered, Mr. Corbin."

"This here is what I was told to deliver."

"You should have checked your ***** load."

"I loaded this ***** load, mister. I didn't have to check it—I loaded it."

"Look at this quality. It's horse***t. Pure horse***t, and you're telling me I'm supposed to use Mr. Rimbauer's money to pay for it? I would ask you to reconsider that position, sir." (I might add that this reference to John inclined me to believe that our presence there to-day may have influenced Mr. Williamson's response, as well as his aggressive nature.)

"I ain't reconsidering no **** position. And it ain't ****, and I'd thank you, sir, not to call it such."

"It is ****."

"It is the goods you ordered. These are them. Right here in Mr. Rimbauer's wagon. Now sign the receipt, get your Chinamen to off-load the wagon and let me get out of this hellhole of a stinking construction site. Never seen so much yellow skin in one place, except maybe the railroad. And I don't like railroads!"

"You will lose your job for those comments, sir. You will never be a teamster again, with that attitude and that mouth of yours. You just wait until—"

"Unload the *** **** wagon. I got me a date with a beer at the Merchant Café, and you're getting in the way of that, and that there is unsettling me a good deal. That there is what you want to do right now, mister. Unload the **** wagon, or prepare to eat some horse***t!"

"That's it! Enough of you! Turn this team around. Return the wagon. It's the last run you'll ever make."

I recall the teamster—Mr. Corbin—reaching into the back of John's wagon, beneath a tarp, almost as if he were digging for something. And then he turned toward Williamson. From a distance where I stood, I saw a puff of blue-gray smoke, like a tiny cloud. Then felt a punch in my stomach as a dull boom filled the air. Another small puff. Another boom. The first of these reports actually lifted Mr. Williamson off his feet. He looked as if someone had tied a rope to the back of his trousers, the other end to a horse, and then slapped that horse's behind. The second of the two shotgun blasts caught Mr. Williamson in the neck and face, a bloody spectacle so horrific that I was immediately sick to my stomach.

He lay there on the porch, as still as a statue, rose-colored and dead. I'd never seen a dead person. I didn't know the effect it would have on one. The finality. The awareness that I too shall follow Mr. Williamson to that place. Heaven. Hell. I don't have the vocabulary. Those two offerings don't help me. I believed in Heaven and Hell before to-day. Now, I'm not convinced there are only the two places, the black and white of afterlife. I'm of the

opinion that gray must exist. Mr. Williamson convinced me. I can't imagine a man with that foul disposition in Heaven as I write; but what man who dies at the hands of another deserves Hell? And what of Mr. Corbin? Where will the afterlife place him?

Did I tell you where they found Mr. Corbin? At the Merchant Café, of course. His beer. They found him bent over that beer, nursing it. They say he didn't know where he was, or what he'd done. Didn't remember any of it. They say he must be crazy. "Half out of his mind," John said to me. But of course he means fully out of his mind. There are many of us walking around with only half a mind. They don't lock you away for that. You need to lose it all before they take you, and Mr. Corbin lost his. And they took him. Off to jail, still wondering what it was he'd done.

I've heard the term "possessed" before. I've heard it used as an explanation for someone "half out of his mind." A Christian woman, I have never given such claim much weight. Possessed by what? I wondered. But—dare I write this, when writing seems so final an act?—now I better understand the term, now I am inclined to accept it. It pertains to the gray in the afterlife. It pertains to tragic people like our Mr. Corbin. Not empty, as "half out of one's mind" implies, but instead filled, but with the wrong element. The bad. Evil. Filled with tainted fish, the stomach is already informed but has not yet signaled the brain to retch. Filled with the gray. The other side. Possessed.

Mr. Corbin was possessed. In this regard, who do we blame for the vicious act perpetrated upon poor Mr. Williamson? The possessed, or the possessor? Was Mr. Corbin merely an instrument of the gray?

It won't matter now. He'll never be back among us. He will hang. Possessed or not, he will hang. And he will die—legs twitching in the wind.

The grand house will never be the same, of course. Mr. Williamson's blood is spilled upon the earth, is mixed with the mud and the mortar, is part of that place. And I can no longer think of it as I have. The blood is spilled. I saw it with my own eyes. Someplace between Heaven and Hell. Some color between black and white. And I find myself wanting a name for the place, seeing Mr. Williamson lying there. He can't have died at the grand house. He died someplace more lyrical than that. I will talk to John about this, for it is his house. But the color I remember so vividly is the color rose. Rose red. Blood thinned by a falling mist.

On the way home in the car, John pulled off the road, came around and opened my door. He apologized for all that had gone before us that day, as if we'd encountered a delay or bad service at a restaurant. I recall being amazed by his apparent indifference to the fate met by Mr. Williamson. He begged my forgiveness for the "aggravation" of that day, whereas I certainly bore him no blame for it whatsoever. Then he dropped his right knee into the mud, and I knew what was coming, and I must admit to both elation and revulsion. John is pragmatic. I told you that, didn't I?

This was on his schedule, and he refused to allow a small murder to derail his plans. As he explained it, he regretted very much the events of that day, but his heart and passion would not allow another minute, not another second to pass without voicing his intent.

He asked for my hand in marriage. Clouded in rose. Clouded in gray. I am to be a wife. John's wife. (For I quickly said yes!) But truth be told, he picked the wrong day to ask, the wrong time. I am quite surprised, in fact, that he could not see clear to delay this engagement. Even a day or two might have helped. And after so long, what difference is in a day?

But there was a difference in John Rimbauer. I wonder if it took another man's death to create in him a desire to extend his lineage, or if one had nothing to do with the other? With life so seemingly fleeting, did he rush to judgment to marry? I feel certain we will discuss Mr. Williamson's demise for many months, even years to come. I believe that I saw in John a fascination with death. I know that for me, Dear Diary, life will never be the same. I wonder where it is that Mr. Williamson has gone. Is there any return from there? So many unanswered questions.

What, if anything, does John's hesitation to include me in his thoughts tell me about the upcoming marriage, this voyage on which I'm about to embark? How far, how smoothly, can this ship sail if Captain and First Mate are not sharing their thoughts? Are we doomed to the rocks? Or is there some lighthouse yet to be seen around the next spit of land? Captain, oh, Captain. My breast swells with thought of my marriage and all the new experience it will bring to me, I tingle head to toe. And yet my heart goes cold at the thought of John's carefully kept secrets and his refusal to let me in. He is so reluctant to share his thoughts. Will I ever gain entry, or am I doomed to live in isolation despite our union? I fear this is how it's to be, and I dread the thought of a life spent in a lie. I dread the thought of this marriage as much as I am thrilled by it.

18 AUGUST 1907—SEATTLE

As the future Mrs. John Rimbauer (it's the only plausible explanation for this) I was invited to join to-day an elite group of twenty-three women, led by Anna Herr Clise, to address a health care crisis in our great city, namely the lack of a facility to treat crippled and hungry children. Over an extravagant lunch at Anna's home, we all agreed to contribute twenty dollars each to launch the Children's Orthopedic Hospital. The press gave us great attention, both because of our sizable personal donations (John provided me the twenty dollars, thank God) and because our board is to consist entirely of women, unthinkable to the bankers downtown.

I have subsequently invited all twenty-two of my fellow founders to our wedding, this November, and expect all to attend. I can't imagine what it would be like to have a crippled child, and I hope and pray (yes, even to my darker god) that I shall never have to endure such a hardship. John and I plan on a large family, and I, for one, can't wait to get started—though not without a great amount of nervousness do I approach my wedding night, quite afraid as I am of the actual physical union of our love. (The idea of a man inside me both sickens and excites me.)

I wouldn't have bothered to even mention the fete at Anna's except as a way to preface my anxiety over one Priscilla Schnubly, a ferret of a woman with an exacting manner, pinched face and scandalous tongue. Yes, I invited her and her husband to the wedding out of proper social intercourse, but my how this woman vexes me! When I mentioned John, Priscilla Schnubly snickered for all to hear. She then whispered into the ear of Tina Coleman, who blushed as rose as the spilled blood of Mr. Williamson and went on to refuse to share with me the exchange that had transpired there between them. And yet I know in my woman's heart that whatever it was had to do with John and the rumors of his nighttime activities.

Do I dare condemn John for actions taken prior to our marital union? Does such an eligible man owe me his chastity before we are officially wed? All these questions circulate in my mind, with me knowing nothing of the truth to begin with. Would I not prefer my future husband sow his oats prior to his promises than to break those promises later? Am I personally humiliated in social circles for his actions, as the snickering Priscilla Schnubly would have me believe? Am I to be the laughingstock of Seattle's prominent women because my husband may prove incapable of being a devoted husband? Am I willing to trade that for the wealth and privilege he is certain to bestow upon me? I am nearly dizzy with consideration. Consternation. Concern.

Is John merely entertaining other women, or, Heaven forbid, is he taking advantage of them? Was this the reason for the snickering? And why on earth do women like Tina Coleman think that their silence somehow protects me? Indeed it does not. I have invited Tina to tea this very afternoon. We shall see.

Tina Coleman is a gorgeous specimen of a woman. Tall. A brunette like myself. Flaming blue eyes. I find myself quite taken by her beauty. She is the wife of an orthopedic surgeon, famous in these parts, and therefore a perfect board member for our new cause. She speaks slowly and calmly, and rarely moves her head left to right, as if her spine were fixed.

We sat down to tea in my mother's parlor. Earl Grey tea was served with cucumber sandwiches and huckleberry scones. I recall our conversation vividly.

"What a lovely home you have," Tina Coleman said.

"I have lived here all my life. When I leave to marry John, it will be the first time out of this house, except for our family travels overseas and six months I spent in finishing school in Brookline, Massachusetts, outside Boston."

"I know Boston well," she said, maintaining her airs.

"Tina, we have been raised in the same city, and had our parents shared the same circles, we might have been closer friends. I've known of you, of your beauty, of your fine manners, your intelligent speech, for many years, as I believe we were both courted by Jason Fine, that most peculiar, insolent man, who in my opinion will be lucky to ever find himself a wife."

"Amen." When she sipped from her teacup, Tina Coleman's small finger raised in the air like a flag.

I said something like, "I would have to have my head in the sand not to be aware of the rumors that circulate concerning the nightlife of John Rimbauer. You need not sugarcoat it, dear friend, but I do ask of you the truth as you know it. What you've heard, and how much credence and faith you put in these reports."

"You find them vexing."

"Indeed. Wouldn't any woman, especially one about to marry?"

"Honestly, I don't know how you cope. I will tell you this: you have the respect of many of the finest women in this city, both because of your strength in light of the rumors you now mention and because of your ability to win John Rimbauer's heart. Some women will envy you, Ellen, and you must be prepared for their vengeance. They will stop at nothing to see you fail. I would attribute a great deal of the rumor to this and this alone."

"But not all," I said.

"John Rimbauer is a respected businessman, a man at the very peak of society. For me, or any others, to color him this way or that without any firsthand knowledge is undignified and without call. He is twenty years our senior, yours and mine. A man of the world. What are we to expect of him? That he spent these past two decades in a monastery? Clearly he did not. I would not trouble myself over his past. His future is with you, dear child, and a bright future I should think. Very bright indeed."

"But you've heard things."

"Words is all. Words can be so destructive, especially when they are just so much fiction."

"But we don't know that. I don't know that," I said.

"I have been married three years. I have given birth to two children in that time. One lived. One did not. My husband is a brilliant surgeon, a fine man and a loving husband. He does not always come home when he says he will. Sometimes it is with the smell of liquor on his clothes. Not perfume, thank God, but a woman's imagination can paint many a difficult picture, can it not? I love my husband, Ellen. He is not perfect. Neither am I. Neither is John Rimbauer. I'm certain of it. But these are challenging times. We live in a challenging part of the country—some still refer to it as the frontier. Can you imagine? I trust my husband's love, even if at times I question his actions. Never to his face. Never aloud. A woman's heart is much stronger than a man's. They are weak creatures, dear. Weak, and often far more insecure than they present on the outside. Trust your love, child. The rest will follow."

"What is it you've heard?" I asked.

"Are you listening?"

"Yes, and I appreciate your sound advice more than I can tell you. But I simply must know what is being said behind my back, behind the back of my future husband, or am I to be the laughingstock?"

"There are women who can see the past, and some even the future. Have you ever consulted such a medium, my child?"

"A séance?"

"They take all forms."

I felt flushed with excitement. "Have you ever consulted such a person?"

"Oh, I do so regularly. Not always with my husband's knowledge, you understand. So you see two can play at this game of carefully guarded secrets. I am trusting you not to betray our friendship and share any of this with John Rimbauer."

"Of course not." I felt giddy. A medium. I'd read news reports, but I had never met anyone who had actually attended such a séance. "What can I expect from such an experience?"

"Remarkable. Profound. Transcendental. You have never experienced anything quite like it. For all my heightened anticipation of the union of a husband and wife, I must admit to you now, dear friend, that I find a séance quite a good deal more stimulating." She showed her teeth when she laughed. She had gold work throughout. She appreciated her little joke more than I did, implying that I would be let down by the culmination of my forthcoming marriage, the anticipated union of which, only here in your pages, can I admit my honest excitement.

"Is it true the mediums can see to the other side?"

"I do not know what to believe, but I imagine they can, yes. That is, I have experienced such a connection myself, during a séance, and I must confess . . ."

I found her timidity provocative. She teased me with her reluctance to divulge all, begging my curiosity. I gripped my teacup with both hands and caught myself leaning into her every breath, wanting more. "Yes?"

"I think it far wiser for you to make your own estimations, dear friend. My experience . . . Well, you see . . . That is, I believe each of us . . . either the connection with the other world is there or not. And for me it was . . . is . . . and as to whether it might be for you."

"But I know it is," I said, clearly startling her. "My prayers are answered, you see."

"Yes, well . . . prayers . . . There is more to the netherworld, dear friend, than one can possibly imagine. And it would be improper and wrong of me to imply it all has to do with angels and prayer. Some of what is revealed is most unpleasant. Not at all the stuff of prayers." She placed down her own cup and craned forward. When she spoke, it was less a voice than a cold wind. Less a woman than a presence. The curtains behind me ruffled as if that window were open, which it was not. The crystal of the chandelier tinkled. I swear the temperature of the room dropped a dozen or more degrees. I could see her breath as she spoke. "Many of the dead are still living. Whether you believe this or not, that is not my concern." She waved her long fingers dismissively. She looked pale, almost gray. "One does not attempt to make contact with the other side without a certain . . . shall we say . . . personal investment." A wry smile. She was consumed. I shuddered from the sudden cold, longing for a shawl or a throw over my shoulders. "One does not approach this lightly." She leaned back.

The curtain stopped moving, as did the chandelier. The color returned to her cheeks and the temperature of the parlor was restored. I am certain I must have looked the idiot, my mouth sagging open in abject horror. For a minute, I swear to you, Dear Diary, Tina Coleman was not in that room. It was someone—something—else entirely. And I will also tell you this: I am a believer. Nothing in that room was of the world I know. Nor can I perceive that place from which it came. But I am fascinated and intrigued, as curious as a person can be about something so unknown.

I wanted to ask her for the name of her medium right there and then, but something prevented me from doing so. Fear? Guilt? Was it John looking over my shoulder and cautioning me that "no wife of John Rimbauer will be found to be engaged in such sinful activities."

For I have no doubt as to its sinful nature. None whatsoever. God, whoever and however He may be, was nowhere to be found in that room this afternoon. And I would be lying if I did not admit to a certain amount of enthrallment, dare I say attraction, to whatever occupied my new friend for those brief few seconds. A power greater than any I have known. A power that both filled me with a numbing cold and an unspeakable heat that penetrated the depths of my soul. This is a friend I long to visit with once again. A power I yearn to feel again. To glimpse such a formidable presence is one thing. To taste it, to drink of it, yet another. To be owned by it—what must that be like? And how soon until I can find out?

12 NOVEMBER 1907—SEATTLE

I am sitting in my mother's dressing room and parlor, a room in which I doubt my father has ever set foot. I am here, in front of the mirror where for years I have watched her brush her red hair before bed. I am perplexed, and nearly in a state, some moments giddy, some pensive, some nearly in tears, clothed in my wedding gown, a garment at once both splendid and lush, yet fetching (or so I hope). My maid of honor, dear Penelope Strait, has gone off to inspect the route of my descent to the front door and the team of two black geldings who shall deliver me to the church in royal fashion. She said she would arrange tea to be delivered, and given this small break, this moment alone, it is to you, Dear Diary, that I now turn.

I feel a bit like the young girlish child who once picked at daisies reciting, "I love him, I love him not." Petal by petal my poor heart labors over my decision to marry John Rimbauer. I feel both passion for John and reservation, cloaked as I am under the uncertainties that rise to the lips of my friends. The caution in their eyes that greets me whenever John's name is mentioned. I fear that in a very short time, I am to marry a ladies' man, I am to be both pitied and scorned by my peers. And I shiver with the thought. "Deliver me from evil and leadeth me not into temptation." Why do I find it so difficult to move on from these thoughts? Why do I weep now at my mother's mirror, knowing I shall never live in this home again?

Following the reception, John and I are to take the Presidential Suite at the Grand, where we shall stay but a single night prior to our departure on the *Ocean Star*, bound for the Pacific Atolls. I am told the native women go bare-breasted there, and the men wear loincloths and the water is as clear as an old man's eyes. Much has been made in Europe about the changing face of fine art, and the influence these islands have had, and

John would like to experience this part of the world firsthand. Oil is not used on the islands, and he claims he might consider starting a small business there, but these islands are said to be rustic and quite taken to debauchery and even open fornication, and I don't know whether to believe this or not. If true, what kind of a place is it for a woman? Why would John bring his new wife to such a place? And is this trip of ours to be made as husband and wife, or businessman and wife? I harbor all these questions, but I ask nothing of John, for it riles him so when I challenge his decisions. He takes it for criticism instead of the curiosity it is. And so more tears fall here upon your pages, for I know not what I have gotten myself into. Wealth. Position. A darkly handsome man who has caught the eye of many an eligible girl. But twenty years my senior, moody and private. About our trip overseas he has only told me "to pack for a long trip. A year or more. Warmth, cold. Prepare for it all."

"But where are we going, my dearest?"

"To the islands first, as we've discussed. India, perhaps. Burma or Tibet if we can find passage. The British have long since installed magnificent rail lines in this part of the world, and how far behind can an oil-burning locomotive be? I tell you, Ellen, Omicron is in a position to be an international supplier. We have the jump on the Far East because of our base here in Seattle. And after that? Persia. I'd like to see Persia. And then on to Africa as the seas blow cold and that continent warms with summer winds. East Africa, of course. Good hunting. And around the Cape and up the coast to Spain, France and Britain, if war doesn't prevent us. New York. Philadelphia. And then by rail again. Chicago? Denver? Who's to know? The world is ours, my dear. Five star. The best cabins, coaches and the finest suites at the grandest hotels, train cars all to ourselves. Six months? A year? Long enough for the completion of the grand house, so that we have that magnificent structure to which to return. A place of our own. A place to raise the children that I hope you'll be carrying before our return. A family, Ellen. Just think of it."

Said with such passion and enthusiasm. Who was I to cut in with the voice of reason? To intrude upon my husband's shining moment. Never mind the insects that came to mind, the disease carried by every living creature in such places, never mind the rumors of bare-breasted heathens (it seemed he had chosen only primitive locations). Never mind that I might have preferred San Francisco, Paris and London. A year in Paris, Venice or Rome—now there was a honeymoon! Long hours spent languishing in bed under a down comforter with room service a bell pull away, hot bubble baths with Parisian soaps and my husband to guide me through the pleasures of being husband and wife. But for him, hunting. Natives. Exploration. Elephants, diamond mines and the Iron Horse.

I kept my thoughts to myself the first time he mentioned the trip. And the second. And the third. Always telling myself there would be plenty of time to set the course straight. That course now starts to-morrow. Pier 47. We steam to Victoria, switch ships and board for the Tahitian Islands. I see in myself this hesitation to confront John, a reluctance to spoil his good moods, or dare to enter his bad ones. He lives on these giant swings, like an ape, back and forth, high to low. Perhaps the great Sigmund Freud, about whom everyone is talking (his publication on the sexual theory is under translation into English but is said by Germans who have read it to be quite scandalous and intriguing), would have some way to quantify John's moods. For me they are difficult to read, and dangerous to intrude upon. At his most elevated moments, he is so exciting and stimulating to be around: animated, courteous and entertaining; at his low points he is sullied, dark and brooding. I fear him. I anticipate violence at times, though have yet to see—and I hope I never will!—this side of him rise to the surface. If John ever does become violent with me, I tremble at the thought. He is a big man, strong and imposing. I fear he could crush me like an insect.

I read the last few paragraphs and wonder that I could put such thoughts to ink on our wedding day, of all days. My mother tells me that she too had reservations prior to her wedding (she told me other things as well, concerning what to expect on my wedding night, but they are best left between mother and daughter), that it is not uncommon for a woman to question her decision and that men go through much the same thing. I must admit that John, bless his heart, has never for an instant voiced anything but total support for, and faith in, our union. In fact, one of the great ironies here is that the concern is all mine. John, for his part, seems absolutely giddy with the marriage. He has been a saint throughout its planning (has financed a good deal of the reception and celebration, a much appreciated gesture from my father) and has often been boyish with glee about the approaching date. Now he waits for me at the church. I can picture him there, in his finest London-tailored tails, white gloves clasped behind his back like a general awaiting his army. In this case my arm, not an arm-me. (I annoy John with my puns, but what liberties I have here!) Standing there at the altar, an occasional grin steals its way onto his otherwise composed expression. He is a man of great vision, and I know that he sees much ahead for us, and I trust him to make the most of it. Yes, it is true that at times I fear he regards me more as a brood mare than a mate, that as a man turned forty with a sizable fortune he is looking more for an heir than a companion. That—dare I say it?—women of pleasure are there to pleasure, and a wife is there to bear and raise children. He will want a son, of course. Will not stop breeding me until I throw one for him. I see all this in his eyes, hear all this between the lines of his reasoning. As long as the love is there as well—and it is, it is!!—I am not deterred by his intentions. Love, true love, provides an abundance of good. I go in just a matter of minutes to profess that same love before God, family and all our friends. And oh, how I do love my John Rimbauer. I go with courage. I go with faith. Great anticipation. I go without doubt or expectation. Let love carry us where it may. I am ready. I am ready. I am ready.

13 NOVEMBER 1907—ABOARD SS *OCEAN STAR*

Oh, my. Where to start? The marriage? The reception? Dare I ever put in these pages a recounting of the marriage night itself? (The pain? The pleasure? The fulfillment of dreams? The fear? The feeling of overwhelming consumption, as if possessed by him?) Another time perhaps, although some things are better left to blossom in memory rather than wither in reflection.

Here we are aboard the *Ocean Star*, a luxurious steamer bound for Tahiti, in a presidential stateroom fit for a king and queen (three rooms and a full bath with WC). We dine at the captain's table tonight (black tie and evening dress) and begin our Pacific crossing. If the rest of the trip is anything like our first few hours, it is to be spent in the union of marital bliss—we have been together twice already, and only on the ship for four hours! John has gone topside for a cigar and to hope to collect telegraphs he's expecting concerning both business and the construction out at the grand house. The complexity of the project has continued to consume him. To my knowledge the only day he was completely away from it was our wedding day, and for all I know he had one of his many business associates keeping him current even then. He has informed me that he wants the house decorated to reflect our travels, to remind him of our various ports of call, and that it is my duty to spend as much money as possible to that end! Yes, he was kidding, of course. But his eyes twinkled in such a way as to tell me he was serious as well. Even now I am only beginning to glimpse how wealthy we are. Comments like the one to which I refer would have seemed something fit for one of the tawdry novels I read, not for a serious comment from my husband. The house alone is costing a fortune—literally. This trip, another fortune entirely. And yet I sense these fortunes are but mere play toys to John. Could there be a bottomless well from which John draws our funds? Is such a possibility anything more than pure fancy? Whatever the case, I am thrilled with this challenge of his. I expect to collect many objets d'art, decorations and furnishings, so that he shall never forget our voyage. (Without John's knowledge, I paid for and kept the sheets from our marriage bed at the hotel, crimson stains and all. I wanted a souvenir of that night as badly as he wants souvenirs of our trip. I carry them with me in one of my six steamer trunks, wrapped in tissue paper and a red bow. Something feels so shameful about this action, especially preserving my virgin blood, and I hesitate to think of John's anger if he were to ever find out. And so it is that we start our marriage with secrets. We start our marriage holding on to some small part of ourselves, treasured and kept private. Is this wrong? I ask myself. Or does a woman have to hold on to something in the face of such overwhelming surrender? He climbs on top of me, and he possesses me in a way I never imagined could be true. Inside me. Occupying me. Pleasure, and pain. And I wonder, will I ever get used to it?)

Teak from the islands; ivory from the dark continent. I have begun to make lists in my head. Thankfully John has brought along a complete set of plans to the grand house, allowing me to anticipate placement of our forthcoming collection. Now, not just John, but husband and wife shall be poring over those plans day and night. Now, finally, the project can consume us both! I have become a part of that great house that owns so much of my dear husband. I feel myself inside its walls. He enters me. He resides in me. I sweat and I writhe in his presence. My walls shudder. My mind reels.

He comes and goes from our stateroom, having not invited me to join him topside. Returning just now smelling of liquor and cigar, he pulls the underclothes from my trembling body, lifts my skirts and drives me against the far wall, the sound of the ocean and the rumble of the ship. He lifts me from the floor, pulling my legs around his waist, and I am carried away to the point of frenzy, the point that any shard of ladylike behavior is lost to his lust, his penetration. My lipstick smeared, my breast exposed and the object of his attention, I can no longer maintain my composure. I cry out into the stateroom, "Oh, John. Dear John!" my fingers raking the back of his dress shirt, "Dear God in Heaven! I have never . . . I have never . . ." And all my shameful release so unexpectedly serves to engorge him, to send him into a fevered pitch, a furious, frantic pace where the thumping of my bare bottom on the wall runs up my spine and fills my ears like drumming. He pins my arms to that same wall, his face a crimson cry, and I wail behind his release like some wounded animal, humiliated and reduced to a trembling, panting state of spent excitement.

And he loves it.

He leaves the stateroom yet again, neglecting to offer me his company. Me, ruffled, sitting quietly on a chair, awaiting his departure so as I can tend to my toilet. He, his eyes flashing, his white teeth grinning at me, and without a word, he departs. The air is no longer tainted with liquor and cigar, but with our commingled scents—dark and somewhat sour. I freshen it with perfume. I open the doors to the balcony. I stand with the wind whipping my hair, flushed with a woman's satisfaction, embarrassed with myself, and yet exhilarated. I am a wife. I have made the transition.

19 NOVEMBER 1907—ABOARD SS *OCEAN STAR*

A brief note in an effort to keep myself company. I have torn out and discarded many of your pages, Dear Diary, small knots of white paper in the trash as I attempt to come to terms with my position. Dearest John is quick to display me at dinner or lunch, or an evening reception offered by one guest or another, but the remainder of my time on board this ship resembles more prison than honeymoon as he confines me to our stateroom, where I must admit, I am taken to nausea in the early winter seas that we encounter. I have begged to go topside to relieve myself of this condition, for fresh air and a firm horizon can do wonders to steady my stomach, but my husband steadfastly refuses me, saying that he doesn't want any "displays" on deck. He points to the balcony off the stateroom and suggests its use for my purposes. He is afraid I might vomit, or show my pale face, I suppose. ("No Rimbauer ever shows weakness!") He uses me as a charm on his bracelet while claiming that the less others see of me, the more mystery, the more power I hold over them at the captain's table, afternoon teas and cocktail parties. When he does visit me in my confinement it is to take of me his pleasure. With no other trustworthy woman in whom to confide, I have no idea if this is normal or not, though I must admit it is thoroughly exhausting, if in no other way in terms of bathing and dressing. I must spend half my day being undressed by him, later bathing and finding new wardrobes to replace the last. What appetites he has!

I find myself at least a bit unstable, with the only attentions his, and these so clearly physical. Only this morning did it occur to me, from something he said, that he is hiding me from the other men on board, the silliest boyish notion I can imagine. John, jealous? The conversation went something like this:

John asked me, "Did you notice Mr. Jamerson, last evening?"

"Notice how, dear?"

"Does the word notice escape your comprehension, Ellen?" His tone immediately sharp and coercive. I feel myself being drawn into a fight, and worse, I find myself willing to go. Why? I wonder. Because he locks me in this stateroom, a captive, readying myself for his next fit of womanly satisfaction?

"It does not. Taken literally, I most certainly did notice Mr. Jamerson. He sat immediately to my right, as you will recall."

"And the captain placed you to his right for the fourth dinner in a row." He pauses, strutting now about the stateroom. "The chair of highest honor on a ship, its occupation to be rotated night to night through a variety of guests."

"I am honored."

"You are the most beautiful woman on this ship, Ellen, by a factor of ten."

"You flatter me."

"I caution you," he said. "A ship is a lonely place."

"What are you saying?"

"You needn't take to their humor quite so vigorously. Your endowments, my dear . . . ," he indicates his own chest, meaning mine, of course, "quite an eyeful when you laugh like that."

I blush, for I can feel it in my face. Not from embarrassment, as he must suspect, but anger. Is he implying that I am purposefully being vulgar in such company? Is this the kind of thing husbands and wives argue over? "May I remind you that it is you, dear husband, who bids me to remove my shawl at the dinner table. Such as my bosom may be, and I might remind you—as if it's necessary—that Miss Pauling, our ship's entertainer, and a guest I notice who has come to address you most informally, John, has a substantially greater bosom than I, and is in a mood to display her wares in what I consider, quite frankly, a most inappropriate and lascivious way. Moreover, my gowns are crafted by the finest San Francisco seamstresses and fashioned to designs created by Paul Poiret himself, and that all of this was at your request. These gowns were ordered because you heard of them, or saw them for all I know, on that business trip last August. I take great umbrage at any implication from you that I have behaved in any way unbecoming. I was born, bred and raised a lady, dear sir, and you will kindly remember that fact before leveling such accusations at me."

"I meant only—"

"You meant to say that when I laugh my bosom is on display, and believe me this fact does not escape me. I have nearly come out of my gown. I am terribly aware of that fact. So perhaps your indignation might give way in favor of allowing a woman to wear her shawl when she sees fit, rather than forcing her into compromising moments of great embarrassment. Now, leave me alone! Go do whatever it is you do on this dreadful ship. But if you return with Miss Pauling's perfume on you, John, as you did two nights ago—oh yes! you thought I missed that? how could I? It's a dreadful scent!—then there will be hell to pay!"

I had lost all composure and found myself shouting at the top of my lungs. At my husband. To my regret. But oh, Dear Diary, the story does not stop there. For I swear it is true that upon mention of the word "hell" did the gas lights in that stateroom dim, and the bedroom door blow open. Behind this door came a wind that lifted my nightgown from the floor and blew my hair straight back off my shoulders—and yet John moved not a hair. His handkerchief did not wave. The curtains did not ruffle. As my heartbeat did subside, so too did this wind lessen. John and I stood perfectly still, a silence between us. The air crisp and smelling as it does after an electric storm, both bitter and sweet all at once.

My husband said not a word, a stunned, apoplectic expression overtaking him. His eyes narrowed, boring into me. He turned and left me then, partly because there was nothing left to say, partly out of fear, if I read him right. I have never seen John Rimbauer seeming anything less than absolutely certain. Stoic, even.

Until now, that is. This evening the tables turned.

I attended dinner without a shawl, just to spite him. And I laughed as never before.

FOR THE SAKE OF EXPEDIENCY, AND DUE TO ANY DIARY'S REPETITIOUS NATURE, THE EDITOR CHOSE TO OMIT VARIOUS DIARY ENTRIES. ELLEN RIMBAUER'S FULL DIARY IS ARCHIVED IN THE WINSLOW LIBRARY OF LETTERS AND MEMOIRS, SEATTLE, WASHINGTON, A COPY OF WHICH RESIDES ALONG WITH OTHER MATERIALS IN THE JOYCE REARDON COLLECTION: OBSERVED PARANORMAL ACTIVITIES, 1982–1999, WHICH RESIDES IN THE WIRMSER LIBRARY, BEAUMONT UNIVERSITY, SEATTLE, WASHINGTON.

—JOYCE REARDON

15 DECEMBER 1907—THE SOUTH PACIFIC ISLANDS

I don't know why they bother giving these islands any name but Paradise. Certainly one is no different than the other, a crust of sand rising from the deep, palms clinging by shallow roots, wind and bright sky and the bluest, clearest water on the face of the earth. The cinnamon-skinned women, as bare-breasted as the National Geographic Society would have us believe, welcoming white strangers with wide smiles and, I fear, open arms. The sun beats hot as we enter the part of their seasons that coincides with spring and summer, despite it being fall and early winter at home. Our world is quite literally turned upside down.

I lock your pages closed each night, Dear Diary, and then, in turn, lock you away in my steamer where I keep my underclothes and my toilet, confident my husband would never violate that sanctity. I scarcely know what would become of me if he ever did. And so it is, with beating heart and a certain amount of timidity, that I once again turn to you as my confessor.

It began more than a week ago now, during a nighttime celebration as the *Ocean Star* crossed the equator. There was music, much drink, a proclamation by the captain, dancing and a gay atmosphere on board. John and I, for all our conflicts, rose from our beds in the morning as if we had not a care in the world.

We had taken breakfast together on the balcony, a peaceful, enchanting hour. I do believe that John has adopted a different attitude toward me, and that this is reflected both in our breakfast and in the fact that we followed breakfast with a stroll on the deck, an extremely social activity where certainly my absence has been noticed. We lunched together, in a smaller dining room I'd not seen before, but one where all the waiters knew John quite well, addressing him as "Mr. Rimbauer," instead of the "sir" and "madam" used on guests less well known. After high tea with several new friends, we retired to our stateroom and "rested"—

John's new term for our husband and wife activities, which falls desperately short of the truth of that time spent together; it is anything but restful!—and prepared for a late dinner at the captain's table and the equator celebration scheduled to follow.

It was sometime during that fabulous celebration, the warm tropical night winds playing over the *Ocean Star*'s rail, the champagne playing with my head, the delicious chocolate mousse still lingering in my taste buds, that the following events occurred.

John, I believe, was dancing with a matronly woman named Danforth, Danvers—I have a devil of a time with all the names!—leaving me to the company of Mr. Dan . . . I can't possibly remember! . . . who rather quickly excused himself to the toilet, one brandy over his limit, if I might say.

"Truffles, Madame?" A creamy warm voice over my shoulder, as welcome as that tropical wind. A woman's voice. Deep and soothing.

I turned, perhaps too quickly for our proximity, and found myself eye-to-eye with a Negro of nut brown skin and enormous olive-shaped eyes. Her face was a perfect oval, her lips thick and sensuous. I felt myself stir in a way no woman should stir for another woman. I am certain I made a fool of myself, the way my voice caught, with the blush I must have revealed.

A waitress, she was dressed in a black costume appropriate to her service, with a white apron and a firmly pressed white collar buttoned nearly to choking. She had a tiny, wasp waist, full hips and strong legs, widely set. The shoes they had put her in were easily a size too large. She had feet more my size. What an idiot I was, just staring into her eyes as I did.

"Madame?" she inquired a second time.

"Well, yes," I answered, having no desire to consume any more food. But I picked one off the silver tray nonetheless, and bid her to remain in my company a moment longer.

What I felt is unspeakable, but I push my fountain pen to write it here in these pages: I wanted to kiss her. To touch that soft skin. Mind you, I did not want to be kissed back—Heaven forbid!—nor touched in any way, shape or manner. But I did want to undress her and see her God-given body in all its glory, to run my hands over her skin and feel it respond to my woman's touch. So horrified was I by this response that I left the celebration early, feigning a headache, and I returned to prayer in our stateroom, kneeling at the side of that bed where my husband and I perform acts of increasing indecency, praying for salvation from wherever it is my mind seems destined to take me. Is this what marriage brings on in women: a heightened curiosity of the forms that pleasure takes? If there were only someone to whom I could bare my soul! The ship's priest comes to mind, but he is a rheumy-eyed man with a proclivity for drink. My one great fear now is that in all my isolation of the forthcoming year I will not find answers, not find release for such sinful thought. For the better part of three weeks I have been shuttered in our stateroom. I am currently ensconced in a five-room suite in the only decent hotel for a thousand miles. Laughter rolls up from the hotel bar, spilling out into the street and then rising like hot air to the room's high ceilings.

Dare I confess this? Earlier this morning a chambermaid entered to service our rooms, to change the sheets that my husband and I have soiled with our activities. (I dare not ask where John has learned all that he is "teaching" me—his term.) She couldn't have been over fifteen, if she's a day. Petite, and fair-skinned with black eyes and a strong back. Oh, yes, I studied every inch of her as she worked. She saw me watching and seemed to take great pleasure in it. Giggling. Provocative. She knows not what she does to me! I had a kink in my neck that I tried to work out—there are no pillows here to speak of, only firm square mats with cotton slipcovers. I sleep fitfully, if at all—in part because John's appetites are insatiable (he drinks heavily into the night and then arrives to our rooms in a desirous state). Our maid took note of my efforts and indicated that I should turn around. She touched my neck with her small, warm hands and I jumped, a source of great amusement on her part. Then, for the better part of a quarter of an hour or more, she kneaded my tight, knotted muscle and sculpted it, restoring it to a state of complete relaxation. I am told this form of massage is Asian, Japanese or Chinese in origin, and spilled down the archipelago over the thousands of years of commerce that has come and gone in this remote area of the world. I was quite taken by the magic of her hands, and I tipped her generously, which she clearly enjoyed.

But listen, Dear Diary, there's more! This young beauty then indicated that I should lie down on the bed. In her unfamiliar tongue and sign language, she first locked the door and then motioned for me to disrobe. (I am certain this was the meaning. It needed no translation.) She indicated with her hands that she would continue her work, the Asian massage with which she had soothed me. She appreciated my generosity, no doubt, and saw clear to the idea that she might expand on that gratuity by increasing the canvas, if I may adopt an art analogy. I declined, of course, thanking her profusely, which I'm sure she understood, and getting out of it as best I could. I suppose she meant for me to remove my dress, and only my dress, so that she could continue her work through my undergarments, but given the level of undress these natives undertake, my thoughts went elsewhere. I had visions of disrobing, becoming naked in front of this young girl.

Even now, many hours past, I find myself excited at the prospect. Dare I confess this? To be touched by another woman, someone of my own sex, who would know the aches and pains of a woman, where to touch, where to relieve the back pain that comes of the corsets, the foot and leg pain that comes from the shoes.

Nothing more than this, you understand! And yet, even this seems a sinful act. One woman with another, one in full undress.

The bright-eyed young girl had such a problem accepting no from me, either being driven by the desire for another tip or being culturally unfamiliar with such a refusal. This island and its simple people are so very foreign to me.

I am troubled by my desires. There, I wrote it down. Perhaps that will help to purge me of them. Perhaps if John included me more, allowed me out more often, my mind would have elsewhere to go other than to the physical pleasures that have entered my life for the first time in these past few weeks. The dark secrets of satisfying a man that John continues to reveal to me. But my days are just this: food and carnal pleasure. The honeymoon is for me more a horrormoon. I have prayed—to both sides—for release from this depravity of thought, for increased independence from my husband, for the freedom to walk the sands and visit the markets. I have prayed for his drinking to temper, for his earlier return to our suite, as some nights he does not return until three or four in the morning, sweating, smelling of liquor and cigars—and—dare I say it, for I am not absolutely certain?—other women.

He snores as I cry. He snores as I long for home, and most of all my dear mother. Her guidance. Her advice. Oh, the ache in my heart this loss causes me. The terror with which I face another day here, for I know it is but one of many that will combine to make up this year of travel.

There is talk of a European war. John believes the need for petroleum will increase dramatically, and with it our fortunes. But what good is fortune without love? And if John loves me, what strange ways he chooses to display it. Is love at the heart of our sweaty embrace? I once felt this—it seems like months ago now. But since our arrival here at the islands, it is bestiality that my husband brings to bed, not love. He takes me, he does not make love to me. It is carnal and awful, and I give myself to him only reluctantly and with great displeasure for fear of suffering badly should I do otherwise.

I know not what I've gotten myself into.

And all I want is out.

19 APRIL 1908—KENYA, AFRICA

Africa. The dark continent. A man's place. Primitive and intriguing. The birthplace of mankind, they say. Eden, they say. Skin so black it's blue. Wild animals in numbers that stagger the imagination. Oh, to have a motion picture camera record this!

John and I, and three other couples, two from Britain, one from Cleveland (ironically he and John share some business acquaintances there), are escorted into the bush by nearly thirty natives, an Australian guide named Charles Hammer and a Negro gun-bearer named Hipshoo—at least that's how we all pronounce it. About ten of the thirty are women, two of whom are assigned to me, one named Sukeena, the other Marishpa. They tend to me like court-appointed maids, at my side the moment I need them. Bright-eyed and filled with laughter, they have greatly elevated my spirits, which had been lagging these past several weeks. Christmas away from home was most trying, and though John endeavored to explain to me that I had a new home now, it only made matters worse.

That home is, of course, the grand house, and what pieces of information we've obtained while away are encouraging indeed. The walls are up, the roof going on. It is said to have thirty windows on the front of the house alone. The glass is being ordered for them now. I have continued to collect, starting in the Pacific Islands with lovely wood carvings, some coral and one enormous fish that John had taxidermied. Its species escapes me, though indirectly he's told me a dozen times as he loves telling this fishing story at nearly every dinner table we enjoy. I believe John caught some two hundred fish during the course of our stay, and with only this one to remember it by, he stretches the story a little longer (the fish too!) each time he tells it.

But John started me thinking about the house, and now I find I am hard pressed to do otherwise. Planning for its decoration and its completion consumes me. I bought a hundred yards of silk for wall covering while in Siam; beige, and exquisitely woven. Another hundred yards of a similar linen, also for wall covering. (We skipped India because of the anticolonial uprisings there.) John keeps encouraging me to "buy, buy, buy," emphasizing the enormity of our future home. To my great relief, the home itself has drawn us close together again. We talk of it constantly, consulting the plans, he inviting my opinion. I can actually see it growing as we discuss it, as strange as that may sound. These "visions" of mine seem a preternatural connection to the house itself, effortlessly reaching across the thousands of miles of ocean—a radio of the mind. (Radio has not yet reached Seattle, but it was all the talk before we left.) I have kept the existence of these "visions" to myself—John has no mind for any of it—while all the time actually "seeing" the house grow behind the work of the hundreds of men now on-site.

A most remarkable thing happened two days ago, worth sharing here. In studying the plans with John, he was pointing out the Breakfast Room, a well-intentioned space left of the Banquet

Hall and below the Kitchen on our plans, and one obviously thought up by a man. I'm annoyed with its placement, as its only windows face west into the garden, and any woman knows that it is the morning's east light that so pleases the morning soul. John argues that I may take my breakfast wherever it pleases me, including the Parlor, which does, in fact, face east and south, but with an uninspired view of the driveway. He reminds me that the home will be staffed with over thirty, and that if I wish to have breakfast in bed every day of my life, so be it. But he misses the point, of course, of the aesthetics of the placement of the Breakfast Room and my belief that it shall go virtually unused because of it. No matter. What was astonishing was this: in the course of our heated discussion, John pointed to a second of the room's windows in the plans. I told him no, that the window had been lost, as the architect had only recently discovered a need to relocate the pantry from north to south, to provide better access to cold storage and the china storage in the basement below, access to which was to the north of the Kitchen. He'd heard nothing of this, he reminded me, even taking the time to sort through his many telegraphs. But you see, I knew, quite clearly, that this change had been made. I had "seen" the wall being erected already, the bricks laid in place, the trowels tossing the mortar. I knew, and no one had ever told me. When John received a telegraph late that evening, he came to our rooms somewhat ashen. He passed me the telegraph and said, "Explain this, Ellen."

"A premonition is all, my love."

"A premonition?"

"Exactly so."

"Concerning the house," he said.

"This particular time, yes."

"You've had others, then?"

"The world is opening up to me, dear husband, just as you

said it would. This voyage of ours has already proved most . . . illuminating. One might even say, enlightening."

"And what else do you . . . 'see,' if I may ask."

"You dare not ask, I would suggest."

"Me? Is it ever me?" He looked nervous, visibly upset.

"And if it was?"

"I don't believe in such rubbish."

"Then you've nothing to worry about, dear soul."

"Do not call me that."

"I see you with women," I answered. "Young women, barely budding. I see you performing unspeakable acts with these dark women with whom we've surrounded ourselves since we left home." I was crying now, but trying so hard not to. I'm sure I must have looked the fool.

He blanched. "Ridiculous!" A hoarse, dry whisper that I fear even he did not believe. Void of the usual flare of temper, he left our rooms in quietude.

To my surprise, he returned later, sober and unusually considerate and polite. That night he was husband to me as gentle as our wedding night. He luxuriated me in my own pleasures as he has never done before, and later I heard him crying in his sleep. It's the heir, Dear Diary, the all-important heir. I am now the vehicle through which to deliver him his lineage, and any other will be bastard. (I fear we have left a string behind us on this trip already!) He needs me in this endeavor, my willingness to take to bed with him, or this dream of passing along his fortune will never take light. It is this need that compels him to treat me with respect and dignity, no matter what the truth of our union be. I do believe I have struck the fear of God in him. But truth be known, it is the Devil, for who else invoked in me such a lie as I told him that night, having never had such visions of him with others. Suspicions, to be sure. But brought forward as images, I do believe that he briefly saw them as well, reliving his unfaithfulness, and that perhaps these memories, so vivid and so clear, afforded him the opportunity to believe that I too had witnessed his depraved acts. Am I to believe he simply invents these things he puts me through when in bed with him? He learned them, of course, and we both know it, and we also know that I am not that teacher.

And so the little games we play continue. Acting out husband and wife. Reviewing our grand house plans as if none's-the-worry. Me, beginning to communicate with Sukeena and enjoying her company so very much. He, taking off on his safaris for days at a time and returning with guilt on his face and a fallen impala under his arm. Me, with my visions. He, with his dreams. And my womanhood the secret that holds the balance for both of us. When my monthly issue does come, he shrinks into the bottle and depression for days, only to return to try again, sometimes tenderly, sometimes desperately. I am the key to his future happiness, and he, in turn, is the key to mine. I am beginning to learn the ways of marriage.

15 MAY 1908—KENYA, AFRICA

I have not made entries in this personal chronicle for nearly a month—three weeks and five days, to be exact. I do so now, only weakly, unable to hold this pen for long, I am afraid. I have been unconscious for some of this time and delirious for the rest, stricken with what our recently departed fellow travelers believed was malaria. I have lost no fewer than fifteen pounds—my rib cage protrudes front and back like some of the native women in our employ. I have suffered from fever for days at a time, a complete loss of appetite, sweats and tremors. Only through the tender care of Sukeena and her bitter teas and remedies she has fed me, and my own endless prayers for recovery, have I survived. For these four weeks I have never left the confines of my tent, quarantined from all but the natives. Even John has avoided contact, standing outside at the far end of my tent and talking to me through a small triangle of light caused by a turned-up tent flap. It is this isolation that has worn on me, driven me at times to the very edge of my sanity. Only my rough conversations with Sukeena, an awkward combination of words and gestures, have maintained my link to this world. In my delirium I have traveled to unthinkable places, at times believing it so real, only to have Sukeena pull me back. I do believe that no less than three times I was within a breath or two of death, hovering in a netherworld where at once I felt both refreshed and fearful. This delicate contact with what I perceive of as the other side has left me far less apprehensive of my own demise, and yet with mixed opinion as to whether I was in Heaven, or Hell, or Purgatory. What I know, and know for certain, is that God saved my life, but that the Devil may have bargained for my soul. The exact conversations escape me now (though they were extremely clear at the time), but I know for certain I made promises that perhaps I should not have made.

Sukeena, who has served me as both nursemaid and witch doctor, as sister and friend, has known the truth all along, that my fevers and infirmity resulted neither from the water nor from the jungle insects that do infest this godless place. Instead my illness was contracted by contact with my husband, for I am plagued by an unmentionable disease carried by men and suffered by women. The remedy for my affliction is most unpleasant, though as I understand it, is far less worse than it is, or will be, for John, who has no doubt undergone, and will continue to undergo, a series of injections to an area of the male body that is also unmentionable.

This, in turn, explains John's sweats of nearly six weeks ago, a lingering illness that put him of foul mood, unable to walk, and accounted for his sending for certain medications, of which I was unaware until Sukeena recently informed me. His recovery, however, appears to have gone much more quickly than my own, for he has returned to hunt and safari these last three weeks while I lay here in my tent. (I am told, again by Sukeena, that the reverse is usually true—that women tend to suffer far less than men from this horrible affliction. What curse on me reversed these odds?)

Husband and wife have not spoken of this, nor will we ever. Of this I am certain. Much have I cried and agonized over my husband's unfaithfulness, his failure to live up to the mutual consent of our marriage vows and the lack of respect he has shown me. Much have I now suffered for his pleasures, and I ache for a way to return such shame and pain to him. It is the heir, of course. To deny him the right to continue his line, but I cannot throw myself into this cause with much heart, for I, too, would welcome the distraction of children. And yet the thought of joining him physically I find so repugnant as to literally make me sick to my stomach. I vomit if any such image enters my mind. I expel it and swear it will never come to fruition. I have now lived the error of forgiveness (for certainly I've known all along what he was up to!). I will never fool myself again. He will be made to beg me. He will be made to cry. To pay, both financially and emotionally, for the trials he has put me through if he wishes to have his heir. This inferno that has lived in my loins and in my head these many weeks has taken root in my condemnation of my husband and my determination for revenge. If it's money that he loves then I shall bleed him. This grand house of his will never be complete. Construction will never stop. No expense will be spared. He will watch as the frivolity of my mood directs the depletion of his funds in whatever unnecessary and trivial manner I can and do imagine. And he will be loath to stop it, to even try—for my legs shall close upon his lineage forever, like a springed trap.

The call for revenge drives me to take the soup Sukeena offers. To allow my sweat-soaked bedsheets and nightgown to be removed and replaced, rather than succumb to the fevers. To tolerate the treatments Sukeena puts me through, at once both painful and humiliating.

I will prevail to leave this tent, to face my husband across the dinner tables erected beneath what appears to be a banyan tree. I will look him in the eye and show him my resolve to right his wrong. And he will know. He will wither under the power I have gained both through my prayers (to both sides) and from my dear friend, Sukeena. She has the power to heal, the power to connect to the other side. Her dolls of black hardwood. Her musical chants and infusions. In what my husband may only slowly come to see, my illness has led to strength of mind, my suffering to strength of heart. He will come to regret his infidelity, ultimately and forever.

And I shall triumph, Sukeena at my side. She is coming home with us. This is the first of many concessions my husband shall learn to make.

15 JUNE 1908—CAIRO, EGYPT

I cannot imagine any place hotter in all the world than Cairo in June. We have sailed down the Nile for days (how strange a world this is that north is downstream?). John is foul of mood, and no wonder: he has not won my affections since late April when he bestowed upon me that horrible curse. And now, in such close company as this small flat-bottomed boat, he cannot find any budding young women to pluck except those of the European families that people this vessel—girls who can speak, read and write—girls who would report him in an instant if he lifted their skirts. He broods and drinks and brags with the other passengers, wisely leaving Sukeena and me to ourselves, except at dinner at a tedious captain's table where liquor is the official language and all but I speak fluently. I hear him tell his hunting stories and marvel at his ability to win friends, and I watch the women swoon, and I wonder if that is how I once looked in his company as well. I want to hate him, but that vexation is slowly wearing off. Calculated or not, he has taken some time to charm me, has helped me pick out several splendid rugs from Persia (bought in Luxor) and a great deal of woven wicker—baskets and hampers mostly, some seventy-five in all. The prize so far is the hand-carved alabaster. We are to have dinner, bread and salad plates, soup bowls of two sizes, all for a table of forty. It is to be shipped to Seattle within the year, each piece carefully packed. John said that if half the cargo arrived undamaged we should consider it a victory, at which point I increased the alabaster order to a serving for eighty, and watched John wince at the increase in price, although these dirt-poor Egyptian farmers are practically giving away such wares. I could have increased it to eight hundred and not taken a week of my husband's income. Indeed, if I am to have any revenge on my husband, I see clearly now that it absolutely must come in the construction of the grand house. That is the only weapon I possess.

I have come to detest the Europeans for their treatment of my dear Sukeena. Of those who acknowledge her presence (precious few, I'm sorry to say), few treat her with any respect above a slave. A French couple was nice to her—the woman offered her some clothes that would fit (mine are far too small for her) and she accepted. A Canadian woman was quite thoughtful and respectful and always greeted Sukeena by name. The rest were brutes. I was glad to be free of the *Sun Ra,* even if it meant the streets of Cairo.

Few cities in the world are as densely populated as this one. Brown bodies by the millions, all covered in long cotton robes of soft browns and a few subtle greens. They look like nightgowns—as if everyone has just woken up. The men wrap their heads in white cotton. The women cover their faces—all but the black eyes that stare straight ahead, unseeing and yet all seeing. Water buffalo drag carts through the streets but foul the sunbaked brick and make a stink that rises with the sun. People wash themselves in the river—this river that is the heart of the land—they wash their babies, their food utensils, their camels. The river is putrid and foul—and they practically live in it.

But to the story at hand! Sukeena and I were bicycled by rickshaw into the city's main market—deep in the center of humanity. We were not, by any means, the only visitors to this city, but it felt that way. We collected some trinkets, a good deal of colorful fabrics and a few more pieces of alabaster, these ornately carved. All our goods were stacked high on the three-wheeled bicycle, our driver never hesitating a moment to add to his load. After about an hour of this, we took tea in a small teahouse where young boys circulated the air by manning large fans. The tea helped me to perspire, which in turn cooled me off. I made the mistake of showing my coin purse to pay for the tea—a practice John has warned me against time and time again, and one I just cannot seem to master. At any rate, I committed this mistake (John is right, of course) and must have shown to all those looking a good deal of bills within that small purse, for John had just exchanged some dollars upon our arrival and had provided me appropriate spending money.

I realize now this must have been staged, but at the time the commotion that arose at the front of the building drove Sukeena and me to the rear, in hopes of escaping the melee. As we slipped out the back, not one, but two very evil-minded men approached, their message clear from the knives they carried: the purse, or our lives. I nearly fainted at this threat of violence, and it did not escape me that as men confronting a white-skinned woman they might want more than just my purse.

I willingly offered the purse, but Sukeena lovingly took hold of my arm, shook her head "no" and made me to hold on to it. One of the two stepped forward—I believe to challenge us, certainly to challenge Sukeena. But that brave woman stood tall. Her skin so dark it shined blue. "Nubian!" they called out in their foreign tongue.

And then I witnessed with my own eyes a side of Sukeena I had never before seen. She stared at this man—a glaring stare unlike anything, impossible to describe. She stepped toward him, her body fluid and flawless, moving more like a wave than a step, a snake than a legged creature. And all the while a deep, low, guttural sound pulsated from her throat and chest. This sound seemed to surround us. The man, increasingly uncomfortable with her approach, took a step back, the first sign she had dominion over him. At this point, the guttural sound evolved into language—a tongue I had never heard, not in all our travels in the dark continent. But this man, and his associate, apparently understood the primitive message she imparted. As she waved her hands the man stopped, absolutely still. As still as marble. That knife carried as an ornament, not a weapon. Both men began to tremble—and I swear I felt the earth beneath my feet rumbling—like a self-contained earthquake. Then they folded in on themselves and writhed in pain on the ground as if stricken by some disease to the stomach or bowels. What began as their moaning developed into cries of terror.

Sukeena took my hand, stepped around the one in front of us and led me down the alley to our waiting driver. As I looked back, the men were still groaning miserably.

Sukeena has not spoken of the incident, and I, for one, am glad of that fact, for I'd know not what to say. But I am less concerned about travel deep into these foreign streets now. I feel protected, defended against the dark side by my African friend. I am more intrigued by her unspeakable powers. Where such powers come from, and whether or not a person can learn them, can adopt them for her own, I have yet to discover. But with Sukeena to teach me, I suddenly feel that anything is possible. Anything my heart desires.

4 JULY 1908—CRETE, GREECE

Our nation's birthday was met by much drinking on John's part. He began his celebrations before noon, partaking in the clear liquor these fishermen drink by the shot, said to be a variation on grain alcohol. The Greeks, of course, have little if any idea of our Independence Day, and must find John's display of patriotism somewhat confounding.

Sukeena and I toured a ruin, an old port city now inland by a quarter mile, rocked above sea level in a seismic shift two thousand years earlier. We visited a row of stone tubs used for washing laundry, so well preserved that all they lacked was a stopper and some soap to be put back into service. This is the land of raw olive oil, squid and goats that climb trees (I saw this with my own eyes!). A quiet, peace-loving peasant people with a rich appetite for café discussion, drinking and coffee so strong and bitter that it turns my stomach.

It was here, this morning, in a spectacular suite of rooms overlooking the rich blue depths of the Mediterranean that my will surrendered to John for the first time since this past April. The morning broke incredibly hot and I slipped out of bed to stand by the ocean breeze at the window when my husband took hold of me from behind, his massive hands beneath my gown before my voice could rise to protest. I grabbed for either side of the open French doors and braced myself, casting myself forward and clearly inviting his ardor, the hem of my nightgown riding on my hips, his brazen intentions driving me to my toes, my knees quivering, my heart racing. My God, I must admit here to the thrill of it all. Our passions mutually heightened by my months of refusal, John's aggressiveness, so masculine and forceful, yet careful and kind to me. I could not maintain my footing, and therefore slowly sank to my knees, my husband keeping us joined and fervently pursuing his climax, to where, in a dizzying moment of unbridled sensation I tried to call out to him, only to hear my voice moan through indistinguishable syllables that he clearly took as a signal. We collapsed in a gasp of satisfaction, he on my back, me with my face pressed to the tile floor. "This is hardly a situation becoming of a lady," I said weakly, winning a spontaneous eruption of laughter from the both of us.

"Our morning ride," he said, and we laughed again.

When we were apart he rolled me over and we lay together again, half in, half out of our bedroom, half in, half out of consciousness, basking in the morning sunshine, basking in our union. I wrapped my legs tightly around his waist and heard myself say, "It's all behind us, yes?"

"I have hope it is."

"Never again."

"Never," he said, gently touching my cheek. "I was a fool, Ellen." And then the words I had prayed to hear. "Forgive me."

"We will not speak of it. Not now. Not ever." From where this capitulation arose, I know not. Perhaps I wanted a marriage back. A life. Perhaps my confidence in Sukeena's enormous powers made John Rimbauer less of an obstacle and more of a game to me. I felt more the cat than the mouse. I had what he wanted: ability to deliver his heir. He had what I had quickly grown accustomed to: position, power and tremendous wealth.

As we lay there, this forty-year-old man grew ardent yet again, and again I capitulated. And for the first time since our marriage, I directed him as to the choreography of my pleasure. With each instruction I gave, I witnessed arousal in my husband, excitement. He would answer each touch I gave to him with a hearty, throaty, "Yes!" and do exactly as I wished. I tell you, Dear Diary: I never knew . . . I never knew. But under my careful instruction, both of the hips and the hands, he did pleasure me, carrying me to new sensations that both alarmed me (for my surrender to them) and overcame me with pure and perfect delight (my every muscle on fire at once!). My legs still gripped around him, I eased my damp head of hair back to resting, my chest a florid pink, my husband panting like a long-distance runner. "Good boy, Johnny," I said, using a nickname I had never dared use before, adopting an attitude—as much a test as a conviction.

He placed his head on my chest, and briefly was that little boy I had complimented. I cannot explain in these pages, but in that moment the tide of our relating husband to wife did shift, wife to husband. I gained the strength and courage to express my physical desires, and in doing so somehow also gained the upper hand over my formerly defiant husband. I didn't want to think about the past, I wanted to command the future.

As we dressed and took coffee on the balcony, I felt another stirring in my loins, and nearly requested my husband's favors yet again. But this stirring was something altogether different from a woman's urges. At first I blamed this awful coffee and then, later, the excitement pent up from my morning discoveries and the accomplishment of one part of my dream.

But then I blamed the act itself (or the acts, if one is counting!). For though I'd never experienced the condition firsthand, could only speculate on the sensation surging through my soul (not my body, but my soul), I sensed the presence of another life. A life within me. I was pregnant.

I knew this absolutely and with all conviction. The first fledgling moments of a human being were growing inside me.

When Sukeena saw me it was all but confirmed. She met me in our rooms, looked deeply into my eyes and smiled widely. "So," she said in her pidgin English, "it has begun."

Indeed, it has.

9 SEPTEMBER 1908—PARIS, FRANCE

I am cursed. Ever since our engagement to marry and the tragic murder at the site of the grand house, Harry Corbin's insanity, events so strange and peculiar as to foreshadow a life so different than a young girl dreams—I should have known! Earlier to-day I lost my child. It issued from me, Sukeena nursing me through it (she says all women lose the children not made for this earth, but that hardly helps). This, following a social calendar here in this beloved city that I begged John to constrain. We have been active every night for nearly two weeks—opera, dinner parties, business dinners. I felt myself weakening under the fatigue, straining to keep awake at times, eating food I found utterly too rich and unappealing. Wearing corsets too tight. I cautioned John, who knows so little of women and their needs. I warned him that if he wanted this child, he could not make requirements of me after this fashion. And now we suffer the agony of this loss.

Such complete devastation I have never known. I spent two hours in Sukeena's arms in hysterics, sobbing and incoherent. My little child that warmed in my belly is gone. A doctor has been brought in. I am to take bed rest for a week to ten days. As if the torture of my loss is not enough, my infirmity now frees my husband for the first time in months to roam this city alone in search of his favorite flower—and don't think I don't know it. He began drinking heavily this morning, the moment he was informed. I can picture her: fifteen or sixteen. Blond. Blue eyes. So much my opposite. My husband lavishing gifts upon her. And she, spreading her honey, a sweetness he cannot resist.

I am sick to my stomach with the thought. Sukeena believes my nausea is related to my loss, but I know better. I am livid with anger and resentment. Again I brood and consult the dark side on how to punish John for never listening to me. Always ordering me around like one of his foremen or ship captains. Again I know that the power I lord over him is the presentation of an heir. Without me he has only bastards. I offer him legitimacy. Immortality.

Sukeena has eyes that smile as I explain this to her. "As long as you angry, Miss Ellen, I know you to live." She wants me to have a raison d'être, afraid that my loss will throw me into a slump (for I am certain she has seen this before in her tribal friends). So I focus on punishing John, on denying him my womanhood, denying him his child. Let him roam the streets for his girls, he will never know love. He will never know family.

I conspire in my mind to hurt him, while at the same time worshiping him. At times I hate myself for my devoted love of my husband—is it the age that separates us? his success and strength?—I treasure him, even while disliking him so fully, so absolutely. If anything drives me insane, it will be these two women who live inside me: one that loves, one that wants to hate; one that prays to God to celebrate life, one that prays to Darkness to punish my husband. How can I ever reconcile these two in the same body, the same woman? I loathe him, I love him. I want his attention, and yet I now grieve because he wouldn't leave me to rest; I want independence, separation, and yet I long for our life together at the grand house—a family. I want to punish him, I want to serve him. Who am I, Dear Diary, that I can be so vexed?

And so, for the next ten days, I shall mourn the passing of this almost-child. I shall beg to be given back the gift of God's gracious blessing. I shall resent my husband, so very much, if he takes my infirmity as opportunity.

I cannot find peace. I cannot sleep. I am not hungry. My body purges. Sukeena nurses me like a sister. My belief builds that if God has allowed me to lose this child, there is some hidden reason behind it. Why else would He put me through such loss and agony, anxiety and pain? Is it perhaps not yet time for John's heir? Are there more tests upon us to come? Or am I deficient in some way, unable to deliver what every other woman delivers so naturally?

How, if ever, will I now find internal peace? How, if ever, will I recover my soul? For I fear it has fled with this almost-child—his little heir running from his father before even entering his world. And as I read back what I've written, I know that the answer to these questions is itself a dichotomy: motherhood. That which I seek to deny him is itself the solution to my grief and anxieties. I am so confused. Tired now, I must rest. I must close my eyes, even if sleep won't come. I will listen to Sukeena humming by my side, those tribal melodies and rhythms. I will fall under her spell, this enchanting woman who loves me and cares for me like a sister. Where would I be without my dear Sukeena? We are bonded now, the two of us. And it shall remain so, forever.

9 DECEMBER 1908—SEATTLE, WASHINGTON

After nearly a year away, John and I returned to Seattle to-day by train. Met at the station by my mother and my former governess (who now works as my mother's secretary), I threw myself into Mother's arms like a schoolgirl returning from summer camp. I had written home at least a letter a week, and so it is that my mother is quite aware of both the pregnancy and the miscarriage. She greeted Sukeena, not like a Negro kitchen maid, as I feared she might, but as a member of the family, with kisses and the warmest of welcomes. This, above all else, meant so much to me.

My mother took Sukeena to her home. We are to live apart for a short time, until John and I are moved into the grand house, an event that is expected to take place within a matter of days but may stretch out a few weeks due to the holiday season. Oh, how grand it is to see this city I love so. Muddy roads and all. Gray, wet skies and all. The lush green is a welcome relief to eyes that have looked out train windows for days as we crossed the wheat fields of Kansas and Colorado and the barren reaches of Idaho and eastern Washington. These endless rains are not without their lush rewards.

John and I took to his rooms. Sukeena met me later in the day and together we began the arduous task of unpacking my twelve steamers. Added to our burden is the job of overseeing the inventorying of the goods shipped home over the past year. They have been assembled in a downtown warehouse—crate upon crate upon crate. Some are to be unpacked, some will wait for relocation to the grand house, but all are to be counted and accounted for. It is a task that will occupy both Sukeena and me for weeks to come, as by my count no fewer than ninety-five shipments should have arrived. Rugs, furs, John's African shooting trophies, urns, vases, lights—the list is nearly endless. Christmas indeed. I have never been so excited as to unwrap these treasures. I am like a little girl under the tree.

The long train trip afforded me the opportunity to refuse John's advances time and time again. I gloated in the pleasure of it. Confined as we were, he had no opportunity to take to the streets. Instead, day by day, he became both more frustrated with me and more subservient. I had him serving my every need, calling for porters, for dining service, acting as manservant to me. What a sensation! I cannot explain it here, it is the first time I've felt so since the loss of the child. He wilted under my glare. He trembled when at night we took to bed and I pressed my warm body against him, only to deny him the ultimate prize. I will surrender, of course. It is hard for me to deny myself his pleasures as well (though I never indicate this!). And now that we return to a place he can find such satisfactions without me, it is time I give in, hoping to stem that tide. I prepare myself for that eventuality.

John and I spent much of the train trip writing a list of guests to be invited to the opening of the grand house. We have scheduled a party for January the fifteenth, allowing several extra weeks in case of a holiday slowdown. (John will devote himself to the house fully when not engaged in his oil business. He has already left for a meeting with Douglas Posey, his oil partner, to discuss the events of the past week, during which time we were isolated on the train.) A packet of photographs awaited us at the Ritz in New York upon our arrival there by steamer. Oh, such grandeur! The facade is brick, the house contained behind a wrought-iron fence and a twin set of stone pillars over which hangs the Rimbauer crest. The driveway hosts an island, home to one of the many statuettes we purchased in Italy. There must be thirty windows or more on the front of the house, a half dozen chimneys rising from its myriad of rooftops. The interior pictures, of the Grand Stair and the Entry Hall, leave me breathless. Oh, to think of this

magnificent place as my home! I can't imagine! (But I shall soon enough!) In the Parlor, I saw that the suit of armor (from England), the brown bear (shot by John in the Swiss Alps) and the pipe organ (from Bavaria) are already installed! How impressive a sight it is—these souvenirs and treasures from our year abroad. I thrill at the thought of taking tea in my Parlor!

The party—our homecoming and the dedication of the house—is to be a lavish affair: local politicians, entertainers, friends and businessmen, perhaps three hundred in all. My mother has been overseeing much of the preparation in advance of our arrival. John sent nearly fifty cases of champagne from France and another several hundred cases of wine, many of which will go to the celebration, the rest to be housed in our Wine Cellar (John wants to boast the largest private wine cellar on the West Coast). Beef has been shipped from Chicago and Kansas

City. Pork from Nebraska. Fresh fish is to be delivered from dockside on the day of the grand affair. Chocolate from Switzerland. Tea from England. Cigars from Cuba. John is leaving nothing to chance. This is a party no one in Seattle will ever forget.

And if I have my way—and indeed I will—it is a party we shall repeat annually. A party to dwarf any New Year's Eve event. The Rimbauer Party. It shall go down in the society pages for years to come. The biggest party in the biggest house.

I feel myself on track again. I am glad our long journey is over.

Another is just beginning.

CHRISTMAS EVE, 1908—SEATTLE

For two painful weeks, John has denied me a visit to our grand home as workers complete the final touches. We shall formally move into our home on January the fifteenth, the day of our homecoming party (John has scheduled our "arrival" with a greeting by the staff on that day). After repeated requests on my part to tour our new home, so that I might orchestrate the delivery of our personal items well in advance of our formal arrival, John drove me up Spring Street in his new Cadillac this afternoon, a trip I remember well from my first journey here so many months ago.

The city is still in the grips of various stages of the regrade, accounting for some very silly sights. Some families have elected to challenge in court the city's right to lower certain streets by as much as seventy feet, while filling in various gulches that make passage nearly impossible. This effort, ongoing now for nearly a decade, has been a bitter battle. Those families that have brought legal suit against the city have not been required to lower their homes, leaving some lots and the houses atop them isolated on forty- or fifty-foot "pinnacles," earthen towers rising from the new street level (muddy as it is). The homes are completely inaccessible, leaving the families without residence. It is quite obvious that at some point these families will capitulate, but oh what a sight in the meantime! It seems as if nearly every building in this eastern part of the city is on scaffolding of some kind, and intermixed, these "pinnacles" rising over five stories into the gray, dreary sky.

Our arrival at the gates of the Rimbauer mansion (for it is nothing less!) left me breathless. All these months of reviewing plans, moving walls, changing windows, even the photos delivered in New York, did nothing to prepare me for this moment! She is spectacular! Pretentious! Gorgeous!

The front of our stone and brick home stretches hundreds of feet, north to south, presenting one with a formidable wall of brick, roof, glass and chimney. If impression is what John was after, impression he accomplished. I could go on and on in my description—and perhaps I will when I am less tired—but for now, I wish to describe just one or two rooms, rooms that as wife to this man will be forever important to me.

The dining room, to be called the Banquet Hall, is magnificent, with the gleaming walnut table occupying its center. I estimate this table can accommodate roughly seventy or eighty dinner guests. Cabinets are built into two sides of the room, all with glass doors, and are soon to contain our vast collection of china. I envision the north wall holding John's family's collection of teapots, representing over sixty countries around the world. Fine paintings from the European masters adorn the walls: landscapes mostly, many of which we acquired on our honeymoon, so our guests can sit and dream of places far away while six-foot logs burn furiously in the fireplace. I can hardly wait for our home-coming party! We will fill this table and more with our dinner guests—what an occasion it is to be!

John's and my chambers occupy the entire West Wing of the second floor, each of us having six or seven rooms to ourselves when including parlors, dressing rooms and our studies and libraries. My bedroom, the Lady's Chambers, is everything I dreamed it to be! It has a big bay window facing the courtyard and overlooking the glassed-in Solarium off the Kitchen, where botanical varieties of every sort are currently being planted. The windows of the room are hung with white silk curtains with over-drapes of heavy green brocade. The bed itself rises up three steps, and I can already imagine the staff making comments about my "throne." No matter—I love the look! The woodwork in the room is decorated with hand carvings, most of which are from the small town of Opede in the south of France, where John and I visited not six months ago. Installed into my bedroom, the craftsmanship looks sumptuous, ornate and quite rich! To the right of the bed, and down the steps, is a three-panel Oriental screen, behind which I can quickly undress. The doors of this screen carry full-length mirrors so that I might view all sides before joining my husband in bed for his husbandly visits. (I must say that sight of this house has erased so much of our ugly past. John is so proud of it, and I of him, for this magnificent accomplishment.) The opposite sides of the screen, those facing into the room, are of a dark green plush reminiscent of the forest behind our home. There are four area rugs, all from Persia, a green velvet recliner, two Louis XIV armchairs and a dresser from the Loire. I am fit to be a queen!

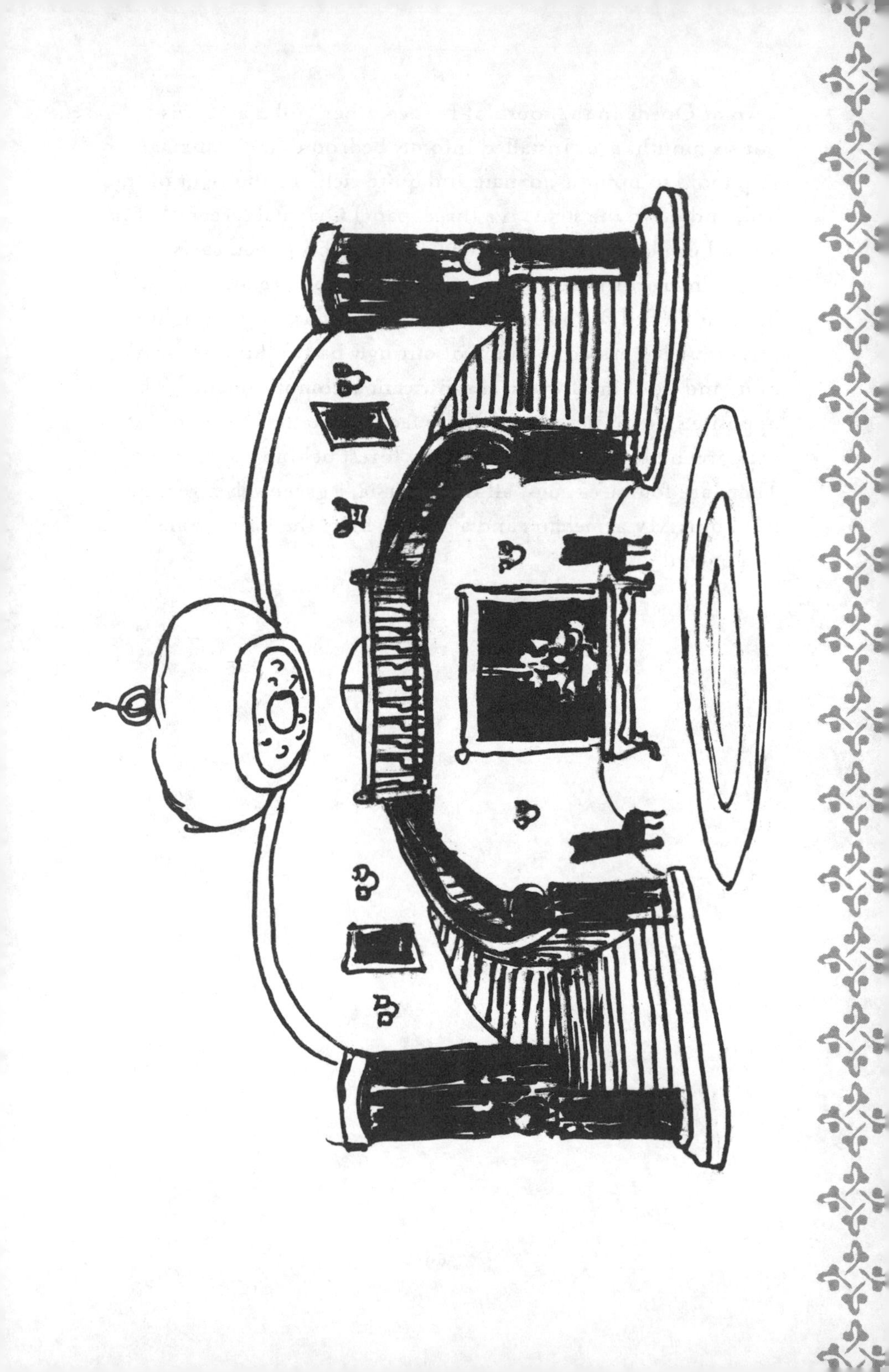

16 JANUARY 1909

I must report, Dear Diary, on the inaugural of the grand house and the night of divine romance that followed.

First, to the weather. We must be being punished for our year away to mostly tropical locations. The heat of Kenya and Cairo is being more than made up for in the most bitter cold Seattle has suffered in memory. The freeze that gripped this city just days ago with a temperature of only twelve degrees above zero, and allowed skating on Lake Union for the first time I can recall, was reversed less than a day later with temperatures in the mid-twenties. The cold-weather fun continued for all of that day, and into the night. And then tragedy as the thermometer soared to well into the forties—a more typical temperature. By early the next morning, the paper reported that over twenty thousand pipes had burst across the city. Miraculously, our new home, perched high on the hill, was somehow spared. We suffered not a single burst pipe—a fact that quickly made the social circles. John claims it is the result of good planning on his and the engineers' part, having insulated the pipes and run them on interior walls. It didn't hurt, I suppose, that the staff has had fires raging in every room, and the steam heat on as well, preparing the home for our party. No matter! Our guests, many without running water in their homes, were delighted to join us that evening!

And now again, to the house itself, for I am smitten with her! Such splendor, such lavish expense has seldom been seen, certainly on these shores. Perhaps only Rockefeller, Vanderbilt or Carnegie has ever built an American home so grand as ours. It is still under construction as I write this (will it ever be completed? I wonder), and yet we were able to tour our guests through some twenty thousand square feet of living space. The front Entry Hall, gallery to John's hunting trophies, is sixty feet long, a stunning foyer of rich, African mahogany that leads to the curving two-sided staircase ascending to the first of four floors. To stand at the base of the stairs, one faces a hallway both right and left, forward and back. Ahead is the Kitchen and Solarium. To the right is a picture gallery and several sitting rooms. To the left is the Banquet Hall, more hallways and parlors, the Breakfast Room. It has taken me days just to learn my way around this palace. One can get lost so quickly and easily.

Our inaugural was attended by over two hundred and fifty. All ate dinner in one of six rooms, and then there was dancing in the Grand Ballroom until well into the wee hours. We had a senator, the mayor, the great Broadway stage actress Marjorie Savoy, a baseball player whose name I cannot recall but is said to be quite famous, the soprano and stunning beauty Jeanine Sabino (with whom John spent a little too much time for my liking) and two Italians and Chinese, all three of whom are rumored to be gin runners or some other form of lowlife and were invited only because John's importing of oil depends on their cooperation. (The more I learn of this business, the more horrified I am. One great advantage of our year abroad was that John took me into his confidence regarding his oil matters and I learned a great deal. He seems constantly involved in secret negotiations to bring refineries and minor oil companies together to extort the railroads for lower shipping costs, to affect supply, to negotiate better labor costs. So much secrecy is involved—I had no idea!)

I wore a white dress that was such a success with the men that I shall wear it each and every year from now on! The women were all dressed so beautifully, rich velvets, silks and wool. The men wore tuxedos—white tie, so elegant and refined. I tell you, we were the toast of the town and shall remain in high regard for years to come because of it. Few could believe the size of the grand house, as close to town as it is. I heard words like "museum" and "royal palace" on the lips of everyone who toured. The decorations are splendid—our long trip so justified now that

I see all that we collected so beautifully coordinated. It is sumptuous without being gaudy, extravagant without being hideous. I am quite proud of both John and myself for what we've accomplished.

I share here a conversation I overheard while approaching the Library (6,000 volumes!) between two men—Tanner Longford, chancellor of the university, and Bradley Webster, head of a bank that competes with my father's. I point out, Dear Diary, that these are not small-minded men—far from it!—and that to hear such talk (taken in confidence, I'm sure) adds a great deal of verisimilitude to the content of their exchange.

Tanner's is a deep voice that reminds one of a storyteller. Bradley Webster is a small man with a choked, nasal exaggeration to his conversation. I heard Tanner first.

"You heard about the murder up here?"

"Yes, of course. Horrible, wasn't it?" Bradley Webster is a bit full of himself.

"I hear the man—Corwin, wasn't it?"

"Corbin, I believe."

"Yes. That's it. Well, the poor man went insane. Totally mad. Sentenced to twenty-five years. He clawed his eyes out in his cell claiming an Indian had made him do it. Said he came out of the hole like the Devil—the hole being the foundation to this house, you see—had handed him the shotgun."

"His eyes, was it?"

"Yes. Died from it, I heard. Bled to death. The eyeless bastard running around his cell screaming 'Go away! Go away!' Claimed that same Indian had visited his cell and told him his work wasn't over."

"An Indian."

"Rimbauer knew, of course."

"Knew what, Tanner?"

"You don't know about this site?"

"I'm afraid I don't."

"Lisa told me," Tanner Langford explained. (Lisa is Tanner's sister, an influential woman and a member of our children's hospital board.) "They uncovered Indian remains while digging the foundation. Goddamned cemetery is what it was. Skeletons by the wagon load, I heard. Some of the Chinamen quit. There was some illness blamed on the graves. Fevers, that sort of thing."

"I haven't heard any of this."

"Lisa knows all the doctors. I think we can trust her reports."

"I didn't mean to imply . . ."

"Some relics were uncovered, I heard. A chief or some tribal head of state. There was looting. Rimbauer ordered several men fired. But word got out. The state was to send an expert. And then he burned the bones."

"He what!?"

"Made a bonfire of them, as I understand it. Had them use a few barrels of his oil—I like that little touch—and burned them to ash. By the time the state's man arrived, there was nothing left. They were going to shut him down, you see, but they couldn't do that now. Rimbauer put it all off to rumor. A clever one, Rimbauer is. But then this man Corbin—what do you make of that? 'An Indian,' he said. Made him do it. Can you imagine?"

"A story is all. Nothing more than a story."

"I agree. I agree! But still . . . an Indian!"

At this point in their conversation someone met me in the hall and greeted me, and my eavesdropping was interrupted. I don't know what followed. What I do know is that John never mentioned a word to me about any Indian burial ground. I never heard the story about Corbin either. His eyes! Good God, I can't imagine such a self-inflicted wound! I hope beyond measure that it's purely sensational rumor—my but how people love to spin tales about the wealthy! John has been the subject of much discussion and rumor for years now. I am a part of that now, and I suppose it will continue as long as he wields the kind of power he does. He supplies this city with some eighty percent of its lighting oil, kerosene and gasoline. Portland as well. Forty percent of San Francisco. Ninety percent of Denver. The Japanese are buying, the British, French Indonesia. He has created an empire (having enlarged it during our honeymoon!), and any emperor suffers at the lips of his people.

I related what I had overheard to Sukeena, who is so perceptive about matters of the spirit. She tells me the house is "powerful" and like nothing she has ever felt before.

One matter of note: several of our guests at the inaugural related to me that they became frightfully lost while touring the house on their own. I found myself amused by this, actually, as I was myself lost just a day or so ago—for a moment I actually believed the hallway had looked entirely different just minutes earlier. Can you imagine? I paid little attention to these reports until Sukeena warned me to stay out of the Billiard Room. At first I thought she meant because John is so possessive about his private time spent there with his cigars and brandy. We did not speak further of it until this evening when I made a comment about how some of the guests could not find their way.

"The Billiard Room," she said.

"I'm not sure," I told her.

"Miss Ellen, I tell you—it is the Billiard Room they speak of. I seen things there. I feel them in here." With that she clutched at her heart, a mannerism she uses only in the most engaging of expressions. (When I lost the baby she sat by my side, holding my hand, covering her bosom in this same way.)

"Feel what, my dear friend?"

She shook her head, not wanting to speak of it.

"What?" I repeated, perhaps a little desperately.

"Not what, Miss Ellen: who," she said. "I feel them. The ones that take us. My parents. My nephew."

I shuddered. Sukeena's parents and nephew were dead. I knew this absolutely.

"The Indians," I whispered.

Sukeena looked at me gravely, and she nodded. "We not alone in this house, Miss Ellen."

As to the romance of this inaugural evening, suffice it to say here in these private pages that the champagne went to my head quite early in the evening, and that by the wee hours, when John and I finally retired, I was not quite myself, given to my desires and overcome by my husband's passions. Our lovemaking was frantic, desperate even, John upon me before my undergarments were removed. His affections are so impossible to resist at moments like this. His strength, his intensity. Had I not had the wine, perhaps I could have found my strength, but as it was I succumbed with little resistance. And then I participated. And then I cried out my demands and drove him to a frenzy—a practice I have learned to time to meet my own needs. We fell to the floor of my dressing room in a tangle of white silk and a mutual hunger that did not abate until the silk was torn and my dear husband carried deep scratches down his back. (My gown will need much repair!) I fear I screamed so loudly that the maids must have heard. Perhaps the whole house. Sukeena gave me a look this morning that informed me at least she had heard. Then she made me to lie in bed with my rump elevated on pillows for nearly three hours, a twinkle in her eye.

"I will give you child, Miss Ellen."

Sukeena knows how badly I want this, how much I fear losing another. But just those words filled me with excitement. John was off to his study early this morning (oh, how his head must throb!) in an effort to read a new contract with the Union Pacific. But before he left, he entered my bedroom and left a red rose on the pillow next to me, the thorns neatly removed with a penknife, the smell so luscious and filling me and my dreams with contentment.

"What color to-day, Miss Ellen?" Sukeena asked from my dressing room.

"Red," I said back to her, naming the color of the flower. "Rose Red," I repeated more strongly. It has a familiar ring to it, though I can't recall from where. And then a realization: my husband and I had just named our grand house.

13 MARCH 1909—ROSE RED

I hesitate to put down into words my thoughts on this day, for I am vexed indeed by what happened here this afternoon. As I write, police are still searching the house. Somehow, by putting this down here on paper, it seems I am giving it power. And I have no intention to do such a thing, for I fear this power (if it exists at all) is formidable indeed. But where else can I express myself? Certainly John will hear none of it, and though I love Sukeena as a sister, her limited English rarely allows exchanges that go beyond the ordinary mechanics of living or the functions of a woman's body.

I am now two months pregnant with child, and I have never been happier. John parades around the house as proud as a peacock, barking orders at the servants to take care of my every need. He stays home at night and reads to me in the Parlor (the site of our unfortunate incident to-day), all the while fretting over me and my every squirm. I have just now begun to show ever so slightly, and John comes to my rooms at night, lifts my nightgown up past my waist and gently rubs my stomach, sometimes with lotions, lays his head there and talks to the tiny child growing inside me. We have had relations quite often—he has never been more tender—and I feel closer to him now than at any point in our brief marriage.

My pregnancy—the news has spread quickly through society—was responsible for a teatime visit from my dear friend Melissa Ray and her friend, Connie Fauxmanteur. I am less personally acquainted with Mrs. Fauxmanteur, although well aware of her husband's lumber fortune and their sizable contributions to city charity. She is five or more years my senior, and as such I never knew her in school as I did Melissa, with whom I have enjoyed a steady and steadfast companionship.

We discussed John's and my year abroad, me carefully embellishing the journey to sound like the ideal honeymoon. There was also great discussion of children, both as infants and older, and the mood was quite elevated throughout the long afternoon.

The Parlor is a magnificent room, just to the left of the front door as one enters. Paneled in walnut, with carpets from the East, it houses a pipe organ I acquired in Germany during our European travels. It is home to landscapes of France, a portrait of John commissioned in England and various other minor treasures, such as a Chinese vase and a set of German marksman pistols. Although a poor cousin to our central Library, the Parlor nonetheless houses among the literature on its shelves five autographed works of Dickens and another half dozen autographed by Rudyard Kipling, a clever writer who has focused his works on India and is becoming quite popular both here and abroad. There is a leather-clad globe of the world, purchased in Oxford, England, in the far corner, guarding the door into the Central Hall West. Mrs. Fauxmanteur was regarding that globe when I last laid eyes on her. Melissa and I were engaged in some gossip at the time about rumors of Tina Coleman's brother's addiction to opium, and I only made a sideways glance in the direction of the visiting Mrs. Fauxmanteur. I felt an urgent need to warn her that Sukeena uses that very globe as a kind of prayer wheel and that she tells me this globe is since vested with extraordinary powers, including the ability to open a portal into the soul of Rose Red. (Sukeena claims the house is alive—that she can feel its presence—an opinion with which I have taken great issue and that has been the source of argument between us.) Sukeena also believes there are many such portals throughout the home and that one must be careful where one moves and to guard one's thoughts in certain locations or suffer the consequences—although she has never relayed what these consequences might be. All this is communi-

cated between us in such a clipped, uncertain way that I'm not even sure I have it right—although I do know, quite clearly, that Sukeena is afraid of Rose Red. Or perhaps cautious is a better word.

At any rate, dear Mrs. Fauxmanteur was in the corner, spinning the globe like a small child with her gloved hand. All at once, Melissa and I overheard the most astonishing language coming from her. She was mumbling as if in prayer, though not in any language I have ever heard (and over the course of this last year, I have heard many!). The globe spun faster and faster, and yet, at least from my angle, Mrs. Fauxmanteur was no longer assisting its motion.

"Connie?" Melissa inquired in a troubled voice.

"Mrs. Fauxmanteur?" I called out, knowing more about that globe than my dear friend Melissa Ray. "You really should not handle that globe."

And now, I swear to you, Dear Diary, did that woman's head turn all of its own accord—as if unattached from the body itself. It did rotate toward us, and that woman fixed her maniacal gaze on us with reddened eyes and twisted lips. But what most astonished us both was the ashen quality of her facial skin. Mrs. Fauxmanteur arrived under the burden of a great deal of rouge she did not need. And yet, as she turned to face us, none of this cosmetic remained. Her skin seemed nearly translucent, the blue veins showing like a tangle of knitting yarn, her lips bloodless and cracking like ice.

"Step away please, dear woman," I called out.

Connie Fauxmanteur did in fact step back and away from that globe. And as she did, the globe's rotation began to slow, and for the first time I noticed a noise, like a single high note of a children's choir, dissipating in volume. I had not noticed this music until it left the room. Mrs. Fauxmanteur left the room with it, stepping through to the Central Hall West (I believe). I thought perhaps she might be searching for the powder room, and so I called out to her that I would be happy to show her the way. At this point, Melissa, I suppose because of my pregnancy (everyone is making much too much of my condition!), rose herself and motioned for me to stay seated. Melissa did not appear in full possession of her senses, I must say, clearly taken aback by that translucent apparition of our dear friend. For a woman of such poise and grace, she did hurry to the door to the gallery through which Mrs. Fauxmanteur had just that moment passed.

I recall quite vividly that I smelled something bitter in the air, could almost taste it—carried as it was with the wind of that swinging door to the gallery. Whatever the source of that flavor, it did give me chills and rose the hackles on the nape of my neck. I had tasted that same air in the *Ocean Star* when the great wind entered our cabin. Despite the admonishment of my friend, I rose from my chair and followed upon Melissa's heels.

"Connie?" I heard Melissa call out.

A moment later, I too stood in the Central Hall West, alongside Melissa.

The magnificent room was empty of all but its oil paintings, cherry and maple benches and some marble sculpture from Rome. Mrs. Fauxmanteur had apparently run to the far end and left before Melissa had herself reached the gallery.

"Mrs. Fauxmanteur," I called out, "I would be pleased to show you the way." For she had it all wrong. The nearest toilet was through the Banquet Hall and off a small corridor that connected the Grand Stair. The far end of the Central Hall West connected again with the Entry Hall and would only serve to lead her in a circle. That is, unless by chance she had ventured upon one of the room's many false panels, one or two of which led to storage, and another that offered "secret" passage between the Central Hall West and the Kitchen, allowing servants more direct access during our entertaining. Now that I viewed the Central Hall West in this light—indeed the whole house is a veritable warren of such false passages—I realized what opportunity existed for a person to become briefly lost in its complexity.

"Connie!" This time Melissa's voice carried the concern that already beat in my own heart.

"You take the Entry Hall," I instructed my friend, pointing to a closed door at the end of the long gallery. At the same time, I stepped to the wall and pulled on the servants' cord, summoning whoever was on duty at this hour. I had my own eye on the door to the Banquet Hall, believing it the closest to the Parlor and therefore, given that little time had elapsed, the most likely explanation for Mrs. Fauxmanteur's quick disappearance.

As I pulled open the door to the Banquet Hall, I found myself face to face with Brian, our day butler, who had responded to my summons. But our timing was of such coincidence that I did jump back and let out a small scream, of no insignificance. This, in turn, set John and the rest of the house to motion. By the time I reached the Banquet Hall, and found it empty, several others had hurried to my assistance. Doors were thrown open, false panels too. It seemed that ten or more of us were immediately engaged in the search for our Mrs. Fauxmanteur. Yolanda and Fredrick hurried up the Grand Stair, believing they had heard someone up on the second floor.

The louder we called, the more our voices echoed. Mrs. Fauxmanteur was nowhere to be found. I felt rather faint at the prospect of her disappearance, and I stumbled toward a chair, Brian at my elbow. As I sank into its needlepoint and oak, the door to the Banquet Hall sagged open, and I could see through the Central Hall West and to the door of the Parlor.

There stood Sukeena, looking vexed and—dare I say it?—terrified. She stood by the globe, still slowly spinning. She wore the same red handkerchief over her head as a scarf, a long blue work dress with a white apron, her blue-black skin shining in the glow of the gas light. She shook her head at me, left to right. She was crying.

This house had claimed a soul, and Sukeena knew better than anyone that Connie Fauxmanteur was not coming back.

The police were much taken aback by the size of our home. Perhaps they had heard the rumors and were surprised to see it for themselves. (I hear tell it's called "the palace" and "the statehouse" by the people of Seattle.) In terms of the way "the other half lives," John and I are the "other half" and at least John makes no apologies for it. He was born to success, or so he says, believing success a matter of pocketbook, certainly not of character.

"What do you make of the disappearance?" I ask over the five-course lunch. (We invited the policemen, but they declined to join us. So we eat in the Banquet Hall—why John insisted on this I know not, since we usually dine in the Solarium or one of the smaller dining rooms at mid-day.) It is just us, and four servants in attendance (all white glove of course).

"I don't believe it for a minute," John Rimbauer replied.

"But, John—!"

"No, no, Ellen. You mustn't be taken in by it, you see? The Fauxmanteur woman simply chose us as her whipping boys, electing to stage her little getaway from our house instead of her own. It's simply a case of a wife deserting her husband and responsibilities—three children, can you imagine?!—and we are made to suffer for it. We are made to bear the brunt of her irresponsibility, and I for one am considering bringing charges against the woman when they catch her. And mark my word, they will catch her."

"No, they won't catch her, John. They won't even find her. And if they do, it shall be in this house, and by now I fear they shall find her dead."

"Good God, woman! Whatever's gotten into you?"

"Rose Red, dear husband. It's gotten into us all."

"The house? You don't subscribe to that garbage, do you? Dear soul, do not fret over this, do not risk your condition in any way. I am so angry at this Fauxmanteur woman, I cannot tell you! You are doing so well of late. Please, my dear Ellen, do not spend another minute thinking about it."

"I want this child most of all."

"Of course. As do I. Most of all."

"But I promise you, she never left this house." I added, "Do you remember the guests at the inaugural? The ones who said how quickly they'd become lost in Rose Red? What of that? What do you make of that?"

"You mean as it relates to Mrs. Fauxmanteur?"

"Yes, exactly."

"I see positively no connection between the two. Besides, dear woman, let us not forget all of our guests at the inaugural are accounted for."

"You're making light of it."

"I'm not."

"At my expense."

"Never. I assure you, it was not my intention."

"Guests complain of getting lost and then two months later, one does get lost. She disappears. Coincidence?"

"I hear it in your voice, dear. Do not trouble yourself over this. I tell you, it is simply that we've been made to look bad by a woman who chose us and our home for her ill-conceived plans. The child . . . please . . . do not trouble yourself."

"The child is fine."

"Yes . . . but before . . ."

"Before I was made seriously ill either by our social calendar or by exposure to an unfortunate malady." I left it at that. I might as well have taken out my bread knife and thrust it through him. I know not why I raised this issue again, so long after we'd both laid it to rest.

John cleaned his chin with his napkin and stood at his end of the long table. He dismissed the servants. I felt the heat of dread and regret. I had awakened the sleeping monster in him. His eyes burned with disfavor for me. We had never discussed this directly.

"At the age of eighteen I joined the Army and remained enlisted for six years. I took certain liberties that many young men of that age take, and I bear the punishment for those liberties even to-day. It is rarely with me, this curse, and I regret terribly my misspent youth. I can only hope that you can find it in your heart to forgive me my past sins, my dear. But I will not have my wife speaking to me in this manner. Not ever. And until you are prepared to apologize, you shall not see me. Not for meals, nor social engagements."

Though I believed little of his explanation, I apologized to him forthwith, before he could leave the room and make even more of this by requiring me to chase him down. I explained that my visitor's disappearance had greatly upset me and that I had misspoken just now. The police wandering the house did nothing to make me feel at ease.

"Then I shall drive them out," John said.

"No, dear."

"Of course I shall. Whatever is necessary to your continued good health!"

As I had ascertained back in Africa: the heir meant more to John than anything in this life.

He stormed out of the Banquet Hall shouting commands at servants, police and anyone who happened to be in his way. (The house is busy with workers day in and day out as the construction continues unabated. No one of society can quite believe that the Rimbauer Mansion, as it's also known outside these walls, is in a constant and continuing state of construction.) Within ten minutes or so, John had used his considerable presence, as well as his keen sense of negotiation, to arrange for all but two police to leave Rose Red. These two remained in the hunt for Mrs. Fauxmanteur, though I must confess I had already given up hope. (Not that I believed John's explanation for even a minute! The problem being that neither John nor I would likely understand the other's position—thus is the scourge of marriage, there are those points that will never be resolved because opposite opinions cannot resolve themselves; they can either be overlooked entirely or tolerated, occasionally respected, though if true opposites, even this middle ground is unlikely.)

I telephoned Tina Coleman to consult her on the disappearance and embarrassed myself by breaking into tears in the middle of our brief discussion. Tina advised me to consult a "seer" in hopes of locating Mrs. Fauxmanteur in places that the police were unlikely to find her. This only served to further upset me, and I ended the call as quickly as possible, somewhat concerned the woman at the exchange may have been listening in, a practice that is rampant these days. Our family was always well off, but John Rimbauer can only be said to be wealthy, and as his bride I have experienced firsthand the loss of privacy that accompanies the life of the rich. It seems someone is always watching, always listening, whether a servant, a maid, a driver or the public. People point at John and me as we leave the motorcar for a dinner or to attend a performance. They whisper, not bothering to even disguise their alarm at having seen us. We live under a magnifying glass, day in and day out, and I find the overall effect of this close inspection exhausting. John, who has lived with it for so many years now, seems either not to notice it or not to care. He conducts himself the same way, in public or not—a bit brash yet charming, smooth yet easily agitated, a man who takes control of any situation the moment he enters it, even parties thrown by our closest friends! It is the consistency in him that I believe makes him such a formidable businessman. This sense of power he bestows that both men and women find attractive, even seductive, though for different reasons. John Rimbauer entertains as he frightens. None would dare cross him; few dare challenge him.

And so it is that he must find marriage to me a considerably vexing proposition.

Tina suggested I consult a medium.

As I hung up from that call, the police collecting outside and finally dispersing some of the press, I came to consider her suggestion more thoughtfully. If a medium was what was required, then what was holding me back?

Dare I confess this? (I think I shall order Sukeena to destroy you, Dear Diary, if I should pass at childbirth, or in any way for that matter, for the secrets I confide here should never reach another's eyes.) I lied to my husband to-day—for what was, I believe, the very first time. (There have been little white lies, of course—telling him I don't mind his coming home late; pretending to enjoy a bedroom encounter when in fact it repulsed me; defending some action of his to his face when behind his back I believe he handled it incorrectly—but never a lie of this magnitude!)

This afternoon I told him that Tina Coleman was taking me shopping for the nursery. Sukeena was to accompany me and we were to return home well after tea, as we planned to take tea at the hotel, or possibly even at the bank with my father. John bid me farewell barely taking notice of my mention, consumed as he was with problems concerning the construction. I have begged to add a central tower onto Rose Red. John has denied me. I will get my way someday. (It is to hold an exquisite stained-glass window I ordered from an artisan while in London. We received a cable earlier this week that the window was put on a ship bound for New York and is therefore on its way. Now, to convince John!)

There was no shopping planned, of course. No nursery in my mind. The truth was that my dearest Tina had arranged for me to meet Madame Lu—a Chinese woman who is said to possess extraordinary conjuring powers. And oh, what a day!

Tina sent her carriage at half past one, insisting we accept this offer as her driver knew the way into the underbelly of the city where we might find Madame Lu. Just the thought of this journey gave me gooseflesh! One hears stories about the China district—the use of opium is said to be rampant, the young women available for pennies, disease and poverty everywhere for those the railroads left behind once the laying of railroad track reached the ocean. The Chinese ended up here in Seattle, tens of thousands of them, without work and desperate. I am well aware that some of our husbands "gambled" here—that perhaps part of that gambling was with their pants down—and that still others took opium, or young boys. But I was completely unaware of any Caucasian women venturing into the China district, much less the likes of Tina Coleman, one of the most respected women in the community.

Sure enough, the carriage picked up Sukeena and me, returned to the Coleman residence where we refreshed ourselves, and then the four of us (Tina brought along her maid, Gwen, a Swedish girl of astonishing beauty) returned to the carriage and set out south of the city.

The dirt road went quickly to a thick mud as we left the familiar part of town, the stone buildings of center city giving way to wooden shacks crowded together, mud, crates and trash in evidence. Narrow, dark lanes of mud ran between these shacks, small children, half naked even in the cold rain, running side by side engaged in games with balls and sticks, their small yellow bodies so thin from hunger. Plumes of wood smoke rose from metal stovepipes and cooking fires open to the air, sheltered from the rain by tarpaulins or woven bamboo. It is a world only minutes from my own and yet one I have never known existed except in places like Egypt and the Indias where John and I have traveled.

My heart was in my throat by the time the carriage arrived at a two-story wooden building deep in the heart of the China district. I expected at any moment for a Chinaman to leap out of the shadows wielding a double-edged knife with a sinister curved blade. (I've read of such people in Kipling.) I expected our purses to be robbed, or worse, the one crime any woman dreads above all others: violation. But to my surprise, no such deed presented itself. Instead, the driver helped us down to a boardwalk, which we crossed, and we entered the building in question.

The air smelled of sandalwood incense, a fragrance I recognized immediately from our year abroad. This first room was dark, lit by candle, not gas, as the gas lines do not run this far south. It was not a particularly sturdy structure; the wind found its way through cracks, moving the small candle flames and throwing shifting shadows across the walls. An eerie and disconcerting environment. Sukeena pulled lightly on my elbow and shook her blue-black face back and forth indicating her disapproval. I trust Sukeena so much in these matters—she has a prescience for anticipating the unexpected. She sensed something wrong here—terribly wrong—and even I could feel this along with her: a dark, foreboding presence. Sinister and unforgiving.

"Are you sure?" I asked Tina.

"A bit dramatic, isn't it?" she said. "I tell you, Ellen, Madame Lu is nothing like this room, this building. I think it to be a matter of commerce. The Chinese, who make up a majority of her clientele, expect ambience, and she gives them what they pay for. They expect something other-worldly, and Madame Lu is only too happy to oblige. I tell you, friend, she is nothing like this. You will find her to be noble, infinitely patient and accommodating. Gwen was most troubled, the first time I brought her." The pale young beauty nodded her agreement. I considered the stark contrast between her and my Sukeena—one so pale and translucent, one so dark and opaque. And I wondered, had this lovely girl's hiring been Tina's idea, or that of her husband? Many a housemaid in this city had bastard children to show for their service. "But now she is as comfortable as I, for she too has met the incomparable madame and knows there is nothing to worry about. Remember, dear soul, that these seers are often as much show as they are reality. Madame Lu is no phony, I'm happy to report. But she must compete with those who are, and that competition requires her to invest in the show along with the best of them."

I heard her words but was not entirely convinced. (Sukeena, I knew, doubted this woman's powers from the start.) This room emanated a heaviness, like danger, whether the result of incense clouding my breath or the shifting shadows accounting for a certain sense of dizziness. Whatever the case, I moved my feet forward with caution along with a great deal of excitement, I do confess. This was not "the place" for a woman, and just the fact that I was here filled me with a degree of thrill impossible to fully explain in these pages. (There was quiet talk among the women of my class that a woman's "time" was coming. I think now, here in this place, for the first time I fully understood that certain boundaries were soon to be crossed. In fact, I felt something like a pioneer just coming here.)

We ventured up a flight of complaining stairs, ensconced in a narrow tunnel of wood, completely unlighted, to a stark reception room where the formidable Madame Lu occupied a wicker chair as fully as a hand occupies a glove. She was easily the size of three or four women, an enormous edifice of flesh and silk with two ebony hairpins containing a curtain of rich black hair that might have reached the floor unbridled. She had a series of chins that cascaded down to the upper seam of the red silk gown, and pudgy hands that appeared bloated and inflexible. Her voice was that of a man's, deep, resonant and filled with fluid. Her words bubbled from her throat.

"Please, sit." She indicated the floor, covered only by a woven mat.

I glanced at Tina, my astonishment clearly showing. She simply smiled back at me, folded her legs and slowly lowered herself, with the help of her maid. (Now I understood her insistence that I bring Sukeena along!) Sukeena helped me to the floor—honestly, I do not believe I have sat upon a floor since a toddler!—and

then our two maids stepped to the side and stood alongside two of Madame Lu's keepers, thin young women who were not yet fully developed.

"You welcome here again, Miss Tina. You bring friend."

"It is for my friend that I come, Great Lady."

"Indeed."

Those beady black eyes surveyed me and I felt a heat pulse through me as if she had reached into me with her fat hot hands.

I felt her robbing my secrets, as if she had opened these pages and had begun to read.

Madame Lu commands a formidable presence. As the smell of incense made me light-headed and, indeed, feeling somewhat under her "spell," she opened an old tin box from which she removed a great handful of ivory white bones, all of them small and glistening with the shine of having been handled a thousand times. "What question you ask?" she inquired of me, in a voice deep enough to be my husband's.

"How many questions am I allowed?"

The big woman rolled her eyes and clearly consulted my dear friend Tina with an insolent glance. Tina leaned over and whispered that as a matter of etiquette, the Chinese will not directly discuss business arrangements, and that Madame Lu charged for each reading. I could ask as many questions as I wished, as long as I understood each reading would cost me an additional fifty cents. I considered it a usurious amount of money, but agreed nonetheless. "Very well," I said to the Great Lady. I collected myself, feeling somewhat indignant about my sitting on a mat on a floor, and said something like, "Is Mrs. Fauxmanteur alive? Unharmed?"

Madame Lu considered me for a long moment, steadied a black enamel table in front of her and dropped the handful of bones there. They sounded more like stones. She regarded the unruly pile in the unflinching fashion of a dog inspecting the unknown: a slight cocking of the head left to right. She nodded, hummed to herself and dug through the small pile of artifacts. Her voice resonated as she spoke. "Many forms to life. Yes? This lady's spirit lives. I deal in spirit. Yes? Her body? Maybe not live as you think of living."

I shuddered. Alive, but not alive? Were such things possible?

To my Christian upbringing this reeked of paganism and sinful talk—but I had crossed over long ago in my prayers. Only now was the world around me catching up.

The big woman collected the bones in a greedy hand and deposited them back into her tin box, one eye cautiously on me, expecting another question. I awaited her.

"Something else?" she wondered.

I glanced over at Tina, not wanting her to hear my question concerning Rose Red. Could I trust her? I decided I must. "Is our home, our house, Rose Red, possessed of spirits?"

The question won Tina's attention. She stared at me, but I would not look over at her.

The ritual repeated itself. Her puffy, fat fingers reached into the dull gray box and deposited a grip of bones to the shiny enamel tabletop. Again, her index finger prodded through the pile, mining it for information. Sukeena let me know with a sigh that she clearly put no faith in our hostess.

Madame Lu said, "You are not alone in this house."

"Spirits?" I gasped, suddenly very cold and shaken. Perhaps I did not want the truth. Perhaps I was not ready for it.

"A presence," Madame Lu answered. "This much I can tell you."

I did not wish to hear anything more. A presence. Why did her confirmation carry so much significance with me? Why did I feel so afraid and chilled to the bone? Worse, Sukeena was nodding her agreement. A presence.

I wanted out of there. I wanted home. That is, until I realized that home was Rose Red.

I pray with all my heart that someone is playing a practical joke on John and me, as this is the day for such tomfoolery, but the woman in me knows better, for we have seen this before, have we not, Dear Diary? I feel nearly mad, delirious with worry.

Another woman has disappeared without a trace.

This time it is a maid by the name of Laura, a dear waif of a woman, quite fetching in appearance, who works in our chambers changing linens, housecleaning and seeing to the cleanliness of our toilets and baths. A colored woman, light-skinned and so radiant, she was one of Sukeena's closer acquaintances on the staff, rather a younger sister to my African queen.

When the "Regent"—a fellow named Thomas—informed John, I thought my husband might faint, an unlikely event for such a man as strong as he. "It's Laura, sir," Thomas told John as the two of us were just sitting down to tea. (Don't think I didn't take notice of the similarity in the time of day!)

"Laura?" John sputtered.

"Our chambermaid," I gasped.

Believing I intended this for him, John snapped at me, "I know who Laura is, Ellen. Hush!"

I felt like slapping him, I was so humiliated. Of course, he knows who Laura is; John has had the last say in the hiring of all the servants, and despite his claim that this domestic charge is my responsibility, it most decidedly is not.

He bit his lip and chewed, thoughtfully immersed in some devilish consideration (of this, I have little doubt given my impression of his expression). It was then, for the first time, that I gave myself open to the possibility that this curse that afflicts us might in some way be John's doing, not mine at all. Perhaps it is John's prayers, not mine, that have reached the beyond. Perhaps, all this time I have prayed to the other side, it has actually been my husband's voice that has been heard. And if so, then to what end was he praying? Certainly he could mean me no harm, not before the birth—the possibility of an heir! Then what? I wondered. And still, I have no answer, though evidence presents itself to support my theory, for this disappearance has vexed my husband greatly, far beyond the vanishing of Mrs. Fauxmanteur.

Upon the news of the disappearance, John and the Regent gathered all thirty-three servants (Laura being the thirty-fourth!) in the Grand Ballroom. A hush fell over all, because word travels quickly in this house, believe me. (There is no privacy left to my life—all is known.) The Regent and Sukeena, as John's and my personal representatives, stood forefront to the rows of attendants. John addressed all in a forceful, dare I say, frightened, tenor.

"I must inquire as to the whereabouts of our own Laura Hirtson, master's chambermaid, in service to Mrs. Watson. Anyone with information about Miss Hirtson, please step forward now."

Thomas is a big man possessing a commanding presence, and with a voice that can carry through walls. Some of the girls were already crying, though doing their best not to show it. To my surprise, a man of eighteen or so, who goes by the name Rodney, stepped forward from his line and replied meekly.

"Sir, if I may . . ."

"Rodney?"

The extent of John's memory never ceases to amaze me. I do believe he could recall each of the servants by name, perhaps even recall their backgrounds, if required to do so. I know many, but not all.

"I saw Laura late this morning in the Solarium. I am not certain, but I believe she was headed out toward the Carriage House."

John pursed his lips, looked directly at Daniel, the master of the Carriage House, and the two exchanged a powerful look. I felt for a moment as if a wind swept through the room. "Is that so?" John paused. "Daniel?"

"I never laid eyes on her, sir, and I haven't left the Carriage House all morning until this meeting here just now."

Daniel and John go back years, Daniel having cared for John's horseflesh for nearly two decades. I knew, having no need to ask, that John trusted Daniel's opinion absolutely.

"The Solarium," John repeated to Rodney.

"Yes, sir. And if I may say so, sir, her being there . . . she seemed a bit . . . suspicious, like. Surprised to see me, you might say. Went about an explanation right off the mark, as if I'd asked. And I hadn't! But that's Laura, isn't it? Likes to wag her jaw, that one."

A few of the men nearby Rodney chuckled over the man's deliberate delivery. John saw no reason for levity and squared his shoulders, sobering the entire staff.

"Anyone else?"

No one stepped forward.

I raised my voice from the side. "It's rather important, to say the least. Please, if any of you at all has seen her." I caught an expression in Linda's face—Linda, who is assistant to Mrs. Danby, and one of Laura's dorm mates. I believe the two close, though I have little to support that belief. Her eyes widened. I thought I saw her hand lift, if not imperceptibly.

"Linda?" I asked.

"Yes, ma'am?" A tension in her voice.

"Were you to say something?"

A quick glance toward me and then John. "No, ma'am."

"Just now, I thought—"

"No, ma'am."

John put me back to silence with one scalding look. This was his summons of the staff, not my own. He divided up the group and instructed them where to search. By his calculation, the thirty-three staff could coordinate to conduct a thorough search of premises—every closet, armoire, storage room, steamer trunk—within an hour to an hour and a half. Two hours at most. (It was there and then, seeing this army assembled before us, and realizing this search would still account for a considerable amount of time, that I came to grasp the enormity of this house that was still under construction—a house that even I, the matron, had lost track of. By way of example, there is a new wing of the third floor open, completed and decorated over three weeks ago now, that I have yet to see for the first time.)

As the staff was dismissed and the search began, my dear John showing a color of pale I had never witnessed, I endeavored to locate Sukeena and to request she in turn find Linda and bring her to me in my chambers.

"But the search, ma'am," Sukeena said in her Kenyan singsong, her eyes wide with apprehension. She sounds British at times. "Mister John."

"Never mind John," I instructed. "I wish to talk with Linda immediately."

"Very well, ma'am," Sukeena replied, her determination to follow my request apparent. One of Sukeena's many wonderful attributes is her ability to remain calm and consistent. Regardless of generation, Africans are quite gifted in this regard, able to leave the past behind—an argument, disagreement or other difficulty—without the slightest timidity, as if it had never occurred. (Despite Mr. Lincoln's intentions, and that awful Civil War through which our parents lived, and many fought, I do not believe the slaves—nearly all of them African by descent—have been provided the opportunity to advance socially as once claimed. Indeed, I believe that history will record Mr. Lincoln's attitudes a result of political pressures rather than philanthropic intention. The freemen seem rarely better off, often unemployed, forbidden to buy land and disassociated with regions where they lived for generations. There is private talk among the women of this city who speak of suffrage that the Negro has as much, if not more, claim to fight for personal freedoms than does the American woman!) As to the moment, Sukeena hurried off, and it wasn't ten minutes before I retired to my chambers in the West Wing to discover both Sukeena and Linda there waiting. As I requested a tremulous Linda to sit, Sukeena retreated toward the door—she never presumes, another of her lovely qualities—and I bid her to remain with us. I then took a chair in front of dear Linda, clasped my cold hands in her own and we spoke.

"Dear girl, what was it you wished to say to me just now?"

"Nothing, ma'am."

"Now, now, dear child, we both know you nearly spoke up. I saw it in your eyes. If you know something about Laura's whereabouts . . . I cannot tell you how important this is. A matter of life and death, perhaps. We cannot forget our dear Mrs. Fauxmanteur's ill fate, now can we?"

The frightened thing looked first to Sukeena, then to me, and her eyes teared.

"Go ahead, child. No harm will come to you."

"I . . . it . . . it is as Rodney said."

"The Solarium."

She nodded, lip quivering, head lowered.

"It's all right, child."

"No, ma'am," she whispered.

I looked to Sukeena and her infinite patience and understanding. Sukeena studied the child for several long seconds and she said, "You saw Miss Laura in the Solarium?"

Linda shook her head "no."

"Leaving the house," Sukeena said. I knew from much discussion that Sukeena believed Mrs. Fauxmanteur had never left the house, as police had speculated and continued to believe.

Linda nodded faintly.

Sukeena asked, "How she dressed?"

The girl looked up with wet, saddened eyes.

I said, "A wrap? Was she prepared for the outside?" It has been cold of late, ocean storms from the north. Not terribly unusual for this time of year.

The girl shook her head.

Sukeena said, "The Carriage House."

I felt a shiver, recalling my husband's questioning of Daniel and the fraternity of these two men. What were they hiding?

Linda's eyes widened. She bit down on her lips and sprang from the chair, removing herself so quickly from my rooms that one could imagine she had never been sitting there before us.

"Oh, my," I stuttered.

"This have to do with him, ma'am."

"Daniel?" I asked, though in fact I knew to whom she did refer.

"No, ma'am," Sukeena said, her black eyes boring into me. "Him," she repeated.

Rose Red was indeed thoroughly searched, top to bottom. Cellar to attic. Wing to wing. Floorboard to chimney. I felt a desperation in John with each further attempt. He took a keen interest in Laura's disappearance, more so, I must say, than with that of our dear Mrs. Fauxmanteur. Perhaps it is the repetition of the event that so vexes him. (I prefer this possibility to the other, more likely consideration that now occupies my every thought!) He became personally possessed with finding this girl, requesting the Regent to reassign the staff to different locations and conduct the search again. At the same time, he put his hunting dogs into the woods behind the manor, in search of this girl's scent—a piece of underclothing was delivered from the dorms. We are now some six hours into searching, and still no sign of our sweet Laura.

What troubles me most is John's decision, only moments ago, to not inform the police. With bloodshot eyes, gray skin and an eerie, calm stillness to his voice, my husband said, "Servants run away all the time."

"Not from this house, they don't," I said. "We've never had one leave. You pay the best in the city, John."

"There's always a first."

"But what of her possessions? Her clothing? Nothing was taken. Nothing so much as disturbed! Who leaves in this manner?"

"It could involve some young boy on the staff, dear woman. Some heartbreak. You know how children are."

"Laura was no child, John. She is barely three years my junior."

"A young man. Romance. A broken heart, I'll gamble."

"But not to involve the police?"

"There is our standing to consider, my dear. Our position in society. The police, twice in the same year? Do you think we would survive such a scandal?"

"If we talk of survival, John, should it not be Laura's whereabouts that concern us, rather than the vile tongues of this town? I can control the tongues. They will not wag to our disfavor."

"How can you be so sure? Already there is the difference in our age. You know quite well that people talk of this—they give us little chance of enjoying our years together."

"We have endured much in our first year." I let my words hang in the air where he could taste them. "We shall prevail, even if Laura is never found."

"Don't say such a thing!" he said, looking nearly dead himself.

"John?"

"What is it about this house?"

"It has nothing to do with this house. Coincidence is all," I said. Secretly, I did not believe a word of my own explanation. I believed either my husband responsible or that the two disappearances were somehow related to the child I carried in my womb. Fear kept me from examining my husband's possible role, so I focused on the latter possibility. Sacrifices. My prayers to the dark side were being answered, but I had yet to understand the language being spoken. Privately, I wondered if another visit to Madame Lu was in order. Or, conversely, had my recent visit with the Great Lady been heard? One thing is for certain, prayer is a powerful weapon, and when wishing one's husband ill will, one must be terribly careful.

"Coincidence?" he scoffed. Spittle flew from his lips as he hollered at me, "She was right here, and now she is gone."

I have never felt so calm. I spoke with reserve. "Right where, John? Did you see her yourself to-day?"

My words flustered him. "What!?" he barked, sounding like one of his hounds. "What kind of accusation is that?"

"I accuse you of nothing. Observation is all. I asked merely if you had seen the poor woman yourself?"

"And if I had?" he roared.

"A question is all."

"And you, so calm, so collected. What of you, Ellen? Did you not see Laura to-day?" His large head jerked left to right, and I thought it might sever from his body. "She is employed in this very wing. Our chambers. She is practically underfoot, this woman. At our call, day and night. She serves us both, equally."

Oh, Dear Diary, the look in his eyes! The terror this man felt. The guilt. A woman knows. A wife, better than anyone. "At our call, day and night." I, for one, have not once called Laura to my rooms in the night. Sukeena, of course—more times than I can count. But little Laura? I barely knew she existed, except to note her unusual beauty. The translucent skin. The noble nose. I realize now that my husband did not overlook this beauty either, and I made a point of it.

"A fetching girl, wasn't she, John?"

"You speak of her in the past?"

"I speak of her looks. So innocent. So young and . . . fetching." I said, "Or maybe not so innocent. Looks can be deceiving."

I saw pure panic in my husband's eyes. There, it was done. *We both knew.*

Perhaps I will have an "accident." Perhaps I shall call upon Sukeena to mix her herbs for me and dislodge the future heir from where it lies curled inside me. This is the only true punishment I can conceive for him. Accident that it may be, Laura's disappearance is not entirely innocent. I will not ask Sukeena if she knows what happened to the girl if she, Sukeena, is protecting me. Perhaps Laura did leave Rose Red of her own accord. Perhaps Sukeena intervened and sent the girl packing without so much as a visit to her dormitory to retrieve her belongings. Increasingly, I am convinced that my dear handmaid has powers far beyond insight and herbs. She is prescient and clairvoyant and somehow divines the thoughts of others. I do not ask, because I do not wish to know. If innocent Laura was not so innocent, then her departure in any form is welcome. I have said so in my prayers before. "Curse the woman who takes my husband for her own." I shall repeat it again to-night as I retire, as I do each and every night. If Sukeena has perhaps overheard this prayer, through her substantial powers or a slip of my own tongue, if she is controlling my destiny in some manner—protecting me—then who am I to complain? Who am I to inquire? Laura has left us. The police are not to know. Many a latch will be locked in this house to-night.

Many a question remains.

I write with weak hand, but I will not be denied the opportunity of recording the most important day in my brief life. Eleven hours ago, in the wee hours of the morning, I gave birth to a son. I have called him Adam, for he is the first. I am told by the women who attended me that it was "an easy birth." Three hours of labor and a swift delivery. But if that was easy, I never hope to experience otherwise! I have never felt such pain, have never experienced that part of my body that is only a woman's in such a way that I did not know myself at all. Muscles and cramps and contractions, in and out of consciousness, screams of pain, cries of joy, and then that damp, pink creature laid atop my bosom and already moving for my breast, some primeval instinct overcoming him before the cord was even cut from our connection. He now lies swaddled in the finest linens in a bassinet alongside my bed, his small blue eyes closed in peaceful sleep, his tiny hands clenched tightly, as if deep in thought. Oh, what a treasure! What joy! I'm told Rose Red is abuzz with joy, that all the servants are smiling and the master has been heard singing from his rooms and has twice ordered champagne to his chambers. A son! When Adam had been delivered, his father kissed me as tenderly as I can ever remember. He thanked me with tears flowing from his eyes and promised me—us—a life of joy and prosperity, and that as a family—"a family!" he roared—we should never know pain, loss or sadness. (He must have been drunk, even then, but his little speech brought me to tears just the same.)

Sukeena acted as midwife, sat by my side through the long night of "warnings" as she called the early cramping, the early morning hours of severe pain, and it was into her sure hands that I pushed for the last time and felt that relief that is only a child-bearing woman's. My nine long months were done. For this alone I would have celebrated.

Now I contend with milk bubbling from my breasts, a discharge from between my legs that Sukeena assures me is normal and an abundance of unnatural amounts of skin where my stomach should be. I am not hungry, and yet I am starved. I drink the coldest water they can bring me, and in amounts I would not have thought possible. I sleep for hours at a time, I'm told, and yet it feels like only minutes. All this is so new. So much a miracle. I look down at his peaceful face and marvel that he was inside me, without air, less than a day earlier. This little boy, this breathing creature. This Rimbauer.

I heard music from the general direction of the servants' quarters, and Sukeena tells me there is much celebration—food and dancing—in that part of the house. John has provided the staff spirits and wine. There is much revelry on my account. (I fear Rose Red will barely operate to-morrow, given the condition of our staff to-night, but no matter.) Word has spread quickly around society. Tina Coleman's coach delivered a card requesting a visit, and I fear I shall be much besieged with such inquiries. I have asked Sukeena to prepare a bath, and for my girls to assist me in washing my hair, but she tells me it is too soon. A sponge bath is all she will allow me until my recovery is better contained. My hair may be washed, though in a bowl. In the morning, we shall make the most of me we can.

Little Adam is so precious. When he drinks of me, I feel so good, so bursting with happiness, that I want to laugh for no reason at all. His hunger comes as great relief as my bosom nearly bursts at times with mother's milk. Already we have found a rhythm of sleep and feeding and sleep again. He has not relieved himself, and Sukeena waits for this event as anxiously as I did my delivery. I don't believe she has slept in the last two days, always by my side when I wake, always holding my hand as I slip back off to sleep. What a dear friend she has become. How did I ever exist without her as a sister? Those hands of hers, inside me, ensuring a proper delivery. So gentle, so kind. So careful and understanding of my pain. Some day perhaps I shall dare to ask for the details, but not now. Now, I drift in and out of sleep, Adam at my breast, in the bassinet, at my breast. Sukeena's blue-black face glowing in the gas flame. I see love in her eyes. I feel her love. I see hope and goodness. I shall remember this day forever—the passing of life from life, generation to generation. My husband is back in the hall outside my rooms. He is shouting, "I have a son! I have a son!" There is joy in this house at last. I only can hope and pray that it will last.

23 SEPTEMBER 1909—ROSE RED

Good God in Heaven, I fear this house has a mind of its own.

For the past two weeks I have strolled with Adam and Sukeena down the long halls of this grand house, just today revisiting the East Wing, an area I feel I have scarcely seen before. Here is located the Grand Ballroom, last used during the inaugural but kept wonderfully fresh and white-glove clean by our dedicated staff. I can still see the dancing, hear the orchestra (thankfully, I cannot smell the liquor, for since Adam's birth my senses are severely heightened—I can hear at great distances and detect my husband's cigar from opposite ends of this enormous Rose Red), recall the dashing band leader, and I am able to envision the women's gowns in all their glory. While Sukeena held Adam I strolled the great room, reliving that wonderful party and beginning to anticipate the second of its kind, now only a few months off. Full preparations will begin in just a week or two, as I will organize the staff and we will begin to conceive decorations, entertainment, cuisine, invitations and all the details that must be attended to prior to this January the fifteenth. This was, in fact, the basis for my visit today: to get a feel for the room again, the walnut-paneled walls of the hallway leading to the Ballroom, the grand oil paintings—portraits and landscapes—that John and I purchased in Paris and London while on honeymoon. I would like fresh-cut flowers in the Mediterranean urns, and this will require our gardeners to work months ahead, as the only flowers available will be forced bulbs, and I shall want them in quantities of many hundreds. (This climate seems especially favorable to bulbs, and I can foresee the day when farmers raise great quantities of them. I have already encouraged John to buy and clear land north of the city for this purpose, and he is considering working a deal with the lumber barons to take over the ground they clear-cut, as this ground is virtually worthless to them once the trees have been taken.)

After walking this wonderful room several times and explaining aloud to Adam where I envisioned the drinks, the seating and the entertainment, Sukeena and I (and Adam, in Sukeena's arms) left the great room and reentered the impressive hall of the East Wing.

That I fainted and Sukeena screamed is the only reason Adam remains unhurt, for if I had been holding him he would have fallen with me.

There at the end of the hall, just prior to the top of the staircase, stood lovely Laura, our missing housemaid. Missing these many months! Her blouse hung open, partially exposing her bare breasts and dark skin. Her skirt was missing altogether, her ruffled underclothes untied and hanging open at the junction of her legs, her womanhood exposed, as I imagine some street whore presenting herself. She looked so terribly saddened—a woman recently ravaged—her hair tousled and her skin blotchy. I did not hear her voice, but I saw her lips move and understood clearly her words, nonetheless. "My skirt," she said, looking at me and then down at herself and making the motions as if tying it back around herself. So pathetic. So ghastly!

It was then I lost consciousness and fell to the floor. Then that Sukeena screamed—less from fear than it was calling for someone to help me. By the time I regained my strength, Laura was gone. Lost to this house—or taken by it—as she had been before.

Leaving young Adam with a chambermaid behind locked doors, I ventured outside of Rose Red this evening for the first time since the birth. John had gone off on "business," which meant downtown, either to a poker game, to a business dinner or to places I had no desire to think about. With Sukeena at my side, we struck out for adventure, following a train of logic so easily seen: if

Laura had indeed been spotted in the Carriage House, and if she was now missing her skirt, then what were the chances Sukeena and I might find this piece of evidence and help the poor creature? Perhaps it was that skirt, and that skirt only, that kept her locked in the netherworld in which we had witnessed her. (For I swear it was so: that woman at the end of the hall was a ghost, not any kind of flesh and blood. Do not ask me how this is possible, for I know not. But it is with absolute certainty that I write this!)

I must confess to feeling a bit like a teenager, my heart in my throat, as Sukeena and I elected to flee unseen from the West Wing via the narrow servants' staircase that deposited on the ground floor between the Parlor and the Central Hall West. From there, with Sukeena as lookout, we crossed to the Gun Room, out to the exterior hall, between the Tapestry Gallery and the structural south wall, and down a long, stone corridor and through a door to the spiral stairs that access the west end of the West Wing, off John's chambers. (I swear he uses this hidden stairwell to enter and leave the house without my knowledge.) We passed through the Bowling Alley to the swimming pool, and around the pool to the east doors that face Rose Red's rear gardens. Sukeena is capable of moving without any sound. My African queen seems to float above the stone, move fluidly around corners and remain unseen, almost invisible. Upon reaching the garden, we both stopped to catch our breaths (me, far more than her) and waited for our eyes to adjust to the darkness. Oh my, but my chest hurt with the tension! Our ears clouded with the sound of the fountain, only a matter of yards away—directly between us and the Carriage House—we remained in shadow along the wall of the Pool House, well off the perfectly laid stone paths, electing a circuitous route through the plants, shrubs and flowers.

"I'll have at it later!" came a male voice I did not recognize. One of the Carriage House staff, no doubt, preparing either to leave the property for a beer or to retire to one of the dormitories we provide.

Sukeena and I had chosen our timing carefully, as the Carriage House staff is usually dismissed and done for the day an hour or so after the return of the last horse or team. John having taken the motorcar to his "business," it followed that the Carriage House would be quiet for the night (although John does park the motorcar in a modified stall in the Carriage House and would be returning at a later hour). I assumed that Daniel, as head of the Carriage House, would make himself available upon my husband's return, but Sukeena had it on good report that Daniel had a game of dice planned at this same hour, said to be under way in the skeet room of the basement—a room designed to launch the clay pigeons for skeet shooting from the Loggia on the north side of the ground floor, just off the Billiard Room. If true, Daniel would be hard pressed to find himself any farther away from the Carriage House and still be on the property. That said, I thought it in the man's nature to have a young scout placed somewhere about, keeping an eye out for the master's premature return. Probably a son of one of his workers—someone paid by a piece of sausage or a few coins for his time. It was this scout that Sukeena and I sought to avoid.

We settled in the shadow of a well-kept rhododendron on the northwest corner of the garden, only a piece of the rose garden between the fountain and our hiding spot. Directly across from us was the dark, looming structure of the Carriage House, now all but quiet, given its four-legged residents. (The pool, the west wall of the house, and the Carriage House combine to form an enormous courtyard, the only escape from the west where we were now firmly entrenched.) We waited for what felt like an eternity, my muscles complaining from the childbirth I had performed, Sukeena as still as a black rock. When we ascertained that all human voice was gone from the place, we sneaked ahead and rushed across a small clearing of mowed grass, making for the Carriage House's west entrance—its only entrance entirely screened from the rest of the house. If we were to confront anyone, it would be someone inside the Carriage House. (I had several rather clever excuses for the two of us showing up at the Carriage House unannounced like this, and even one or two that might help cover that fact so my husband would not find out. As it turned out, we didn't need them. At least not right away . . .)

Sukeena led the way across the short open space and into the shadow of the Carriage House. I tell you, my heart felt ready to burst as I ducked and hurried through the garden and out across the short expanse of crushed stone driveway that accessed the Carriage House. We pressed our trembling bodies up to the building's cool wall and tried to catch our breath. I glanced at Sukeena and nearly burst out laughing, I was so nervous. She remained stoic and impassive—hard to read. I don't know if she enjoyed it half as much as I. Perhaps she feared losing her job—and it was only then I saw the difficult position I had put her in. She would not refuse me—not ever, I'm sure of it—and I had placed her in the awkward position of leading me into the mouth of the lion. (It is not that I am forbidden to visit the Carriage House, but to search it for a woman's missing garment is another matter entirely!)

After a moment of collecting our courage, together Sukeena and I calmly turned and entered through the massive open doors at the west end of the Carriage House, as if we had not a care in the world. The doors had been left open, presumably to allow for the return of John's motorcar later this same night. It afforded us easy access as we stepped onto the wide redwood planks, a dusting of straw beneath our feet, the gorgeous Carriage House flooded in dim electric light, not a soul in sight. I have always loved the smell of horses, and entering the Carriage House brought me back to my childhood. The stall doors are made of wrought iron and carved redwood and operate nearly soundlessly. (Daniel is the finest stable master in the state, by some accounts.) It is a two-story barn, the bottom occupied by horse stalls, room for several carriages, a tack room and a saddle room and Daniel's office. The upstairs loft is primarily for straw and hay storage, though several large rooms were constructed here for cold storage as well. I assumed most of these to be empty, as we had occupied Rose Red for less than a year, and these rooms were intended for "overflow" storage. (Mind you, I can't imagine ever running out of basement storage in Rose Red—it's the size of a school playing field.)

Sukeena and I stopped many times, trying to discern the sounds and to separate man from animal. Thankfully, we heard no one, and so continued into the depths of this large barn. I will admit here, where I share my innermost secrets, that I was imagining the worst. If Laura was missing her skirt, I feared a man responsible. Need I say more? I feared Daniel's participation in this matter—his allegiance to my husband is unquestionable. I did not forget Daniel's disclaimer concerning Laura, made in front of all the staff. He had not seen Laura—or so he said.

We passed stall after stall of some of the finest horses in this part of the country: Summertime and Rex are my favorites for I helped buy them, but all the horses here are extremely ridable and elegant examples of their breeds. John knows his horseflesh.

In the middle of the building, we found the tack room and the saddle room locked up tightly. Disappointed, we continued on. Daniel's office was locked as well. We moved silently down the center hall, Sukeena careful to check behind us every few seconds, looking back toward those wide open doors at the west end, fearing someone might find us out and beg an explanation. The stalls were bigger in this east end of the Carriage House, large sliding doors accessing one carriage after another—six in all, three to a side. The first two were ornamental carriages—one a single-pull;

the other intended for a pair. We peered inside through the wrought iron. The pony carriage and the sleigh were next, followed by two large hay wagons, the last of which was rigged to hold a fire-fighting pump, if ever needed.

I can offer no explanation for why Sukeena stopped in front of the door to the second to last storage area, no reason for her choosing the hay wagon, except to say that she is a woman of uncanny perceptions, an almost magical ability to "see" beyond where we mere mortals see. She stopped there as if striking an invisible wall, her head angled on her shoulders in a most unusual way, her eyes locked intently on the darkness beyond that door. "Is here, miss," she whispered, in a nerve-grinding monotone she elects for only the most dire of discussions. That tone alone won my full attention.

"Sukeena?"

"I think we look here. This place here."

"All right."

I helped her to roll the large door open on its tracks. Intended to double as breeding stalls, these east stalls are substantially larger than those on the west end of the Carriage House. One learns not to question a sister's instincts, and I had absolutely no intention of engaging my dear Sukeena in any such debate. The door opened nearly silently, and we stood facing a hay wagon that I knew well, for it was of sentimental value to John, having been in his family many years. I found myself transfixed by the realization that this was also the wagon that had been driven by Mr. Corbin the day he shot and killed the foreman. It still carried bloodstains from that gruesome event. I shuddered as the door ran on its track again, and Sukeena pulled it shut behind us. Only the small viewing window, barred by wrought iron, communicated to the stable's central aisle. I wanted out. I wanted to run from there. John spoke of this wagon often—it seemed many a childhood event surrounded the cart, including the first few dollars he ever earned, won from a neighbor for hauling away refuse. (John entertained dinner guests with the story of how he'd started out as a garbage collector and ended up an oil tycoon!)

Sukeena moved closely around the wagon as if it possessed some power over her. She touched it, closed her eyes, and I saw the hair on her arms stand on end, as if she'd thrown a window open to the cold. When her eyes reopened, fixed now on me instead, I felt a wave of fear flush through me to my toes.

"What?" I gasped.

"We in the right place, Miss Ellen," was all she said. Moving around the wagon, she came to the back where one could load or unload its flatbed. She laid her wide, black hand down onto the neatly fitted planks there and I believe for a moment the entire wagon trembled beneath her touch. Her face broke out in a shine as fast as anything I've ever seen, as if a fever now possessed her. Her jaw hung down. From her mouth came the unmistakable groans of a woman in pain. And I swear this is true: it was not Sukeena's voice at all, but that of another woman entirely. I covered my ears against that cunning agony, for it is nothing a woman should ever be made to hear. Sukeena—or whoever she had become—snapped her head so quickly then I feared her unreal, for it was with the degree of movement an owl might demonstrate, and it turned straight back behind her.

There, hanging from a stout hook, was a thick horse blanket, or perhaps a quilted throw used to separate delicate cargo while in the back of the wagon. A deep forest green, that blanket was stained darkly. Sukeena moved toward it as if in a trance, grabbing its bulk in both hands and jerking it away from the wall. As she did so, the bed of the wagon began to move again behind us all of its own—up and down, up and down.

There, beneath the blanket, hung a woman's black skirt.

With the squeaking of the wagon, we both turned around at once—and I for one was paralyzed by fear. There, on the wagon's wooden flatbed, vulgarly exposed to us, a spectral image of young Laura lay, her blouse torn open, her breasts exposed, her arms held back as if pinned, her legs spread wide, rocking her hips in a most ungainly and ugly manner that was not to be mistaken. She was being attacked—forced into this act—though her assailant remained invisible to us.

Sukeena, God bless her, kept her wits about her. She snatched the black skirt from the hook on the wall and threw it toward the wraithlike creature undulating there on the bed of the wagon, a grotesque expression of pain plastered on the girl's face. She threw the skirt as if covering an open fire. As the skirt landed, both it and this poor girl vanished and the wagon came to rest. I swear I saw this with my own eyes! A moment later we heard voices approaching, male voices, deep and foreboding, and I do believe that this was when I fainted, the rumbling of a motorcar also approaching from far off in the distance.

Sukeena shook me awake, having caught me as I fell, one hand clasped gently over my mouth to keep me from speaking and revealing us. It immediately became apparent that Daniel and one of his Carriage House staff had witnessed the approach of John's motorcar and had returned to the Carriage House to help secure the vehicle for the evening and to greet the master of the house, my husband. All this occurred nearly simultaneously—the boisterous, lively discussion between the two men who argued over a dice game, the soft putt-putt and clatter of John's motorcar pulling down the long drive and past Rose Red and into the center hall of the Carriage House, the oily stench of the car's exhaust. The sudden silence.

"Hello there, Daniel."

"Sir. Earlier than expected."

"A visit to the docks and a brandy is all. I tell you, Daniel, there's nothing as satisfying as seeing those barrels of oil safely put to bed and on their way to the Pacific Isles. Money in the bank for little Adam is what they are. Money in the bank. Providing she has safe passage."

"I'm sure she will, sir."

"Expecting any 'visitors,' Daniel? Should I stay?"

"You might find the view from the tack room entertaining, sir. If I do say so."

"Who is she?"

"A blonde, sir. A new one. Kitchen hand. As young as a green apple, sir. But lured to my company by the offer of pure Irish whiskey. Be along any moment, sir."

"Very well."

I overheard the exchange between the two men, and I knew Daniel had been the one atop Laura in the back of the wagon. Perhaps my husband had watched—for I know so well how he enjoys voyeurism. (Sukeena has found two mirrors in the house that, from hidden spaces, one can use to look in on both the women's dormitory and the baths attached to it. Needless to say, these hidden chambers were not in the house plans that my husband shared with me over the course of our honeymoon!) How desperately I clung to the notion that it had been Daniel with young Laura, not my John. These were Daniel's stables after all. Perhaps my husband knew—perhaps he was attempting to protect one of his most loyal employees.

Sukeena moved us to the rear of the wagon as the voices drew closer. John and Daniel stopped immediately in front of the door to our room. In the dim light before us, the ghost of Laura reappeared. She had redressed herself, though her clothes remained torn and tattered. She stood at the driver's bench, pointing in the direction of the two men as if accusing them. *She could see us!* She wanted our help!

John looked up, sensing something. And I swear he looked right at me, right into my eyes. Right through that ephemeral girl. He looked right at me, but not expecting me, did not see me. Or if he did, convinced himself it was illusion.

I felt hot with anger—this waif of a girl used up, her disappearance lied about. That awful spectral image from the bed of the wagon haunted me. Perhaps he had intended to throw her a few coins for her service. Perhaps he had promised promotion. No matter. She was gone now. Swallowed by Rose Red, the same as Mrs. Fauxmanteur. It was then that I understood for the first time not only what I would come to know for certain but what I intended to take advantage of for many, many years to come. Rose Red was on my side.

Rose Red was my friend.

I take comfort in my dear child, Adam, his sweet innocence. So new is his existence in the world. What a blessing to start with a clean slate. I find myself thinking about Mrs. Fauxmanteur and the beguiling Laura almost to the point of torment. Mr. Corbin's flirtation with murder and insanity. What kind of place is this? Rose Red, it would seem, discards men while stealing women. Sukeena and I talk often of it now, as she worries for me. (I am troubled to the point of nervosa—my hand shook so badly at supper to-night that I returned the soup saying I didn't care for it, when in truth I couldn't hold my spoon steady. John catches none of this; Sukeena sees all.)

We wonder aloud, Sukeena and I, why and how the grand house makes its choices. Why have Sukeena and I been passed over in favor of our two sisters? Why not take all the maids of the house—there are some twenty of them? Why not "accidentally" kill a gardener or a groomer? Why the construction foreman and some of the workers? I look for a message in all this while Sukeena states very definitely her own beliefs.

Rose Red, according to Sukeena earlier to-day:

The house is inhabited by the souls of the Indians whose graves were disturbed during its construction. The foreman and others were held responsible for this atrocity, but now that the house is built and here to stay in all its enormity, its inhabitants shall pay, and pay dearly. It looks kindly upon me and Sukeena because we are victims of the men who built it as much as Rose Red herself. The truth of Mrs. Fauxmanteur may not yet be known, but Sukeena believes Laura was chosen because of her indiscretion with either Daniel or my husband. Rose Red has chosen sides in the age-old war of husband and wife. It does not dare kill John because he is the engine behind its continuing growth—he is making it bigger and stronger; it will not claim me because I am the one demanding this construction of my husband. Together, John and I represent its only chance at life—that is, according to Sukeena, its continued expansion. The souls of the departed Indians have no room for warriors—and men, according to Sukeena, are all seen as warriors in the eyes of tribal leaders. Women, on the other hand, represent little threat, and few would dispute that a tribe's true history is known only by the women, for they survive much longer than the warriors. Sukeena says Rose Red is not only punishing John and his mistresses but capturing the women to learn from them, to have them as company. She believes that as long as the construction continues, as long as John and I live here together, Rose Red will gain strength and that more men shall die, more women disappear. She advises me to order my husband to stop the construction and to sell the home. "No good can come of dis place, Miss Ellen. A woman should not raise her children here."

Over the course of the past two years, Sukeena and I have rarely argued. Our occasional disagreements have instead taken the form of informal debate, one point following another, with no raised voices or harsh expressions. But when she put forward her theory of Rose Red earlier this morning I expressed my anger in the form of a tantrum (which I now regret!). I told her she was meddling in African witchcraft, and I left her and the Drawing Room abruptly, without explanation. Since then, I have not seen her.

Dear Diary, what a fool I have been! To risk my friendship with the one person on this earth who understands me, when deep in my heart I know my resistance comes more from a fear that she speaks the truth. Each part of her explanation haunts me, for it makes so much sense. And yet for it to make sense, I must concede that a house—a structure of brick, stone, wood and glass—can somehow be possessed of spirit, and this is a leap of faith that perplexes me, for though the eye does see, the heart will not accept. A living house? Even one of this size, even built upon a hallowed graveyard, can surely not exist in the spiritual realm! Or does it? I ask, feeling myself haunted and without stability. My mind wanders. I am unable to hold a single thought for very long. Is this motherhood, or does Rose Red own me even now, while I remain unaware?

My temptation is to call upon my dear friend Tina Coleman and to arrange another consultation with Madame Lu, and to present this possibility to the Great Lady (in ambiguous terms, of course) in hopes of establishing her opinions and guidance. Madame Lu's connection to "the other side" could, quite possibly, provide me insight as to the validity of Sukeena's suggestions. (Without mentioning Sukeena! The Chinese do not look kindly upon the Africans, of this there can be little doubt.)

Underlying all this suspicion of reason on my part is the consummate belief that Sukeena possesses a wealth of knowledge that even Madame Lu may not match. Sukeena is my dark angel. She not only nursed me back to life in the African bush but in the process became part of me, a friend, a sister. There are times—I must confess here in the privacy of my writing—that I glimpse the small of her back or the curve of her hips, and I am taken back to my shameful lust for my Indonesian chambermaid. She rubs my tummy with oils in an effort to return it to its former shape before the birth, and I long for her strong hands to wander my body. (My husband and I have not been with each other in months, and since the birth I am loath to even think of our joining.) So sinful are these thoughts that I hardly dare write them here. But if not put down here, they are left to linger inside my thoughts, and that is far more destructive. (You will never know, Dear Diary, what a help you are to me. Once my thoughts find their way into your pages I am free to start over. I am purged. I am certain, for instance, that once I lay my pen down by your side here to-night, I shall call for Sukeena and she shall come, and all shall be forgiven. There is much talk in society of this foreigner Freud, and his formidable insight to the human condition—but I see no need to share with others that which I can place in your pages. You save me with your listening!) So it is with Sukeena and I—a mystery that has yet to fully unfold, not so unlike this house and the people who inhabit it.

I return to your pages now after a brief and wonderful reunion with Sukeena. She made no objections to my suggestion of visiting Madame Lu, and to my relief will make the arrangements herself, having struck up something of a friendship with Tina's handmaid, the woman named Gwen who joined us before.

27 SEPTEMBER 1909—MADAME LU'S

I can see now that John's fascination with his heir is fading. He finds the smells, the crying, the spit-up, even the breast-feeding a bit too much to take. (This, despite the two nannies—one, a wet nurse who feeds Adam at night.) I suspect that when Adam is eight or nine—an age for hunting and fishing and the like—my husband's affections may rekindle, but for the time being he is absent, showing no interest in the boy whatsoever. His dawdling attentions lavished on me during my pregnancy are a thing of the past as well. I have carried his child. His firstborn was a boy. My purpose is served, I fear. Were I to have known that this was the life destined for me, I might have expressed reservations in consummating this marriage. Now, however, it is far too late for such decisions. I can only make the best—or the worst—of the situation. I labor for the higher ground, fearing the results if John and I entrench ourselves for a protracted battle.

I will ask my husband back to my bed as soon as I feel my body recovers fully from childbirth. I see now that my joy and happiness in life is to come from the children. (Adam gives me more joy in my heart than I have ever felt. He is nothing short of a miracle. I have reason to live. Reason to love!) If I am here to make babies, make babies I shall, even though I alternate between loving my husband and despising him. Adam Rimbauer holds a place special and dear in my heart that no other person shall ever come close to occupying. I can't imagine this feeling multiplied by four or five! I can't wait! I long for the sound of many small feet scurrying about this house! Damn John Rimbauer. I shall make a life for myself in spite of his womanizing ways.

My arrival at Madame Lu's felt considerably different today than it did when I viewed this part of town for the first time. I will not go as far as to say I'm comfortable with Chinatown, but I am at least familiar with this area of it, thus reducing my anxiety. Madame Lu, for her part, was most welcoming and accommodating. Again, I was in the company of Tina Coleman, and again Tina was responsible for much of the social talk to introduce us (the Chinese insist on this social exchange before any business is discussed). Finally Madame Lu glanced in my direction and spoke to me.

"You wish 'nother visit, child?"

"Yes, Great Lady." (I follow Tina's lead wherever possible.)

She looked me over. "Something much troubling you."

"Our home," I answered. "Our house."

She nodded. That enormous head falling forward like a stone. She wore a good deal of her hair in a bun at the back of her head, and yet the tail that spilled out of this nest was easily two feet long. All told, her hair must run five feet or longer—as tall, or taller, than she is herself. "I in contact with people, child, not houses."

"Two women have disappeared in our house. One, a chambermaid. A young girl. She's there still, but no longer flesh and blood. I saw her with my own eyes. My handmaid saw her as well," I said, indicating Sukeena. But the Great Lady would hardly acknowledge Sukeena's presence.

Tina Coleman gasped. Until that moment I believe she thought my entreaty might concern my marriage or my childbirth—at worst, the disappearance of Mrs. Fauxmanteur. A second disappearance (previously unknown to her) and subsequent ghost sighting appeared too much for her to bear. She engaged her fan, swiping the air with such force that some of her hair stood up on end.

The big woman said, "I be little help to you, child. Not in house. Need be in house, speak to missing women."

"A séance?"

"Need be in house. Not for me. Madame Lu never leave neighborhood. Dangerous outside neighborhood."

"But I could send a carriage," I said, immediately protesting.

Tina leaned over and whispered, supplying quickly that Madame Lu would never leave this place—any of the powerful Chinese caught outside their own fiefdoms were subject to the whims of city police. Madame Lu knew better than to challenge these long-held principles. The city's political structure is said to be rife with corruption, favor-peddling and nepotism. The city runs exceptionally well for its businessmen, and no one is prepared to challenge its structure. I didn't like hearing any of this—I wanted to understand the goings-on at Rose Red—but I also recognized that despite the influence of my husband's name in some circles, in the world of Madame Lu we barely existed.

Tina spoke to the Great Lady, inquiring after someone who might perform the séance.

"There is one I know," Lu said. "Madame Stravinski. Only one. No other. Come Seattle not often. I write letter and see."

"I would be most appreciative," I said.

"You suspect husband," she said bluntly.

I felt my breath catch in my throat.

"Tell me why," Madame Lu said.

I glanced at Sukeena, who looked as surprised as I did. Tina would not look in my direction. I wondered if I could speak freely in front of my friend. I saw no other course to take. I told Madame Lu about our recent experience in the barn and young Laura in that awful state of undress, legs spread on the bed of that wagon. Sukeena throwing the skirt. Laura gesturing at my husband and his stable master.

Madame Lu's face never changed. She looked at me impassively. "Has been dancing or celebration at house of late?"

"My husband is generous with the dispensation of spirit, at week's-end, there is often music heard in the servants' quarters."

"Place where husband or stable hand might seen young girl dancing like this?"

"The servants celebrate. It sometimes goes on all night, I'm told." Again, I checked with Sukeena. Again, Madame Lu did not let on that Sukeena even existed. My throat constricted.

"Other lady missing. She know husband or stable hand?"

"Mrs. Fauxmanteur?" I said. "Certainly not. She was a friend of Melissa Ray's," I said, pointing to my dear friend to my left. "Tea, was all."

Tina Coleman looked over at me with a face I took for the dead. It held no color whatsoever. Her lips looked yellow despite her application of color there.

"Dear friend?" I asked.

"I wish to contradict this notion of yours, sweet Ellen."

"Tina?"

"As to the nature of the friendship between your fine husband, John, and my dear friend Melissa Ray."

"They knew each other?"

She found her color as she blushed. "John . . . well, he's been to the house on business, you see. Many times. My husband is an investor with your John. Did you know that?"

My head was spinning. "Perhaps," I mumbled. It seemed to me I did know this, though I still did not make the connection that I should have made.

"They had met, several times. Mrs. Ray and the widow, Fauxmanteur. Your husband."

"Widow!?" I exclaimed.

"They make friendship," Madame Lu informed me, as if reading Tina's mind. "Your husband understanding man, yes? Feel badly woman lost husband. Make friendship."

Tina confessed, "There were several dinners . . . while you were with child, and not feeling well . . . dinners John attended without you."

Madame Lu closed her eyes and added, "Husband offer his carriage."

"And Melissa's visit to our house?" I asked, my whole body numb. "For tea. It was her idea to bring along her friend. Tell me it was so."

Tina's lips quivered. She looked to the floor. "Connie Fauxmanteur asked Melissa to arrange it. John . . . it seems John would not return Connie's notes . . . and since it seemed unjust to Melissa that he should . . . for you see, she had confided in me the nature of their . . . their friendship."

"My husband and Mrs. Fauxmanteur?" I gasped. "Are you saying what I think you are saying?"

Tina was in tears. Madame Lu looked carved from stone. The Great Lady said, "One must not look for that which one does not wish to see." It sounded to me as if she were quoting. I'd never heard such a complete statement spoken by her.

"I . . . want . . . the truth," I said. I swear I heard my words echo in that room.

"Madame Stravinski," Madame Lu said without hesitation. "In Europe. I write note. I call for her."

"Do we wait weeks?" I asked. "Months?"

"Years," Lu answered. "Patience, my dear. In matters of the spirit, time is of little consequence."

16 JANUARY 1910—ROSE RED

This day follows another extraordinary celebration at Rose Red, this time marking the second anniversary of our inaugural. To my great delight, the grand house remains under construction, at great cost to my husband. The facade of the house is much the same as a year ago, and so to the casual visitor little would appear different than during the inaugural a year ago, but in fact much has changed. I have ordered the complete remodel of the East Wing of the third floor, an area of some six thousand square feet, now designated "Adam's Wing." Once complete, there shall be a child's library holding some two thousand volumes, a recreation room, a train room (John's contribution), a small gymnasium and a classroom.

I wore the same gown as last year—repaired to look like new—and hope to make this a tradition. (I was so pleased to show the other women that I had recovered my form a scant four months following Adam's birth! Some women never recover at all!) The gowns were among the most beautiful I've ever seen, blue velvet being the most popular. We served nearly seventy-five more couples than last year, the invitation list growing with the popularity of the event. Thankfully no one got lost or disappeared—how ridiculous that looks on your pages, Dear Diary, but oh, how I worried! I was in a frightful state all night, pacing the halls, escorting guests on tours, believing Rose Red might spoil our fun, and although the guests seemed to enjoy themselves, it required three tall flutes of champagne before I fully relaxed. Alas, our grand house allowed us to enjoy its existence. (I wonder if it feels the presence of all the guests, if it celebrates along with us?)

There is little to tell, other than the usual rumors of mistresses and misconduct. What ills society spawns! Our head chambermaid, Mrs. Watson, reported to me this morning that a woman's full set of underclothes was found kicked under the bed of one of the guest rooms in the East Wing. (She apparently left the party with nothing beneath her gown but that she was born with!) Such stories abound at all the best parties. John stayed by my side most of the night, and I know even he is not rogue enough to attempt such a tryst at his own party, so I'm greatly relieved to know he had no part in this, or any other such assignation.

In fact, after the guests were gone (nearly four in the morning), my husband—a bit tipsy—found his way into my chambers and occupied us both until the sun skimmed the horizon. He is quite the spectacular lover, my husband, and I must say it was time we came together as husband and wife once again. I know that he harbors certain reservations about my womanhood, well aware of the suffering I underwent at childbirth, and since then he seems to find it even a bit repulsive to think of touching me as a husband touches a wife, but the brandy apparently did the trick. He showed no reservation last night, and I returned a great deal of enthusiasm for the rite so that I might indicate my own satisfaction with his decision to visit my bed. Hopefully another four months will not pass before he elects to do so again. I will admit here to your pages that I am ready this instant. Just the thought of John's embrace fills me with ardor. (I detest myself for succumbing to this power he lords over me. After all his transgressions, and there I lie in my bed hoping—dare I say it? trembling!—to hear his knock at my door! What kind of sickness accounts for such behavior in a woman? I dare not broach the subject with my friends, although Tina would be safe now that she knows so much!)

Our party was perfect. Following that, our time in my chambers was perfect. I wonder if things are on track again. I wonder if whatever force brought tragedy into this home is suddenly gone. Perhaps Rose Red is a house, a building, and nothing more.

There is nothing to be afraid of. I repeat this phrase in my prayers and yet do not fully believe the words, the memory of Laura's ghost lingers so boldly in my imagination.

I want so badly to believe: *Nothing to be afraid of.* If only I could!

10 JULY 1910—ROSE RED

John's partner in Omicron Oil, Douglas Posey, and his wife, Phillis, attended dinner to-night. We hosted six other guests, but they were inconsequential to the telling of this story. Our guests were invited, in part, to help us celebrate the amending of the state constitution in support of the suffrage movement. This week, Washington became the first state in the land to allow women the right to vote. It has been a hard-fought campaign, led by many of my friends on the hospital board, and John has brought out the champagne to lift our spirits! We dressed the table in American flags and will eat off red plates (from the Far East) set on blue linen, with white napkins. It's all very festive!

I sensed tension between John and Douglas from the moment the Poseys arrived. (Douglas has purchased a splendid new motorcar that I know incites some envy on John's part.) Within moments of the arrival, John took Douglas rather forcibly by the arm and escorted him into the Gun Room off the Central Hall West. I heard raised voices—as did all the guests. The Gun Room is a small, masculine space, wood-paneled with long glass displays containing John's collection of rifles. They started in the Gun Room, but within minutes their voices were coming from the Smoking Room. One passes through a stair landing to reach the Smoking Room from the Gun Room, and John must have taken Douglas by this route, or Phillis and I would have seen them pass through the Parlor. Our other guests were being served smoked salmon, Wisconsin cheese and drinks in the Tapestry Gallery. Phillis, as it turned out, wanted my ear as badly as John wanted his partner's.

I believed the tension between Douglas and John arose from a European contract that John had approved but Douglas had tied up in legal negotiations. Spain, it might have been. By delaying the contracts, another firm—Standard Oil, of all companies!—

had negotiated a separate deal, essentially reducing Omicron's share of that market from eighty percent to less than five, and costing John and the company tens of thousands a year. It is funny how you can be so sure of something only to find out how wrong you are. I could not have been more wrong about the cause of their squabble. Yes, Douglas Posey had delayed the contracts; yes, it had cost John plenty; but the source of their disagreement was to come out in my secret and heated meeting with Phillis, Douglas's distraught wife.

She is a wife in name only, being some fifteen years her husband's senior. (In some ways they, as a couple, are a direct opposite of John and me. While Phillis has the business acumen, Douglas is the socialite. Phillis, previously married and the mother of five grown adults, knows the ways of the world. Douglas is new to marriage and parenthood, just as I am. Beyond that, all comparison stops.)

Phillis is a homely woman, wide of girth, deep of voice. Her black dress could have fit me twice over. She is in the habit of cupping her hand behind her left ear when one speaks to her on this side, the result of a childhood injury when a young boy struck her with a snowball that proved more ice than snow. She smelled too strongly of perfume, and though a pleasant enough perfume, I'm sure, it played bitter in her company—tangy and sharp on the back of the throat. (She would have done better without it.)

"I am vexed," she said, a big gush of wind as from a bellows. "And I have no one to speak with, excepting you, dear child, for I do believe we are quite good friends."

I hardly knew the woman at all. This told me quite a bit about her social skills. Her husband was the one with the smooth tongue. She should have been business partner with my John. If society had allowed it, John might have considered this possibility.

"What is it?" I asked, somewhat anxious to get back to my guests in the Tapestry Gallery.

"Did John tell you? Oh, my, I can see he did not . . ." She is a bit frightening when worked up—I think it's her size. "John . . . It's Douglas, you see. Perhaps my fault, when you get right down to it." She looked at me, blushed and looked away. "Oh, dear."

Agitated to be kept from my guests, I was more forward than I might have otherwise been. "If there's nothing to discuss . . ."

"Oh, but there is!" She produced a handkerchief from inside her sleeve. Dabbing her eyes, although I saw no tears, she continued, "It's our ages, I'm sure."

"You're a young woman, Phillis," I said as kindly as possible. She looks a bit homely.

"Boarding school, when you get right down to it."

"I beg your pardon?"

"Douglas . . . well . . . you see. He's always preferred the boys' locker room to the girls'—if you follow me, dear."

I did follow her. I hope I didn't turn too grave a shade of red. There had been talk. This was the first Phillis had ever mentioned it.

She said, "It was a young man in the company." John, Douglas, everyone associated with Omicron calls it "the company." "An accountant," she said. "A bookkeeper." She lowered her voice to where even I, as close as I was, could barely hear her. "John walked in on them, you see? Compromised, as they were. Douglas's office, of all places." She adjusted to her confession rather quickly, suddenly quite herself again. "I've known since before we were married. He was quite up front about it, dear man. Needed a wife to make the social circles, to be your husband's partner. I fit the bill quite nicely, despite the years I have on him. For my part, I don't ask much. I take a young man myself every now and again." She winked, and I found myself about to laugh. The idea of this woman with anyone was laughable. "An experienced woman knows to marry for position. One's more physical desires are quite manageable outside the confines of that agreement."

Was this how my own husband felt about it? Was our marriage made to suit the situation, while his appetites were another matter entirely? I did not share this attitude with my robust friend, but I kept thoughts on the matter to myself. "Go on," I said.

"Well, it's just that. John caught him. Them! This very day."

It explained John's foul mood. Usually, on the advent of a dinner party, he is quite entertaining and enjoyable company. To-night he had been snarly and gruff.

"I do believe he has a mind to punish my Douglas," she said, her jowls quivering. "And what I've come to say to you . . . to ask you . . . to explain . . . is that Douglas is quite helpless in all of this. It's a bit like me and the gardener," she said with another of those disturbing winks. "I hope John isn't too hard on him . . . in terms of the business, Ellen. Douglas works so very hard."

"To let him go?" I blurted out.

"They're partners. He cannot fire him!" she protested. "Not for walking the other side of the street."

I can tell you this, Dear Diary, my mother and her friends would have never discussed such things. Not ever. Not even cousins would discuss such transgressions. A man taking a boy was nothing new—except when he walked in your front door. They were stories, is all. Your friends did not do such things. But having had my own devilish temptations with the dark-skinned chambermaid, I knew that such lusts surfaced. I knew that fervent prayer was the only lasting answer. (I knew that I still secretly looked at Sukeena in ways and at times that were more appropriate for a man.)

When Phillis laughed at her own jokes, she looked pitiful. I reached out and held her hand. I assured her I would talk to John.

"You are a dear."

"But I warn you, John's his own man." I doubted this was news to Phillis Posey. "Especially when it comes to business. And as to this other matter . . . the accountant. I rather suspect John will be more upset that it involved an employee, and that it was . . . that they were in the office . . . and all." I didn't need these images in my head. "More that than whatever choices Douglas has made."

"But it isn't a choice. Not for Dougie, it isn't. He's been this way since he was a young boy. He took to swimming, diving . . . The suits, you see?" she said, as if this explained anything. I did not want to think about it. "All that bare skin." I assumed her amusement stemmed from anxiety, from her nervousness about approaching the subject, for she dealt with this problem of her husband's in a most unusual way.

For me, the conversation was far more revealing of my own situation than that of Douglas Posey. I could not influence John in this matter, nor would I try to do so. John is outspoken about homosexuals and has told me so often. He seems less troubled with women finding mutual romance than men. He has expressed openly to me the "indecency of one man touching another in any such intimate manner." This, from a man who installs hidden mirrors in the lady-servants' quarters. I can just imagine him lustily looking on as one girl soaps the back of another!

But Phillis's explanation of their marriage of convenience reflected foully on my mood. Had I, in fact, been viewed as nothing but a brood mare—a fear that had lingered in my heart for far too long already? Had John justified his unfaithfulness by qualifying our marriage as one of convenience: good family, good pedigree, breed her and keep her on to raise the children while he takes to the streets to satisfy his more pressing needs? Disgust welled in my heart, a bitter taste at the back of my throat.

I spent the dinner as something less than a gracious hostess, as preoccupied by these new concerns. I drank a little too much wine.

John and Douglas Posey had emerged from the Smoking Room with their contempt barely disguised. I don't believe they shared another word all evening—not even so much as a handshake good-bye. I retired to my room where Sukeena helped me get ready for bed, and I nursed dear Adam. (I think he may walk any day! He crawls—he's fast as lightning—and pulls himself up and looks at me with the sweetest face as if to say, "Do I dare, Mama?" Sukeena and I encourage him: if there's one thing a Rimbauer needs, it's independence and strength!)

The air was still, the night terribly hot. I lay naked on my bed, debating whether to wear a nightgown on such a stifling night. (The night nurse had returned Adam to his room.) Sukeena had gone to my dressing room to put away my silk hosiery and the black heels I'd worn to dinner. I felt the wine as a penetrating heat.

John knocked and opened the door before I answered, and he saw me exposed there on the bed. It is odd, but rarely does John see me without my clothes. On those nights he comes to my bed, it is already dark as he slips in beside me. During our honeymoon he afforded me privacy, believing me modest, I suppose (and indeed I did blush quite a bit in those first few days with my husband). But last night he threw open the door and saw me there, fully exposed as I was, and something came over him. He has rarely shown me the level of interest as he did in the moments after his discovery. He locked the door behind himself and was half undressed by the time he reached my bedside. I opened my mouth to warn him of Sukeena's presence, but his mouth was on mine before those words found their way out. My God was he excited!

I must confess my attention was not fully on my husband, knowing that my handmaid was basically in the room with us, and the electric lights still on! Sukeena had no escape, for there is no exit from the dressing rooms other than through my chambers. She could not have escaped our union if she had wanted to (and I'm sure she did!). As John unleashed more ardor toward me than perhaps ever before, we had a witness. Was he trying to erase the thoughts of Douglas Posey's fascination with boys? Was he drunk to the point that a naked woman prone on fresh linen was too much to bear? (Even if it was his wife!) Whatever the case, his advances . . . the lengths to which he went (which will certainly not be discussed here!) reminded me that a man and a woman can still make discoveries about each other well into a marriage. I bit down on my wrist and finally took to stuffing a corner of a pillow into my mouth before I woke half the city. In the midst of our most excited moment, I glanced over John's shoulder only to see Sukeena's dark face staring out from the doorway to the dressing rooms. Sukeena, smiling back at me. And though I cannot explain it, the knowledge of her there looking on drove me to a heightened passion. Finally, I slumped back to the headboard, sweating and panting, and flushed from my chest to my knees.

Without a word, John redressed, kissed my forehead, and left my chambers.

A moment later, Sukeena slunk from the shadows of the dressing room and made for the door.

"Don't go," I said.

"Sukeena sorry, Miss Ellen."

"I'm not, dear friend."

"I should not have looked."

"I don't mind that you did."

She looked at me timidly. "Sukeena sorry," she repeated.

"It isn't always like that."

"The heat, Miss Ellen. The heat do strange thing to a man." She moved toward the bed cautiously, for though she had seen me fully undressed a hundred times, never quite in the state I was. "A pillow, Miss." She indicated my bottom. "Use the pillow, you want the child."

Another child . . . My heart skipped little beats. Use the pillow you want a child. I used two pillows, though I suspected none was needed. Never had my husband been quite like that. I imagined that if ever there was cause for a woman to be with child, I had just experienced such a moment.

And I know that I am right. I am with child. If true, it will be a spring baby.

9 APRIL 1911—ROSE RED

We will call her April, for that is the month of her birth, but the Devil delivered this child and the Devil's she is. The childbirth was unbearable, the doctor working at my bedside for nearly seven hours to save my life and that of my child. She has been born with a withered arm, and I'm told that arm would not allow a proper birth, and so they cut me, and then cut me some more and finally took the baby by a means only ranchers use—but thankfully my doctor was raised on a sheep ranch. She lives—little April with bright blue eyes and John's sturdy looks. She will be my last child, I'm told, and I've been sick with grief over it. They saved my life, but not my womanhood. Whatever accounts for a woman having babies, I am now without. Barren. Just the thought of it prevents me from getting out of bed. I have not left my bed in a week (April was born on the first day of the month—the second anniversary of Laura's disappearance!), not that the doctor would let me get up, but I wouldn't have even if he had allowed it. No more children. No more reason to be in this family with this man whose seed is so foul as to wither the arms of his young—for Sukeena explained that my illness in Africa is to blame for April's deformity. I hate my husband. I hate my life. I hate this house that holds us all like prisoners. I shall stop writing now, for I hate even you, Dear Diary. I hate reading back and seeing a time where a choice still existed in my life. What have I done? Who is this creature I have married who would—intentionally or not—poison our children in conception!? Who are these whores he takes up with that their venom ends up in the roots of our family tree? I hate them all. You, them, everything.

21 MAY 1911—ROSE RED

My mood has improved in the weeks since my last entry. I could not even look at these pages for so long. Could not review the decline of my life and the tragedy of my marriage. Today, in the blossoms of spring and the music of the songbirds, I sit in the garden with Adam playing ringtoss with his nanny, with April at my side, your pages open on my lap, a pen in hand.

I am delighted to say another maid has gone missing. Giddy even. It is a girl identified by Sukeena as having had intimate relations with John prior to that hot July night when April was conceived. It is a girl I wanted fired, but one whom Sukeena suggested remain in our employ. And then I understood. It was then I fixed my prayers to this girl. Prayers made to the other side. I begged for her demise. I offered my April's withered arm as example of evil. And I waited patiently for a response. Sukeena made a doll. She covered it in black paper and hid it in a drawer.

To-day, we have our answer. While John and the rest of the house mill about anxiously searching for the young waif, I sit proudly quiet in the sunlight of the garden, a wry grin allowed upon my lips. Let them bring on the police. Let them bring on the dogs. They will not find her. Let them ask all the questions they like—they cannot conceive of the truth (ah! there's that word "conceive" again, appropriate as ever!). The police have no idea of the spirit that inhabits this place—if they did, they would burn her to the ground. Burn her like a witch. Rose Red has claimed another disloyal subject. And I swear she feeds off it! She looks bigger to-day. She does! More impressive than ever. Or perhaps it's just me.

Such a fine, fine day is this. I mark it here in your pages for little April to someday know that her arm has been avenged. At least partly.

I'm not sure I'm done with my prayers just yet.

I laugh into the sunshine. Little Adam looks up and laughs along with me. The nanny looks slightly disturbed at this levity, given the disappearance. But I laugh just the same. Let them call me crazy if they want. I've connected to Rose Red.

I do believe that I'm beginning to understand her.

23 JUNE 1912—ROSE RED

With dear little April over a year old, and young Adam growing like a weed, I reflect on the year just past and how our lives here at Rose Red have finally settled down. Perhaps this can be attributed to the fact that John took nearly four months in Europe and the Far East, opening up new business for the oil company. (His geologists believe there is oil to be found under the deserts of Saudi Arabia—of all places!—and John has put this and neighboring countries under contract to allow Omicron to explore.) With John gone, the house seemed to take a rest, and once again I found myself discounting my suspicions that Rose Red could be thought of as a person.

To-day I have dreamed a horrible thing. Just how it will affect those of us at Rose Red, I have not the slightest. In my dream, a bridge collapsed. It was very high, spanning a torrent of water not unlike Niagara Falls, where John and I visited following our return to New York from our year abroad. This bridge fell into that torrent and killed dozens of people, their screams swallowed by the roar that engulfed them. It is not my first vision. It shall not be my last.

I admit to you, Dear Diary, that I have not felt terribly stable since praying that young tart into the clutches of this grand house. Sukeena, God bless her, has gotten to the truth of the young vixen, Delora (the Christian name of the girl), and it was nothing like I thought it was. (I bear the burden of a tremendous guilt over my prayers now!)

According to one of our Oriental maids, a girl named Kathy, Delora White had complained to her about her situation with the carriage master, not knowing what to do. It seems that like young Laura, one of her assignments took her to the Carriage House at least once a week, sometimes twice. It was here that Daniel began to ask questions—often just following a visit (an arrival or departure) by my husband, in motorcar or on horseback. The questions seemed peculiar to Delora—how often she got out, whether or not she had boyfriends on the staff, where she came from, how often she spoke to her family. But the real questions that stung her were about loyalty to "the family," the Rimbauers. To John and me. To John. She reportedly replied that she owed the family everything and would do anything for us.

This is as much as Sukeena knows, but I fear I have done this child wrong by my prayers to remove her. It sounds to me as if Daniel, at the very least, and quite possibly John himself, has been working with the minds of the young housemaids, testing how far their loyalty will carry them. To what end, I need not guess. What else could Daniel be asking of girls like Delora, but to submit to a man's needs? Theft? This house does not need money. Deceit? To what end? No, I think it is quite clear what Daniel asked of her.

What intrigues me now, however, is my mistaken assumption that my prayers were responsible for Delora's disappearance. Perhaps not. Perhaps I do not know this house as well as I thought. Perhaps Rose Red herself feels sorry for these young girls, holding them in her arms, as she does, while they are in the midst of unspeakable acts demanded of them by their employers. Perhaps these disappearances are missions of mercy, not of condemnation! What if she is protecting them from within? What if their blind loyalty to this house later causes guilt on the part of the very house to which they've sworn their loyalty? What choice would Rose Red have but to save them from themselves, to transport them through her walls to rooms where they will live safely forever? This might further explain why men die and women disappear in these halls.

Now, more than ever, I wish to commune with Rose Red, to enter within her and divine answers to these outstanding questions. Madame Lu once offered to put me in touch with Madame

Stravinski, and I am remiss for not following up on this offer. Whether a month or a year away, I feel the absolute necessity for a séance. Here. On this property. With my husband in attendance. (I am amazed that John has expressed an interest in both he and Douglas Posey attending. He's openly curious about the event.) Perhaps Laura is there and can speak. Delora? Maybe the grand house, the lady herself, would condescend to communicate with those of us responsible for her birth and growth.

I feel light-headed with just the thought! A séance. The chance to hear the voice that lurks behind the walls of this enormous edifice. Rose Red. Here. In person.

I shall not make another note in these pages until that day does come!

24 JUNE 1912—ROSE RED

Reading back, I see I lied! (Here I am writing again already! I can't leave your pages!)

Oh, Dear Diary, tell me this isn't happening to me! First, my daydream about the bridge, during yesterday's nap. Then, to-day in the paper, front-page news that the bridge at Niagara Falls collapsed yesterday. Forty-seven people fell to their deaths. How did I know? How did I see this as it was happening? What power lurks inside me? What is happening to me?

I know the answer: Rose Red has found her ways into my dreams . . . into my soul . . . and I am powerless to stop her.

23 JULY 1912—ROSE RED

John is quite excited by the possibility of war. I will never understand men, except to say that John believes it will expand his oil business considerably, and if there's a way to gain riches, John Rimbauer is ever aware. There are reports to-day that the Brits have ordered their powerful Navy into the North Sea, in a buildup against the Germans. These same reports say that the Germans attempted to corner the Brits into signing a mutual declaration of neutrality, but the Brits would have none of it. John believes a business trip to Europe is imminent, perhaps for as long as six months or so, and has asked that the children and I join him! To be free of Rose Red!! I accepted his offer immediately, until he informed me that Sukeena would have to stay, to make room for the children's nannies.

I am unsure how to interpret his request. Is it that he has come to fear Sukeena and her insights? Does he know about her questioning some of the staff about Delora's disappearance? Does he wish to leave her behind, with me away, so that harm can come to her? Or is it that he's lifting the skirt of one of the nannies, with me unaware? I withdrew my acceptance immediately, and John stood his ground: the offer for a European trip stands, but Sukeena is to remain behind.

I postponed my answer for a day or two. Meanwhile, I must make Sukeena busy. There is more here than meets the eye.

10 NOVEMBER 1912—ROSE RED

I write with little Adam about to fall asleep on my lap, pressed against my bosom, his small face warm, his little hands twitching as he can't decide whether to sleep or get up and roam the room. I have dismissed his nanny, Miss Susan McConnell, for the present, content to be alone with my child, the heir to Rose Red. Oh, heart, how can I love so? My children fill and occupy a place in me that sings of contentment and satisfaction. If only I had known life could be so fulfilling and whole! I fear I married for all the wrong reasons—society and wealth—when in fact one should marry for family and love I know now.

I am driven to these thoughts, no doubt, because John is still away in Europe. I considered taking the children, traveling with him, but used the excuse of an epidemic influenza in that part of the world to remain at home (in protest of his refusal to allow Sukeena to attend me on the voyage). I pray for my husband's health. I have had a letter or two. He writes of business and the likely expansion of war, one of a very few who might benefit by that prospect. I hear little of his social activities beyond the mention of the occasional dinner with a few of our acquaintances, and my wife's heart fears the worst. I know the man he is. Live and learn. It troubles my imagination to think of him alone in his five-room hotel suite, his chauffeur-driven motorcars, his late dinners and his brandies.

As to events here at Rose Red, I am saddened to report the death of our stable master, Daniel—one of my husband's most devoted employees. I have written John of our loss (I know this news will devastate him!), but he will not receive the post for another several weeks at the earliest, and by then Daniel will be buried and all but forgotten.

One can imagine such accidents are commonplace enough for stable hands, and thanks to some quick thinking on the part of

Daniel's staff, this house was spared another round of scandal. But mark my word, this man's horrific death was no accident! In point of fact Rose Red reached down and took another man's life—the fourth such "accidental" death in a little over two years' time.

Officially, the police determined he was trampled to death, found as he was in the stall of a young stallion who is known to get quite high of spirits when fed straight oats—a misfortune of inexperience on the part of one of the stable boys, who fed him a bucketful. In point of fact, Daniel was found in the very same wagon stall where Sukeena and I witnessed the ghostly specter of Laura's misfortune. Mind you, Dear Diary, *there is no horse in this stall* to have trampled poor Daniel to death, and as stated earlier, only the sharp wit of a stable hand (who moved Daniel's broken corpse to the stall occupied by Black Thunder and then relaid straw in the wagon stall to cover the spillage of blood) saved us from the undue attention of the police and society. This house and its employees have seen so many bizarre events that we have begun to protect one another. The fast-thinking stable hand, a boy named Dirk, shaken as he was by the events of the evening, was provided several bottles of claret, subsequently drinking himself to unconsciousness. (Sukeena's remedy, as she wisely suggested I quickly buy this boy's silence while formulating a plan. In John's absence the running of this house falls firmly on my shoulders. In the morning I plan to offer him a month's wages and promotion to stable master for his silence.)

I once believed trouble comes in threes. Now, I simply believe that trouble comes. One learns to get out of its way. Daniel invited trouble and was, at least in the opinion of this great house, expendable. My husband, who may or may not be guilty (all evidence suggests he is!), is too valuable to Rose Red to be sacrificed. No matter what others may believe, it is my conviction that Rose Red is behind all of this: she brings out the worst in men, she gobbles up women—she judges, sentences and condemns. (I am told that Daniel was so badly trampled that only his belt and boots lent to his identification. He was not killed, but executed.)

Another life passes through Rose Red. Another life is claimed. The scriptures have never been more accurate in their promise of Hell for those who sin. Just ask Daniel. Why this pleases me so, I do not know. I feel guilt over the pleasure I take in such matters. Yet whatever force did spirit Mrs. Fauxmanteur and the others away (to points unknown) also left the corpses of four men behind (five, if you count poor Mr. Corbin who will rot in jail!) to pay for their part in whatever activities occupy the long nights at Rose Red.

She is watching us all. And though John may claim the title, or even pass the mantle to me in his absence, we would all be well to acknowledge that there is only one master of this house. It is a mistress, indeed. It is the house itself. She governs all. No one leaves without her permission.

4 SEPTEMBER 1914—ROSE RED

The events of the past several years are too numerous to recall. Concerned that my writing this diary somehow contributed to the disappearances and deaths here at Rose Red, I have abstained from these pages for far too long, especially given that two more women have vanished from our grounds—one a gardener, the second a "gypsy" child whose very presence here is questionable. This second disappearance brought the police once again—this time at John's urging, since accusations included that John had been seen with the woman in the docklands the night before (thankfully this rumor was put to rest!). John was nowhere near the docklands that night—he and I had attended a hospital dinner, not returning home by motorcar until well after midnight, both of us retiring to our chambers.

Now, with the war raging in Europe, with John away more than he is home, with Sukeena claiming that several times she has seen *all the missing women* dancing together in the Grand Ballroom, I find I must pick up my pen and write. You, Dear Diary, were never the cause of any of this, and I was a fool to think so. Once again, I entrust my most private thoughts to your pages, confident that only my eyes shall ever read these words. (Woe be to anyone, anywhere, at any time who violates the privacy of these pages! May a curse be upon you. If you have read any of this, you know these pages are for me, and me alone.)

They picked a new Pope yesterday in Rome. Benedict XV. I am Protestant, as is John, but I wish the Pope would visit our grand house and explain what or whose spirit it is that possesses it. The Indians? I fear it is them. They have graves to fill—graves that we dug up. Surrogates will do, I suppose. "Please form a line . . ." Like a ticket box office for a show.

Sukeena tells me that the staff thinks I am crazy, that I have lost my mind (we chuckle at this together). I do spend a good deal of time in my chambers, for my African fevers reoccur, sometimes for days or even weeks at a time. The rest of my time is spent in the gardens or alone with the children—rarely taking dinner with John or showing myself around the house. The children occupy my every well moment, my every well thought—and let the servants think what they think. No person should be made to endure such fevers—and I fear my April, who also suffers horrible ills, shall die of my husband's vile poison if I don't seek a solution outside of what medicine can offer.

For her part, Sukeena is my sister now—having taken the place of your pages these past several years, listening for hours on end to my complaints, my fears and my loves. It has brought us closer than I ever imagined two people could come. She knows my every thought before I think it, anticipates my every need before I voice it. If I did not know better, I should think this dear woman is reading my mind.

The reason for my taking up my pen, the news that I write of here is this: after nearly three years of waiting, three years of repeated appeals, my wishes have been heard. Madame Stravinski is to hold a séance, *in this house,* this very evening. I am so excited! We have invited eight guests including the Poseys. John has resigned himself to participation (I believe the curiosity is killing him). Needless to say, of those invited, all women save John and Douglas, some may believe such an endeavor foolish—a necessity, in my opinion, for I wish to judge their reactions. Should Madame Stravinski connect with the other side, I wish to measure my own beliefs against those around me. Sukeena has openly expressed her hostility for the Madame Stravinskis and the Madame Lus of this world. (Sukeena's powers and abilities in this regard are beyond question.) Partly because of Sukeena's distrust, I have invited only dear friends whose opinions I can rely upon, whether believers in the supernatural or not. Time will tell how we judge this enterprise. Excitement fills the air. All but four servants have been asked to remain in the dorms or dwellings. (Madame Stravinski does not want any human disturbance inside this house when she attempts to make contact.)

I await this evening in the way April or Adam awaits what lies beneath the Christmas tree.

4 SEPTEMBER 1914—ROSE RED, EVENING . . .

I had to run back upstairs and jot down this note because I do not want to lose these thoughts to the séance that is scheduled to start momentarily. The event is to take place in the Ladies Library, to the north of the Grand Stair, beyond which lies the Billiard Room (we should have never designed such a feminine space to adjoin any such male haven, even if not connected by a doorway!). Sukeena and I were checking up on Madame Stravinski, a withered old woman dressed in colorful silks and shawls and wearing excessive jewelry about her wrists that clatters with every twitch of the hand, as she had asked to spend time in the room alone "preparing" herself for the séance. (Sukeena suggests she is "preparing" the room as well, the implication of fraud apparent.) As we reentered to check up on her, I did overhear my husband's shrill complaints to Douglas Posey through the bookshelves and wall that are shared with the Billiard Room. John made it quite clear to Posey that their "interests" were no longer the same, that war presented unparalleled opportunities, and that not to exploit such times out of a fear of being seen as ruthless was to miss the point of war entirely. "War is born of profit and loss," he thundered, "in varying degrees, whether speaking economically or in terms of human life. Profit and loss! Which side of the equation would you suggest we fall on? Yes, we're strangling the competition. Yes, we've cut deals with the Europeans. But not the Germans, Douglas. We are not turncoats! We are businessmen. Holding down supply, on the one hand, while profiting greatly in the other."

"And costing our own military in the process," Posey complained. "Profiting by denying a free market, profiting from government war money while controlling that market for ourselves. I won't have it. I won't be a part of it."

"Business! Profit and loss. An oil company is in business to make money."

"I want out. I'm going to sell my shares."

"No."

"I have every right. Read the partnership papers."

"You sell your shares now, and people will question the stability of the company. It's always the case. Now, of all times. No, Douglas. You mustn't."

"You can't stop me."

"I'll buy them from you."

"What?" Posey's shock registered.

"The partnership also provides for that."

"With what? We have every cent into that Texas pipeline."

"Leave that to me," my husband said. I confess, I feel John is making a huge mistake. Douglas Posey's shares have to be worth millions. John will have to go to every banker he knows. He might bankrupt us. "I will pay cash, and though we must report the sale to regulators, we will make nothing of it in the press. Neither you, nor I. You owe me that, Douglas. Where would you be without Omicron?"

"A good deal happier, I expect," Posey said. "I owe you nothing."

"You owe me your shares," my husband said in a voice that brought chills even to me, a room, a world away. I expect had it been the Gun Room instead of the Billiard Room, one or both would have laid dead on the floor.

"And you shall have them," Douglas Posey said.

With haste, Sukeena and I made it into the Central Hall East in advance of my husband and his partner leaving the Billiard Room, the click of the door opening behind us. We hurried the length of that splendid corridor and ducked into the Grand Ballroom instead of allowing ourselves to be spotted loitering at the base of the Grand Stair. John would not take kindly to even the possibility of eavesdropping—he guarded his business dealings in the cloak of extreme secrecy and attributed his success in part to this.

Winded, and out of breath, Sukeena and I pressed our backs alongside the great oil paintings that dominate the Grand Ballroom. We could reach the Entry Hall to our right, and the Parlor just beyond, where my guests were waiting the commencement of our séance.

I have sneaked up just now "to powder my nose" to make note of this encounter in your pages. I shall now return to the Ladies Library to meet our guests and our guest of honor.

I know not what lies in store, but it has been an eventful evening already—and it hasn't officially started!

5 SEPTEMBER 1914—ROSE RED

I could not wait until the light of morning to put to pen the events of this evening! I shudder with fear and delight at what I have just experienced and shall endeavor to put it down here just as it happened, from start to finish.

Madame Stravinski is seated when my guests and I are summoned to the Ladies Library. A little giddy, perhaps apprehensive, as it were, we were directed into our seats by the wizened woman and told to remain silent. Only Sukeena stays standing in defiance of the instructions (directly behind our guest of honor). The two exchange furtive glances, Sukeena winning the day, and Madame Stravinski makes no more of it. At this point, not to be outdone, my husband stands from his chair and starts an energetic pacing that continues from this point forward. Madame Stravinski, understanding from whose pocket her hefty fee was to come, proves in no mood to challenge John, and a good thing too, given his obvious agitation and disapproving nature. This leaves Douglas Posey the only man at the table. I sit facing her, at the opposing head of the table. Between us, in the center of the great oval table, rests her crystal sphere, a glass object the size of a human head, which sits upon a jeweled base of gold, or similar metal, and proves to be within the extended reach of the medium.

She calls for the lighting of candles and the extinguishing of all electric lights in the grand house. Thankfully, she made these instructions earlier, upon her arrival, for it required three of our four staff on hand and nearly forty minutes to render the house in darkness. Alas, it is but a minute or two to secure the various rooms of the ground floor and for our staff to return to light the candles and dim this room's electric lamp for good. At that time, our medium calls for total silence. Only our breathing and John's impatient footfalls disturb this peaceful blanket.

Next, Madame Stravinski calls upon us all to connect by hand. Only Sukeena refuses this instruction. Even John joins in the fun, moving his chair between me and Tina, taking my hand, but interlacing his fingers in hers. (This was my first experience with jealousy where Tina is concerned. What was it I sensed between my husband and my best friend? Dare I think such a thought? Are such suspicions founded, or do I see deceit and deception around every corner now?)

With all of us holding hands, and only the dim flicker of candlelight shifting shadows on the walls of books, Madame Stravinski closes her eyes, asks us to bow our heads and speaks in a chilling, unvarying tone. "Great house that does surround us, open your doors to a visitor who has come to greet you." She speaks in Russian or German next, perhaps repeating herself, I cannot be sure. My husband speaks a little of both, perhaps he understood her mumblings.

I must admit to a certain degree of awe. Whether it was just my own body or an effect divined by Madame Stravinski, I swear to your pages that the temperature of the room did drop substantially. I also swear that the flickering flames of those candles did dance from the wicks as if a door had been thrown quickly open and a gust of wind had entered the room.

Madame Stravinski is, by now, locked in something of a trance, her head bowed slightly, her eyes closed. I see across the table to my guests, my friends, and observe their astonishment—for clearly they expected a hoax, not the events we have just witnessed.

The medium's mutterings gain volume and clarity as she speaks to no one, her words gaining speed to where they pour from her mouth in a waterfall of syllables and half-formed sentences. She is calling upon the house, the "grand house," and requesting she be allowed through its doors, through its walls. In the midst of this chanting, she opens her eyes at half-mast and reaches out for the glass orb before her on the table. She looks different, not at all herself, younger perhaps, yet frozen in time. Again a great gust of cold fills the room and runs up my legs. That glass orb begins to glow—*I swear it!*—and tendrils of light, like a goo, climb up out of it and stretch for the ceiling. At once, the candles are extinguished by this wind, the only light from the swirling blue and green tendrils overhead and that glowing specimen of glass held between her withered hands. I think of my daughter, April, and her poor withered right arm, I think back to my prayers so many years ago as I was forming the children's hospital that I would never know what to do if one of my own children was born deformed. Did I bring this upon April? Or did my husband, by passing me the African curse? Can I save my children? Mustn't my husband pay for his sins? Question after question is running through my head, as I sit perfectly still while confronted with the agitations of my guests. Only Madame Stravinski, Sukeena and I remain unmoving and unflinching. Even John is visibly upset as he breaks his handhold with me and jumps to his feet.

As he does, there is great chaos in the room. The shelves rattle and books start slipping to the floor. Only one or two at first, then a score or more. The next score of books take flight, sailing across the room, aiming themselves at John and careening into the opposing wall of letters.

"Sit down, please." It is from my throat that my husband receives his instructions, and yet it is not of me. This voice, dark and clouded, jumps from me to Madame Stravinski, and then back to me again. "Sin is where it starts, sin is where it stops. Build me to the heavens, or the next man drops." First from my mouth, then Madame Stravinski's. A moment later, everyone at the table is chanting in unison, and my husband shakes in his chair, to which he has returned. Douglas Posey stands to leave the room, and a volley of flying books strike the door and push it shut before he can escape. I tell you, Dear Diary: all that I write is true, as far as it is from any experience on my part.

The room's twin electric lamps begin to swing. Slowly at first. Then huge sweeping arcs, back and forth, back and forth. And there's that wind again.

"Build me to the heavens or the next man drops." We are shouting now, loudly, all of us. Even John, whose jaw appears to move independently of him, to move in spite of him.

Without warning, Madame Stravinski seems to shed a skin of dark shadow, like a snake in season. This darkness rises out of her, and over her, part ghost (like that I saw in the barn, only black not white), part alive. It looms over the table, and we all stop chanting at once, for it seems about to do something, to attempt something, and it's quite clear that whatever it intends involves those of us surrounding the table. "Come to me . . . ," says that darkness in a dry, deep voice that raises my hackles.

Sukeena steps forward and grabs Madame Stravinski's glass globe, attempting to wrench it from the table. She is consumed in a sudden burst of light, she appears to be nothing but a vague shadow as she strains to remove it.

In an instant, Sukeena is thrown back off her feet, sailing through the air like the books only moments earlier. Crashing into the closed door, she sinks to the floor, out of breath and dazed. I leap from my chair—ducking from the books I expect to attack me, and am surprised when none flies.

If this wasn't enough, it is only as I break from the séance to rescue my dear friend that the wind and the sound of it stops—stops as if a window were shut—and, here's the impossible part to believe, the candles reignite themselves. Silence settles over us all. That dark shadow that loomed above our medium is gone. Madame Stravinski is awake. Eyes wide open, she stares directly at John Rimbauer.

"What?" my husband calls out, dangerously loud, for his ears have not yet lost the singing of that cold wind.

The medium merely stares at him.

"What?"

She does not answer.

John storms from the room, Douglas Posey immediately on his heels. "Rubbish," Posey says, though not terribly convincingly. He's as wide-eyed as the rest of us.

"My God!" I exclaim, feeling the knot on Sukeena's skull. "What have you done to her?"

"Everyone out!" Madame Stravinski declared. "You two stay," she added, indicating Sukeena and me. "The door," she said, once the room was cleared (the guests were only too happy to oblige).

"You've hurt her!" I complained.

"She interfered," Madame Stravinski explained without remorse. "But I heard the message just the same."

"What message?"

"The message for you, child. The message from Rose Red."

I glanced around the room at the devastation. A full half of the books were now on the floor—the wind had driven droplets of wax from the candles, spilled them onto the bookshelves. I shuddered. That spilled wax made the wind very real to me.

"What message?" I asked, though more weakly this time.

"It has promised you life. Life forever. Life without fear of death. Life without fear of illness. Your fevers will never return. As long as you keep building, so you shall live. This, I believe, answers a prayer once made by you. Your prayers are answered now. Life without death. Life . . . without . . . fear."

The medium collapsed in her chair, sagged across an arm, half on the table, half on the chair. She appeared unconscious.

"No listen, Miss Ellen." Sukeena muttered her first words. "No listen to this evil."

"Life without fear," I whispered. "Life without death." I looked around the tossed room again, held my friend tightly in my arms and squeezed. "Rose Red has answered my prayers!"

10 OCTOBER 1914—ROSE RED

To-day, as Lyman C. Smith, of Smith-Corona typewriter fame, dedicated the tallest office building in all of Seattle, the Smith Tower, construction on the newest wing of the largest private home began. (I often think Lyman and others are jealous or envious of John and challenge him with these engineering accomplishments!) Here at the house, horse-drawn teams dragged plows and broke the earth while hordes of Chinamen shoveled furiously, filling wagons by the score. It is as if my former fevers—I have not taken ill since the séance—have spread to the project itself. I have hardly slept in the last month, working tirelessly around the clock on the plans and the arrangements to continue the construction of Rose Red. I fear I am leaving the children a bit too much to the governesses—I am told that April will sit for hours sometimes in front of the great working model of Rose Red and talk to the house in words that no one but she understands. They have called this state a trance, though I am loath to accept that. All children spend time in their make-believe worlds, April just a bit more than most. She's an unusual girl. Nothing wrong with that. More important now is that I live on for my children, that I live to help them through this life, and Rose Red has made her promise, and I am not inclined to dismiss it as lightly as my dear Sukeena. (She remains infuriated with my acceptance of the séance and Madame Stravinski's "performance" as she refers to that captivating evening. We were the talk of the town for weeks!)

Hour after hour the workers outside the window toil. The new wing is to extend beyond the Pool House and Bowling Alley so as to not be seen from the approach, to not damage the continuity of the look of the grand house. It will add some six thousand square feet on two floors, twelve thousand square feet in all. A pittance of what is to come! We are adding three visitor suites, a four-room home for Sukeena, complete with her own kitchen, a Bird Room, a Map Room and more schooling facilities for the children, as well as a Projection Room so that we might view motion pictures in the comfort of our home. There is to be another pool—a hot pool this time, with salts from Europe, for cleansing of the spirit and treatment of arthritis, from which I suffer since the birth of our second child. This pool will be made available to my women friends—women only!—for those who wish to purge the ills of city living. John has no doubt arranged for another of his viewing closets to overlook this women's pool, and though loath to accept it, I see no way to stop its construction, given that the final say with the foreman is John's and John's alone. (This condition I could not negotiate with my husband.) I know such a room will be built and that I shall never find its entrance. I can imagine my husband enclosed there, my dear friends without garments (for the salt will harm the fabric), seen as God will have them. My husband leering. And him not knowing that I know. (If possible, I may try to arrange an act or two to stun his curiosity! I am not without a sense of prank when it comes to John.) I will not blame him for these transgressions. I have brought it upon myself by denying him any access to my chambers. Those days are over. With motherhood prevented by April's unfortunate birth, I see no reason for union with this horrible man. He can find his pleasure elsewhere. (And he does, I'm sure!) I take my pleasure from motherhood. It suffices for me. It fills me as a man never could. As a man never will again.

The new wing shall rise from this hole in the ground now being dug. It shall rise and give me extended life, as promised by Rose Red herself. I swear at times I hear her. Not just the creaking of an old house but the voice that inhabits it. A woman's voice, low and foreboding. A voice I heard utter from my own mouth. A voice that perhaps my little April hears too as she sits playing with her model.

As to that, take note, Dear Diary. With these complaints of my daughter's continuing meditation on the brilliant model of Rose Red, I elected to take tea on the upper Loggia. I instructed for April to join me, and that her model be placed there as well, so that I might see her playing with it, might come to understand the nature of these complaints from the governess.

Daughter and mother did spend a lovely afternoon basking in the fall sunlight, warm and pleasant on the skin. I had tea and scones, and April ate a scone or two herself, a rare treat for me since it is difficult to get April to eat anything at all. She played with the large working model of the home while her mother angled her wicker chair to face west, where the new wing's excavation was partly to be seen. I must have spent the hour there, April just behind me and to my right, explaining to my child the construction yet to come, how the new wing would rise from where once only lawn existed, would rise to fulfill our dreams and to hold our love, one to the other.

Finally, the sun cooling and my fever beginning to rise again as it does so many late afternoons, I turned to instruct my little wonder with her withered arm that it was time to move inside for the day. I turned to offer my hand to her, to help her stand. I turned, my voice catching in my throat.

There on the red Italian tile of the Loggia's floor, I looked down upon the architect's model that April had so long ago claimed as her dollhouse. I reached out for my daughter's one good hand. And I gasped at what I saw beneath my child's pointed finger, a devilish grin owning her face.

The working model of Rose Red had a new addition, complete and perfect, every window, every chimney in its place. The new wing, exactly as I imagined it in my mind.

That wing had not been there on that model when our tea began. Under my daughter's care, that model had grown the wing all of its own. The model of Rose Red is alive, and the grand house along with it.

12 OCTOBER 1914—ROSE RED

It is with heavy heart that I report the latest tragedy. As wife and mother of his children, I appreciate John Rimbauer's business acumen, the wealth he has accumulated, and I avoid, as much as possible, contradicting him in this regard or offering unsolicited advice; this, despite the fact that I do not hold the man himself in much regard. Today, however, I am desperate with dread over his treatment of his former partner, Douglas Posey, a man whom others continue to view as his partner despite secret negotiations that have reduced Douglas to an employee (though a rich one at that!), for I fear my husband's actions were motivated by disapproval of Douglas's private choices rather than the man's business wherewithal. Oh, if that's not the pot calling the kettle black! While John lifts the skirts of his dockside whores he condemns Douglas for taking up with his pale young men.

This morning Douglas appeared at the front door of Rose Red and was announced by his footman there. A butler hurried through the house searching out John and found him in the vast library and study off his chambers, where my husband puts in much time. John took his time responding, finally descending the Grand Stair in a slow procession that I am certain was intended both to make Douglas wait as well as to indicate John's regal attitude as concerns his former partner.

I had made a rare visit to the Kitchen, just beyond the Grand Stair, to sample a soup to be served at a ladies' luncheon (I am hosting the board of the children's hospital lunch) and so was in a position to overhear the Lord and Master of Rose Red as he greeted our guest.

"What is it, Posey?" John Rimbauer called out, still sixty feet down the Entry Hall. Lined with his African game trophies, the Entry Hall is a very masculine, very ominous place, all those glass eyes bearing down on one. The dead heads of former predators.

Dead souls. I hate the place at night—being watched like that. Teeth glaring. The architect's working model of Rose Red has a home on a corner table by the front door and is only moved at April's request, shuttled around the house by butlers each day for her entertainment. We keep a bouquet (nine dozen fresh flowers) on a sideboard in an Egyptian urn halfway down the Entry Hall, a new bouquet every three days, and the flowers throw color into the hall where much is needed. I bought that urn the same day the bandits tried to rob us in the market, the same day Sukeena reduced them to cries of abdominal pain as we walked past to our safety. That urn serves as a reminder to me that to pass by it is to acknowledge such powers as Sukeena possesses. Nothing is as it seems. The African maid is a witch doctor. The house is alive. The lady of the house is half crazy—or more than half, depending on the day.

My husband stops halfway down that long hall, his eyes as dead as those of the beasts overhead. "Servants' entrance is in the back."

"I've made some mistakes, John," a quivering voice acknowledged. "I would like to talk to you about coming back on."

"Not possible. I've a company to run. I'm busy."

"You cheated me!"

"Nonsense!"

"You convinced me to sell my stock. And now, in just six months—"

"You threatened to sell your stock, Douglas. Is your memory so poor? I offered to buy it from you—above market value, you may recall—in order to keep that transaction, those shares, from flooding the market and setting off a selling spree. You were only too happy to sell. That our shares have doubled in six months is tribute to a good product and firm management—management of which, as of today, you are no longer a part. This, because of your own despicable actions and promises made that were broken. End of discussion. Walter!?" John summoned our doorman, who appeared miraculously through the doors of the Grand Ballroom. "Show our guest out."

Walter obediently opened the door. It is cold this October. Colder than I remember.

Douglas did not move. "I've gambled some in the market, John. I could use some help."

"Our guest will be leaving."

"Please."

"Now!" John said sharply.

"Go to hell," Douglas Posey mumbled, not really meaning it, I fear.

Young Adam is five years old, April three, and for the first year both children understood the significance of Thanksgiving. John was delightful with the children, telling the story of the Pilgrims and the first Thanksgiving. The sun blessed us with a fall day to remember. It had been cold of late, but not today.

The servants had their own gathering in the Carriage House—nearly fifty for Thanksgiving dinner. John provided them seven fresh turkeys and bushels of yams, carrots and peas. Cases of wine. The day was one of much celebration and served to remind me how peaceful a place this can be when in high spirits. I think that John's break with Douglas Posey has proved to be a wise move. He has been much calmer these past several weeks, less given to unexpected outbursts of temper. He even played with Adam—something unheard of these past several months. (He has arranged for the construction of a giant toy train to occupy an entire room in the children's wing. Complete with mountains, forests, bridges and stations, it is to be an exact replica of the Seattle area and to utilize some nine hundred feet of toy railroad track, a quarter ton of modeling clay, a dozen gallons of paint and six thousand toothpicks—in one bridge alone. Adam is to have the Christmas of his life!)

Oh, Dear Diary, thank you for the good times that outweigh the troubled. Thank you for Sukeena, for the children, for our good fortune. Bless those who have gone missing when inside these walls, and give them rest.

We have had no grave tragedy within this house for some time now. I hope and pray it shall stay this way. Perhaps Madame Stravinski saved us. Construction continues unabated. This house is growing daily.

This family continues to pay for the sins of its father. I fear my children may never recover from this latest incident, and I am loath to prevent it, to stop it now for it has already happened. The events of this story were not personally witnessed. Instead, they are put here in ink through my own interpretation of Sukeena's having spoken in confidence with young Adam. (He would only speak to Sukeena, and no one else.)

This afternoon, Douglas Posey came to visit. He did not announce himself at the front door, was not greeted by one of the doormen. In fact, if the events of this day are to be explained—sawdust was found on his shoes—it would appear that Douglas entered the house via the new construction to the west. His motorcar was found parked alongside the main road, pulled off into the trees. From there, he hiked the hill and crested to the west of the new construction, approaching Rose Red from a side where he might go unnoticed, as alas, he must have so done. His next accomplishment baffles me, as mother to our children, for we employ no fewer than two governesses, Miss Crenshaw and Miss Dunn, and three other dedicated nannies, including April's wet nurse, Miss Helms, whom we held over to care for the children when her primary purpose had been served. The sole responsibility of all these women is to watch over the children. Nonetheless, for reasons that are not immediately explained, the children went unattended on this day, at the particular hour that I now relate here to your pages.

Somehow Douglas managed to make his way from the new construction through the Pool House and the Bowling Alley to the south stairs. If one goes down these stone stairs, one is led to the Game Room, where John butchers and hangs his deer and elk after a hunt. Up these same stairs leads one to the West Wing and our chambers—John with five rooms including his private study, and me with seven, including my dressing and fitting rooms. It was a cunning move on the part of Douglas Posey, for excepting the chambermaids who clean and service the linens, and the butlers who attend our fireplaces and chimneys, these rooms and hallways go unoccupied—except when I am infirmed, of course, more often than not these days, but as it happens, not on this day when I felt quite well.

Particularly vexing is that had any of those under our employ encountered Mr. Posey, he or she is not in the position to report it. John has long had installed in this house a strict rule of confidentiality, as he carries on secret business meetings (or at least that's the reason he gives!) and can't have word getting out. (He is, in fact, said to be investing in an aero company with his good friend Bill Boeing. I think it's a waste of money, personally, but John says aeroplanes will be important to the military.) So had any of the servants seen or encountered Douglas Posey, they would not have mentioned it anyway. They would be loath to do so. Whether anyone did see Douglas as he entered remains unclear. We all saw him leave.

It is no easy feat to reach the Parlor undetected, especially from where Douglas Posey began his surreptitious entrance into our grand home. He understood the house well enough, and its internal politics, to increase his chances. The Parlor's window looks out on the U-shaped pebble driveway, the Fountain Garden, which offers a welcoming splash of color year-round, thanks to our busy staff. He has been to the second floor plenty of times himself, to partake in one or another of John's many secret business meetings, and even knows several of the staff by name. One can only imagine why a person would go to such lengths as did Douglas Posey, but if there is one thing I have learned from my time in the company of John Rimbauer, it is that there is no predicting the human condition. The man Freud can make all the claims he wants (he is said to attribute nearly every phobia and fear to the physical intimacies between man and woman—sex!—disregarding in the process the drive for sustenance, survival and power). I trust someday his findings will be disproved, despite their apparent accuracy where my husband is concerned. What I will never understand, since I once imagined Douglas took a keen liking to the children, is why and how he chose the Parlor, knowing how fond Adam is of playing there. Perhaps his decision stemmed from the presence there of an oil portrait of John that hangs over the fireplace. My portrait hangs in the Entry Hall, along with John's game trophies—the similarity of our situations has not escaped me. These portraits were commissioned while we were in London at the end of our honeymoon, and I must say they seem lifelike, the work skillful though unimaginative. Indeed, John's portrait—looking so dignified—hangs with a view across the Parlor and out an opposing window toward the drive, as if surveying his domain and contemplating his dominion over same.

I can scarcely write the words, and without the high spirits that fill my glass would feel helpless to do so, but the story must be told, and so, what I have been told of it follows.

Adam was the first to enter the Parlor, on one of his "safaris" where he encourages his sister, April, to forage ahead of him in the great hallways and make like game, as Adam attempts to track her. (Little does poor Adam see or understand the significance of this practice to Sukeena and me—like his father, the game he stalks is a young girl! He must wonder why we discourage it so.) He had missed a cue and lost April as she dodged into the Smoking Room—a room she is forbidden to enter, but girls will be girls. Adam swung open the door, his popgun held at shoulder height and ready to "fire," and apparently looked down that rifle barrel at Douglas Posey, who was himself halfway up a small wooden stepladder that is kept in a closet off the gallery to assist in the positioning and hanging of the artwork. Around the man's neck was a length of hemp rope fashioned as a noose. He stared at young Adam, the boy's physical similarity to his father impossible to miss.

A moment later, dear April with her withered arm clutched tightly to her spare frame ran in behind her brother, in anticipation of surprising him and winning their little game. She too was confronted with the sight of John's former partner up that ladder.

Douglas Posey tossed his hat to the boy (for he had come to our house dressed head-to-toe as a cowboy!). Then he saw the girl and made a gesture toward her as well. Through the air floated a long-stemmed red rose. (Douglas is very much aware of the nickname of our grand house.) April's one good hand swiped the air and stole the rose from its descent, the thorns tearing her flesh and eliciting from her a sharp cry of pain.

Douglas Posey stepped off the ladder and bounced in the air, his eyes never leaving my little girl until they bulged from his florid head, a blue pallor overcoming him. Adam claims he heard a loud snap, like a limb succumbing to the wind of a northwesterly blow. He pulled the trigger of his popgun and its cork flew through the air and struck Douglas square in the chest, for Adam is a crack shot like his father before him. Adam said Douglas "danced," his legs "jumping like when the Negros do the tap at their parties." His tongue sprang from his mouth, a swollen stiff mass, which was when both children screamed at the top of their lungs.

April was found with her hand bleeding slightly, the rose still clutched firmly in her grip. Her eyes had never left the body. Adam was called back from his hands and knees where he tried unsuccessfully to retrieve his cork from just beneath the body, fearing he had somehow killed Douglas himself and not wanting anyone to find the evidence.

Across the Parlor from where Douglas swung from the hemp, his distorted eyeballs nearly bursting from their sockets, he stared

(if the word is appropriate here) at the life-sized portrait of his former partner, my husband, who, it just so happens (and some say that Douglas surely knew this), was at that very moment pulling into the driveway and up to the house returning home.

From his vantage point in his motorcar, John saw Douglas Posey, his stated enemy, swinging from his neck in the large expanse of window that fills the center of the Parlor. Douglas offered him only his backside, stained as it was with life's final excretion.

I think every servant on the property heard April's scream. She hasn't spoken a word since.

26 FEBRUARY 1915—ROSE RED

For the last week I have devoted every waking hour to my children, dividing my energies between Adam and April, though spending far more of my time with my daughter. I do not know how the male mind works, but suffice it to say Adam's recovery seemed almost immediate. Whether there will be longer-lasting effects of his witnessing the suicide I do not know, and I do confess to these pages that I am fearful Douglas Posey's death will linger within him and surface for some time to come. Little April is another matter altogether. Neither John nor I, nor the governesses, nor Sukeena, can get her to utter a single word. She sits, for endless hours at a time, staring at the architect's model of Rose Red. She dragged it in front of the fireplace in the Parlor and there she sits. She screams wildly if anyone attempts to move it, or her, for that matter. The staff has been directed to work around her, to leave her alone, and not to address her unless instructed, for her outbursts are paralyzing. I am apparently the only one she will tolerate even near her. So, mother and child occupy the Parlor, the hissing of the logs, the sharp popping of the pine sap combusting the only sounds. I have taken to knitting, for I find reading impossible in this state. In truth, I stare at my daughter's back, awaiting some sign of a return to normal. Twice I have lost my temper, though not for several days now, finding her silence insolent and enormously frustrating. I also, for a time, felt her prisoner, as if she had concocted this state of hers, taking advantage of the poor man's suicide as a means of capturing me into her web. I have spent more time with her in this week than in the previous six months combined. (I fear this reflects on me poorly when viewed in the written word, but one must be reminded of my own infirmity.)

I have secretly ordered Abigail, one of the children's understudy nannies, to photograph the Rose Red model each night before retiring to bed. This, on account of my troubling impression that it is subtly changing in appearance. I could swear that wings appear and disappear from one day to the next, and that the degree of these changes directly reflects the amount of time April sits staring. (I fear, Dear Diary, that she is, in fact, not "staring" so much as "sharing" herself with the model, with Rose Red. As absurd as this sounds, I tell you it is true: she enters a kind of trance in the company of that model and does not come out until the fire dies and the room goes cold.)

This leads me to another entry here in your pages that I have resisted putting to ink for several nights now. It is time, for I fear the results if I keep such things locked inside me:

My dear Sukeena came to me the other night with a look of pure fright on her deep blue face. I inquired immediately what was ever the matter, and she would not speak to me until we found ourselves sequestered in my chambers, with the door fully bolted. Our conversation went something like this:

"Sukeena! What is it?"

"It's her, Miss Ellen."

"April?"

"The house. Her! Rose Red."

I awaited her, expecting to hear more. When she was not forthcoming, I prodded her, compelling her to speak. She appeared spooked—there is no other word for it. "Please," I finally obliged her.

"Maybe not the Indians," she said.

"What is not the Indians?" I asked.

"Me thinking, miss. Me listening. Listening to April, miss."

"But April has not spoken for nearly a week."

"Not to us, miss."

"Sukeena?"

"It like a wind, miss. A wind all 'round that child. A wind like a voice . . . like many voices. Whenever she 'round that toy . . .

that Rose Red dollhouse. It why she no want me near. She knows I hear."

"What are you saying?" I felt exasperated. "My daughter is . . . is, what? . . . speaking to this house?"

"The house speaks to her, miss. Me think maybe not the Indians."

"You're speaking of the disappearances."

She nodded, still afraid. It is not often I have seen her afraid. Not Sukeena.

"What if . . . miss. If you think of it as fire. Fire, miss. Fire on our insides, Miss Ellen. Like that."

"Life?" I gasped.

"The power of life, miss. Yes. The fire. And what if . . . what if the house needs this fire for itself? The way you and me need our food. Like that. Fire, like that."

"Not Indians."

"No, miss."

"Not the burial ground."

"Not saying the Indians aren't here as well, miss. This place feels crowded at times."

She was right about that. We'd all felt it. Even the servants. We weren't alone in this house. The occasional, unexplained Indian artifact surfacing in our collection seemed to support this spectral presence.

"Are you saying . . . ?" I found myself grinning nervously. I felt terribly uncomfortable. I did not want to express what I was thinking, but we had come too far for such reservations. No walls exist between Sukeena and me. "Are you saying the disappearances . . . ?" She nodded, knowing exactly where I was taking us. "That Rose Red is *feeding* on these disappearances?"

"Sucking the fire out of them, miss." She nodded solemnly.

I sputtered a little laugh, not at all comfortable now.

She said ominously, "I think it has to do with you, miss. No question about that. This house loves you. But I think it takes them others for the fire that's inside them. It living off that fire, Miss Ellen." She added, "And the bigger she gets, the more she need to eat."

I shuddered. "But we're building her bigger," I reminded her, willful of Madame Stravinski's decree.

"Maybe that woman," Sukeena said, meaning Madame Stravinski, "she working for the house. Maybe that was the house talking, not her."

"I don't believe that," I whispered. Construction on the house is scheduled years ahead. "As long as I keep building . . ." I did not say it, but I was thinking: *then I'm immortal!* What I did say was, "I trust Madame Stravinski and what she told us about Rose Red." I added, "My fevers are gone."

Sukeena knows me well enough to leave it at that. I suppose I should not have been so heavy-handed as I was, for I fear I put to an end any further discussion on the subject. Sukeena rarely glares at me, but on this occasion she did just that: a wide-eyed leer of contained anger. I attempted to begin again.

I asked, "It's living off the life of the girls that have disappeared?"

She would not answer me.

"And what of the men who have died?" I inquired.

"That between you and the house, miss."

"Me and the house," I echoed, feeling a chill. A window open? I wondered.

"The house protecting you."

"Mr. Corbin was not protecting me," I objected. "We had never met."

"That man done shot the one man running the construction, Miss Ellen. That man Corbin—he been sent by the gods to stop this house being built, stop her before she ever started." She added, "He done his best."

It was true: Corbin had shot Williamson on the day the first stones had been laid. Coincidence? It added fuel to Sukeena's theories. "Maybe that was the Indians," I suggested, knowing full well Sukeena remained suspicious of the Indians' involvement in the goings-on.

She did not look pleased. "It sucking the fire out a them young girls, ma'am. The bigger she grow . . . the more girls be disappearing. Sukeena know this . . . in here." She placed a wide hand across her bosom.

I experienced another spike of cold—like a draft. Sukeena rarely committed to her convictions with such words. She had done so when she had been convinced I was pregnant, and again when convinced young Laura would never be found. And now this.

I fear I have grown susceptible to such suggestions, and I wonder at the woman I have become. Would the girl of nineteen have believed a house could be alive? Could she have envisioned her closest friend being an African high priestess capable of divining truths where no others could? A mother of two: one mute, with a withered arm, one admiring and emulating a man of questionable convictions? In just seven short years my life has so drastically changed to where even I do not recognize it. I cannot discuss such matters with my mother, for she is certain to misunderstand—to label me intemperate and harebrained. It leaves me in the care of my dearest Sukeena and her keen observations, her frequent connections with the "other side." It leaves me wanting.

I want my April back. I want her arm to be right. I want Douglas Posey to die someplace else, to leave this poor house and all of us in it alone.

What if that model of Rose Red is growing? What if my daughter's voice has been lost to its greed? What if April is trapped, half in, half out of these walls that surround us? What is to be done about that? How do I return her to her mother, her family?

I feel the need to shower even more love and attention upon the poor girl. I have ordered that she is to sleep in my bed alongside of me. I want her to find her mother's warmth when she seeks it. To hear her mother's voice when she awakes. If I am made to fight for her, I will. (If you are reading these words, Rose Red, mark my word on that!)

I want to leave, but I know that is not possible. You will never let me go. Any of us, for that matter. We are your captives here. Immortal captives, but captives nonetheless. Whatsoever does it all mean? How long can I tolerate being under this roof with John Rimbauer? As powerful as he is, as rich as he is, I feel none of his love anymore. Adam has replaced me in his eyes. He brings presents for Adam. Builds rooms for Adam's train. Takes Adam on his business trips (along with the prettiest nanny! This does not escape a wife's eye!). I am condemned. Rose Red owns me, not the other way around. I am a prisoner here. I must get April out at all costs. Her grandparents, perhaps. Ah . . . why had I not thought of this?

What have I waited for?

The cruelty of marriage! It has been several weeks now since I mentioned to my husband my desire to get April out of this house. This morning I intercepted a letter delivered by a most unusual postman: well over six feet tall, a bum right leg that caused him to limp and the thickest of glasses! He came to the front door, mumbling something about a town in Italy . . . Florence, was it? No, Pisa. That was it! He said something like, "Pisa for Rimbauer." I have no idea where the postal office obtains its deliverymen! (I hope our regular man, Floyd, returns to our service.) The letter was posted three days hence from the Cheshire Academy, Portland, Oregon. I opened it immediately (with steam, so that I might reseal it) and saw it to be a letter of acceptance—for Adam. It appears John is far more interested in protecting his precious lineage, his heir, than his daughter with the withered arm and silent tongue. (He believes April's "difficulty with the language" to be a reflection upon her intelligence, and probably her gender, if truth be known; John suffers behind a single-minded, simpleton view of a woman's purpose on this earth—to provide men certain unspeakable pleasures and to bear children. Nothing more.) I am a tangle of anger and grief, for I know my arguments will be lost on his ears. April will remain. Adam will leave us to attend the first grade. April is condemned with the rest of us; Adam is to be saved.

I prepare myself to defend my precious daughter, but I know in advance it is not an argument I shall win. Nonetheless it is a fight I shall give him. And if he ever returns to my bed with other matters in mind—which he's bound to do at some point—he shall find young April under the covers with me. So it shall remain, until he entertains a change of heart.

Two can play this game. Three, if one counts Rose Red. And woe be to him who discounts her. Woe, indeed.

9 SEPTEMBER 1915—ROSE RED

It is with heavy heart that to-day I said good-bye to little Adam as he and his father left to deliver him to the Cheshire Academy. A mother's heart cannot bear such loss, especially in the face of my increased (and failed) efforts to evoke some manner of speech from my daughter, who remains in her nearly comatose state.

To my horror, any attempt we have made to photograph the model of Rose Red has failed, as the images that are developed show a glowing white light where the model should be. It is as if the model itself were emanating some energy, some light, that spoils the photographs. (In one, dear April was captured as well—these same white clouds extended from her hands and fully surrounded her head. If a trick of the people developing these photographs, it is no laughing matter, and I pray for them to stop. John blames it on "dodging" the images while they are being developed and claims they are nothing but a practical joke. April's "condition" is known all over town.)

The European war is all anyone can talk about. John travels incessantly: Denver, Portland, San Francisco—even Cleveland and New York, his exports growing rapidly. The more he is away, the easier life is at Rose Red. (So much of the tension here arises out of John's presence and the staff's fear of the man.) The newspaper's front page is covered in worldly events: Germany offers not to sink ocean liners, a little too late for the *Lusitania*; another city in Poland falls to the Austro-German army; Haiti is in rebellion; Switzerland hosts a meeting of the European Socialists. Our lives here at home seem to have such little purpose any longer. There is war everywhere. The German submarines sink dozens of ships every week. President Wilson is under pressure to join the fight. I know not where any of this might lead, but none of it looks promising. In terms of our lives, there are fewer social events, as so many of our husbands seem overworked by the run-up to war. Although the heads of staff and I have had our first meeting concerning the annual January Ball, there is less excitement this year. The guest list is much larger, as John has added dozens of business contacts to the list. I have used my friendship with the Mastersons in order to arrange the invitation of a famous opera singer, Elizabeth Paige, who will be in the city at that time. Miss Paige, along with the film star Charlie Chaplin, should make it an interesting evening. John says William Randolph Hearst may attend. But he is most excited about some general he plans on inviting (this general has business with Mr. Boeing, and John, being a major investor with Boeing, is attempting to connect the two men socially prior to any discussion of business).

My larger concern is Rose Red herself. She has been "quiet" for many months now, content, I suppose, to use her energies to grow with the construction. (Just listen to me! How foolish this sounds!) This construction, however, is scheduled to slow substantially, though not stop completely, this winter, as John believes the winter will be particularly severe (he reads the almanac and believes every word!) and sees no reason "to fight old man Winter." What, if any, effect this may have on Rose Red I cannot be sure, but my instincts tell me that a woman in want of attention will attention receive, and after all this frantic building these many months, how will she react to her workers leaving her, her men deserting her?

How will her mood affect our annual inaugural? Will she leave well enough alone, or will she seek some company? With John gone so much, a part of me says that Rose Red has nothing to fight for, that her dormancy results from the lack of a need to protect me; but if Sukeena is right—and who am I to challenge her understanding of such matters?—then it seems possible our house may find herself in need of substance, the subsiding construction no longer stealing her attentions. If so, to whom will she turn, and when? I am reluctant to invite a soul into this house. I am of a mind to call off the party altogether for fear of guests disappearing. But never mind, Dear Diary, my attentions, my energies remain focused on my sweet child April and my attempts to win her back from wherever she has gone since Douglas Posey's cruel departure from this earth.

Why has it taken me until this very moment to realize what must be done? How could I be so blind? Why must I write my heart to these pages in order to see clearly the way of it all? Sukeena would never suggest it, for she doubts the powers so, but where have I been that I did not see this sooner? I must call Tina at once! For I now understand the course of action required to free my dear daughter from the slavery of her silence: Madame Lu! Madame Lu! If anyone can unlock this mystery, it is the Great Lady herself.

We must go at once!

With John still in Portland getting Adam settled at Cheshire, I took advantage of my independence, and telling the staff we were headed to Sunday church, we were off. Sukeena snuck through the back forest and out to the road where, with me driving a two-horse, the three of us squeezed onto the carriage and headed off for Chinatown! Sukeena, God bless her, had made the arrangements in advance, delivering a letter for me that was posted to Madame Lu. This morning, by return post, I welcomed confirmation that we would be received by the Great Lady at our earliest convenience. The wording of Madame Lu's note, and the steady hand that did write it, implied a translation, for the English was most correct and sound. (I am under the assumption that one of her young, lithe attendants is also quite versed in the English language and came to her assistance in this matter. This, in turn, warned me that the conversations taken between Tina and me in this woman's presence were probably better understood than we believed possible or likely. I made note to myself not to say anything to Sukeena that I didn't want overheard.)

I must say that fear is entirely connected to familiarity. That is, when I first arrived at the door of Madame Lu's establishment, I can remember nearly shaking from vexation, given the condition of the place, and feeling intimidated and more than a little afraid. On this, my third visit, I felt no such apprehension whatsoever. To the contrary, I found myself excited, enthralled even, at the prospect of seeing the Great Lady again. Now it is that I can understand Tina's calm that day, the almost perverse peace she demonstrated upon our arrival.

For her part, April demonstrated no enthusiasm for the change of environment (something I'd secretly hoped for!). I suspect the condition of Chinatown must have registered in her to some degree, but this failed to manifest itself in any facial expression or noticeable change. Sukeena, April and I (hand in hand) climbed the dimly lighted stairs to the pungent odors of incense, ginger and tea. The Great Lady occupied her throne like a monarch and bid us to take rest upon her woven straw mat. As before, Sukeena remained standing, slightly behind the two of us. A level of formality had developed between her and Madame Lu, if not outward respect.

"So this is child," Madame Lu said.

"April," I said.

"Pretty name. Pretty child."

"We . . . I—"

She cut me off. "Come here, child. Sit with Lu." She extended her pudgy, swollen hands behind stiff arms that looked like tubular balloons knotted at the elbow. To my complete surprise, my daughter stood, walked the distance and scooted up into the large woman's lap. For a moment, she seemed to get lost in the Great Lady's garment, like stepping behind a curtain and then peering out again. I smiled at her. Then my heart stopped: my daughter smiled back at me. It was the first such expression since Douglas Posey's suicide, and it brought tears to this mother's eyes. (I am softened by the simplest gifts!)

The bearing of the Great Lady was formidable. She seemed to fill the entire room all of a sudden. The flames of the candles in the room (and I swear this is true!) *all* bent toward that throne as if victims of a dozen simultaneous winds, as if water were running past them and down a drain directly beneath the Great Lady's lacquered chair. The room filled with added light, and for a moment my heart danced in my chest, and I thought I might be faint. She said, "Mother tell me child, that you seen a man take his life." No beating around the bush for Madame Lu—this was the first that anyone, to my knowledge, had spoken so openly about Douglas's tragedy, and I feared repercussions. Again to my surprise, April nodded. "Madame Lu understand you no talk since this day. You hold your tongue. Madame Lu think smart child. Good girl, little April." April looked up at the woman's swollen cheeks and beady, slit eyes. "You no talk because the question not answered, isn't that right?"

I bubbled out my surprise and began to sob as my precious little girl nodded right along with the Great Lady—this was, by all accounts, a conversation, and as such, nothing short of a miracle.

Lu said, "No one here answered the question for you, did they, Child?"

April looked over at Sukeena and me and shook her head.

"Until question answered," the Chinese woman continued, "no sense in risking anything and ending up like that man—dead as dead can be. Am I right?"

April nodded vigorously.

"Oh, yes. Oh, yes."

The candle flames stood straight up again, the wind suddenly lessened, or perhaps it was gone completely. I worried immediately that Madame Lu had missed her opportunity, and my heart sank like a stone. She read me from her chair and flashed me a look that urged I reconsider, and I realized this woman was inside me: she heard my every thought. I forced an awkward smile.

Lu asked, "Do you know the question, Mother?"

I shook my head no.

"You, Darkie?"

Sukeena remained impassive. I wasn't sure where Sukeena was at that moment—I had a feeling that she, too, was inside me, also reading my thoughts. Perhaps protecting me, standing sentry at my door. I struggled to stay conscious.

"The question," Madame Lu said privately to April, "is where did the man go? Isn't it, Child?"

April looked shocked. I let out a yelp and again was reprimanded by the big woman's glance. "If he were no longer, where he gone? If still here, why he not talk?" She said quietly, and calmly, "So you no talk."

"Where did he go?" April said, speaking for the first time since the tragedy and causing me to sob with joy.

"To the other side, my child," Madame Lu said, still calmly. "You seen him there, yes? You talk, you and this man. Talk, with no need to use mouth. He the one tell you no talk to others, yes, Child?"

"He said they'd never understand."

"Ohhhh," I sobbed into my handkerchief, so overcome with grief and joy that I failed to hear the rest of what was said. It was over quickly, Madame Lu grinning, showing gaps where her teeth were missing. April hopped off her lap, cheerful as a bug, and scurried over to me. We hugged, and she must have thought me queer for my display.

I waved over Sukeena and requested she complete the business with Madame Lu—I would pay anything, offer anything she requested. Sukeena promised to relay the message. April and I descended the dark stairs, my sweet, loving child already telling me all about the "awful man who jumped from the ladder."

If ever I doubted the power of the other side, to-day this mother's heart was convinced. To-day, I became a convert.

For the last eighteen months, suspicious again about your role, Dear Diary, in the strange and entangled events of this grand house, I have kept thought and soul to myself, never sharing them with your pages, no matter how great the temptation. No ghosts to look over my shoulder, goes my reasoning, if nothing is being put to paper. Alas, my plan has had little consequence. I sit down here to write in an act of desperation (this is not one of Poe's gory inventions of fiction: no young girl who can set schools afire; no dog that behaves as if possessed; no giant pendulum swinging to cut one in half!). If there exists some wraith, some bodily spirit here in this room with me, if he or she can hear my thoughts as the wet ink travels from my pen to parchment, if in fact said entity has any modicum of compassion still held in reserve, then you—it!—must certainly heed a mother's cry: my sweet child has gone missing. *Help me!*

I offer anything in return if sign be shown to indicate such an exchange. Money? My own soul? My life. My husband's. "What's that?" I ask . . . a voice in reply? A wind? (It is at this point I notice my east window has slipped open, and I fear the woman's voice I did detect was nothing more than nature's idle callings from the forest that surrounds these walls.) Nonetheless, Dear Diary, I do speak again into the privacy of my room, after securing this window shut and locked. "Did you speak to me? Is anyone there?"

Again—and I swear this on my life—a rumbling grew from beneath my trembling legs and swept through my ears like a whisper. "Hello?" I call out.

Another window open! This time in my reading room, a lovely place for meditation and study just off my bedroom chamber, opposite the first of my two dressing rooms. I hurry through, about to shut it against the swirling wind and rain that engulf this awful tomb, when I think that perhaps this is how you speak to me, Rose. A mother's hysterical anguish? I ask myself. Or is there reason behind this assumption? As your "voice" grows stronger I can picture my sweet April in the bed behind me so vividly, her golden curls thrown back against a pillow, her high little voice whispering to me: "Whales don't have noses." Or is it you? "Are you there?" I call out into my chambers. "Are you with me, Rose?" Nothing comes back at me. No sign that I can take to heart. No indication that my girl has only been borrowed, not stolen instead.

I tremble, my head unstable. I swear I hear the words return: "T . . . h . . . e d . . . o . . . w . . . e . . . r." Though these words make no sense to me, I am grateful for any sibilance, any sustenance to what previously was discerned as only wind. "The dowry?" I wonder, reminded of my marriage. "The dowager?"

"Help me, I pray." I return again to the empty reading room, my head spinning as I turn on my heels, a blur of the books' leather bindings floor to ceiling, the stained-glass lamp I bought in Venice, the carpet from Constantinople—all these and more I would trade in a beat of the heart for even a sign that my child has been spared, never mind what I would surrender for the child herself—this mother's life in an instant! Just give me a sign!

I stand now, the window thrown open to the storm, debating throwing myself to the slate of the garden path below in sacrifice. All I await is the sign. Give me such a sign, and I am yours! A flash of lightning. A cry from the forest beyond.

I see instead the unsteady flickering of the policemen's flashlights as they patrol our woods, and wish it were a sign. I hear the thundering voice of my husband, a world away, in the Entry Hall below: "Find her! Find *my child!*" He is in a fit of rage, ordering staff and police alike (there are fifty police here searching for my April). I fear that like me, John, too, is making his prayers heard to your spirits, Rose, making offerings for an exchange. How this parent's heart breaks at the thought of any harm coming to my April.

The main focus of the search began in the Kitchen, where April was last seen playing tea—the enormous architect's model of the grand house just out of reach. Sukeena reports that the child was playing by herself and seemed quite content at the time. (I fear that John has directed his fears to Sukeena herself, for I am told by Millicent that Sukeena has been sequestered in the staff kitchen, where she is being questioned by the police. Try as I might to intervene, to free her from this unfair suspicion, John sent me to my chambers, and this is one time I dare not challenge my husband, for his mood is aggressive and even frightening.) April was left for a moment as Sukeena neatened the pantry (she believes the pantry another of the house's portals). When Sukeena turned around April was gone. Oh, how my world is turned upside down all of a sudden! (Indeed it has been quite askew for some time, but only now do I admit to the full effects of such behavior. I would never doubt Sukeena's explanation of events whatsoever. I trust my friend beyond any other.) She explained also that at no time did April leave the Kitchen nor did she call out. Nor was there any cause for alarm, nothing whatsoever out of the ordinary. When next she looked the Kitchen stood empty, only the tea set and that model, a grotesque representation of our grand house, planted firmly in the center of the kitchen table, the house's wings and extensions growing from its original form like some tumorous root. Not a lock of hair, not a fiber of clothing. Just the empty room and, of course, Sukeena.

A moment later a scream: John claims it was Sukeena; Sukeena says it was the house itself.

I stand at my window, eyeing it as my escape from this pain. I never imagined a heart could endure such torture. I never understood the depth of this great love, how encompassing, how whole and complete. Dare I say it here? Yes, there were times I wished the children would go away. Yes, there were times I longed for that simplicity of husband and wife in the cabin of the *Ocean Star* with nothing but time between great lavish meals, the best wines, and the intrigues of physical discoveries. But now! Just the thought of such selfishness is enough to make me sick! How gladly I would recapture the slightest whisper of such wishes! How simple that window looks to me. How effortless to end it here.

I drag the Louis XVI settee to rest before the window and think to remove my shoes before stepping onto her pink and green silk upholstery, my dress held high around my thighs, and I awkwardly squeeze myself into the open frame, looking down between my feet at the looming darkness. I teeter there, half in, half out, whispering prayers repeatedly, the drumming of my blood in my ears, as images of sweet April swirl and fill the void in my chest where once my heart resided. Oh Wind, talk to me now. Summon me now! Say but a single word—J . . . U . . . M . . . P—and you shall own me forever, or what is left of it. I can see beyond the slate rooftop of the Pool House, to the rising wing I commissioned at the instruction of Madame Stravinski. I would haul it all down in a second for the affirmation of life in my precious child. I shudder at the thought of immortality that fails to include my children, fails to include those I love: Sukeena, my mother and father. Who would wish for the curse of the endless extension of a life without family, a life without love? If Rose has taken my dear child, is it because I built too slowly, or because I built at all? Is it because I have shared my bed with the sweet child for nearly two years, or because I allowed my husband to send the boy away to school? How much is a product of those things I control, and how much those I do not?

Do I confess my sins now, from the pious mount of this open window, the fireflies of flashlights blinking in the woods? "He is unfaithful!" I shout from my pulpit. "I am unfaithful!" I hesitate. I hear a voice. Rose Red? I wonder. I shout, "I live torn by lust, corrupted by a woman's gentle, loving touch." I want Sukeena to hear this. I want her to understand. The guilt has been too much to bear. Rose Red has punished us for what we've done in secret these many months. She has taken my child to show me the ways of such wickedness. Such sweet wickedness it was! Love, as I have never known. I want my husband to hear, to pierce his heart the way he pierced mine so many years ago.

Alas, it is not to be. My rumblings from my perch echo from the acres of rooftops and I spot Sukeena through the glass roof of the Solarium. She has broken free of her interrogators and is appealing in cloistered silence to me, with the pained expression of the only one who cares. "Don't do it!" her expression calls out. "Don't jump!"

I look on as a uniformed policeman approaches her in the Solarium, the policeman not seeing me but me seeing him. I look on as Sukeena spots his arrival. She lifts her arms like a musical conductor and throws her head back in a haunting display of the quiet powers she possesses. He retches, gripped by a pain in the stomach, and I am reminded of our encounter in the Cairo market, all those years before. I watch, as impossibly the thorny vines of Sukeena's remarkable indoor garden, lush as it is with African creepers and exotic botanical varieties from our year abroad, come alive with alarming speed. I watch as that dense greenery runs up the glass as if a thousand snakes, sprouts racing from the soil demonically. I watch as that policeman, already halted in his approach, is suddenly tangled and overcome by the twisting, creeping choke of that instant jungle. As he is consumed. Sukeena shaking her hands invitingly. The density of the tangle overcoming even my view of the events below as the glass is obscured.

And then, I see the policeman no more. My maid's delicate hands fall back to her sides. In stunned amazement I watch as the overgrowth recedes as quickly as it came, suddenly alive with color

and bloom—a paralyzing red of bougainvillea, orchid and, dare I admit it, roses. More red roses than I have ever laid eyes upon.

With that canopy removed from overhead, my friend dares to look once again in my direction. We are quite some distance, and yet her face is close enough to feel her warm breath, to drink her earthy perfume. She shakes her head in denial. She will not allow me to jump, will not allow me to end it. Will not leave April unfound and Adam without a mother, only that monster of a father, my husband, to help him fashion a life, to control her destiny. I am condemned by my love. Of this blue-skinned woman. Of my magical son. Of a driven man I once allowed to impregnate me with his seed and thus spoil my fertility forever. What a fool I feel, exposed like this in an open window, as several of the officers break from the forest with their lights, called by my shouting and ranting and raving.

And then I see him. John. Below me and to my left, at one of the many doors leading to the garden. Sukeena sees him too, though he does not take note of her. The three of us. Me on the ledge. John, blithering and drunk and terrified he has lost his daughter to this tomb we call home. Sukeena, surrounded by her murderous blush and bloom of a thousand red blossoms.

I laugh wildly. Hysterically. Maniacally. I laugh for the policemen to hear. I laugh for my husband to be sick. I laugh at the moon and the clouds, the wind in my ears speaking as Rose Red. "She lives," says the wind. "She lives in the dower . . ."

Only then do my ears forgive me, only then do clarity and alacrity impose themselves, a comprehension by the ear prepares me for the understanding that is to follow. It is not "dower," as I once supposed. The word I am to hear is "tower," and Rose Red is whispering clearly that this is where my daughter's future lies—where my daughter now resides.

The Tower.

A tower not yet built.

3 A.M.—ROSE RED (SUKEENA'S CHAMBERS)

I shudder to relate to you, Dear Diary, the tragic events of the past several hours.

Not long after the dramatic occurrence in the Solarium, and my brief encounter with my husband, did a sense of dread invade me that rivaled the disappearance of my dear child only hours earlier. I knew in an instant that this dread involved Sukeena and that my own intervention was required to spare my sweet friend. I have suffered much infirmity these several years, nearly always cautious in my walking about not to lose balance and fall to the floor like some invalid. Yet on this night the eyes I must have raised with the staff as I ran down the West Wing's second-story halls and flew down the Grand Stair, my feet barely lighting as I descended. Drastic action was required of me—I knew this without so much as a single thought. My response was born from within me, having little or nothing to do with any kind of thought process—and for this reason I trusted it, I suppose, or at least I followed it without question.

"No, John!" I heard myself calling out in an unfamiliar tone, a tone a wife should never use to address her husband. Especially in public. (I tell you, Dear Diary, it was not my voice at all, but one given to me, just as the quickness of limb was given to me. Just as the voice in the séance was given to me. This, in turn, begs a greater question upon which I hope to expound at a later date: that is, if not my voice, if the voice of Rose Red, as I firmly believe, then why was she speaking through me in an attempt—vain, as it turned out—to save Sukeena? Has this house come to listen to my handmaid? To talk to her? Do they share some connection about which I am previously unaware?) "You let her go!" I roared at him in a voice that was not mine.

John knew that other voice. He is smarter than other men. Wiser. More experienced. He recognized that voice immediately

as being the voice of the grand house. Paralyzed, he stood, flat-footed, as I ran—ran!—toward him, my dress rising behind me like a shadow. Two policemen had Sukeena by the arms and were dragging her toward the open door, beyond which I could see a car waiting. The police in this city are a model of corruption and influence peddling. (Mayor Gill, now in his third term, has attempted to change our image by closing the bawdy houses and saloons that people the water frontage. He would not dare touch the police, for they control this town, including the actions of the mayor!) If Sukeena was placed in that car, I knew well that I might never see her again. As I approached my husband at full speed, a thought sparked through me: what if April had not disappeared at all? What if my husband had ordered her removed briefly by one of the loyal staff? What if this evening's anxiety was nothing more than the result of a deftly scripted act of deceit intended to lay blame on my maid and win her forcible removal from our home? What if his plans called for her beating, her jailing and the pox or other illness that seemed to claim the lives of so many of this city's jailed? April is removed for one night, and John reclaims the power over his wife and destroys the one person in this house who has more power than him. (Discounting the house itself, of course!) Had my husband tricked me, tricked us all, including the police (whom he may have bought off) in an effort to regain his single authority?

John caught me unawares. He extended his arms in advance of my fast approach and knocked me off my feet, throwing me down onto my behind, where I skidded across the polished wood and came to rest against the wall, directly beneath my own portrait.

"She . . . heard . . . her . . . scream!" he roared. "The only person to claim to hear anything!"

"She heard the house scream," I cried, for I was quite aware of Sukeena's firsthand report.

He snorted derisively at me. "It was our daughter, Ellen. Our daughter's last sounds. And this woman must answer for it."

"Answer for it? This woman? Does she answer for the disappearances? For your partner's suicide?" I caught him with my defiance. "It . . . is . . . this . . . house. And you know it!"

"I know nothing of the sort."

An officer remained in the open doorway. Beyond him, I saw Sukeena violently thrown into a police wagon, her head striking the frame. She glanced back in my direction. It was the last I saw of her. I have not seen her since. John nodded toward the officer—my husband clearly giving his okay—and again my thoughts of conspiracy surfaced. John had a greater hand in this than I thought. The man pulled the door shut.

"No!" I cried out.

"A cop has disappeared, Ellen," my husband said.

"The woods," I said, making no mention of the sudden bloom in the Solarium. "There are dozens of them in the woods. One is lost is all."

"They found a belt—a policeman's belt—on the floor of the Solarium. Sukeena was in the Solarium at the time. I think it's time you faced up to the fact that your . . . what is she exactly? . . . your friend . . . grew jealous of your time with our daughter and has brought her harm. Indeed, has removed her from the face of this earth."

"You bastard, John Rimbauer."

He bent down and slapped me across the cheek. Tears leaped from my eyes, like beads of juice from an orange slice.

"I'm sorry . . . ," he mumbled. In our ten years together, my husband had never laid a hand on me in this way.

Perhaps it was the jarring that this blow caused me—my husband unleashing his anger. Perhaps it was simply the right time for me to see the truth, as unadorned as it so often is. For me, that slap of his was like sunlight through a magnifying glass—directed, fierce and intense. A light so bright as to be blinding.

Surprisingly, my husband had it half right. He had nailed it on the head: jealousy. The clarity of that thought! I thought I heard the voices of choirs in my ears. Jealousy. But half right was all. He was wrong about the source of that jealousy—felt over the past two years as I focused my every waking moment on the love and progression of sweet April. Not Sukeena at all. But Rose Red.

She'd grown jealous. And she'd fed off the substantial life force of my child as a way of extending her own longevity and striking out at me all at once. Two birds with one stone. Rose Red has claimed April. She has removed Sukeena as well.

She has me all to herself now. And I shudder at what that means.

Horror of horrors, do I dare relate what I know now about the events of the past three days? I know not how much of what has happened was the result of my husband's instruction, his determination, and how much simply the result of a corrupt and bigoted police force. Naturally, I would prefer to believe the latter, as I must continue through this lie of a marriage to the former, and thereby, perhaps, the blame for it all should be laid at my feet, and mine alone. When I think back now to what I might have done to save my dear Sukeena . . . Had it not been for fear, had it not been for grief over the loss of my sweet April, perhaps I would have been in the presence of mind to formulate some plan, to articulate my degree of concern, to make demands upon my husband and those clearly under his control.

Sukeena has failed to return from the police station, or wherever it is they have taken her. Three full days have passed since April's disappearance, and I am teetering on the brink of suicide, haunted by my husband's continued stalking of this house like a cat after a mouse and his approval when the police hauled off my handmaid late that night in a pitiful rainstorm. Finally, about an hour ago, I received word, through surreptitious means that I dare not go into, not even in your trusted pages, Dear Diary (except to say that one of the staff is close friends with a young woman whose brother serves on the police department, and that through this connection I have been privy to information that otherwise should have never reached my ear). The word is this: Sukeena has been under lock and key in a basement room in City Hall for the past three days and nights. She has been denied food, sleep and even the common decency of a toilet. I am of information that she has been beaten, berated and quite possibly violated in the way only a woman can be violated, while her captors continue to demand and await her confession—a piece of fiction she has quite properly, steadfastly, refused to provide them. I am of a state, so wrought with grief and overcome with anxiety that I am in one of my fevers, confined to bed, and only weakly able to make this account in your pages tonight. Immediately upon hearing of Sukeena's treatment, her predicament, I wrote my husband a brief note upon my personal stationery and had it delivered by Yvonne, a woman I trust implicitly. My note read something like this:

Dear Husband,

It has come to my attention that persons unknown (namely, the police, or persons masquerading as the same) are torturing and mistreating my dear friend and African handmaid in their pursuit of the truth as concerns our dear departed daughter. I am quite aware that you continue to attribute the random spirits of this house to Sukeena, and to place her in the blame for events here. This, despite my many objections to such an attitude. You now apparently harbor suspicions that include the disappearance of our dear April. I beg you to review the events as they stand.

What I hope to remind you of is that Mr. Corbin's actions predated my even meeting Sukeena by over a year. Furthermore, during the séance with Madame Stravinski, it was Sukeena, and only Sukeena who attempted to stop the events of that evening—to disconnect us all from Rose Red, not to encourage us to listen. On the night of April's disappearance, only Sukeena heard this wretched house scream.

Your suspicions are incorrect and ill founded, and I beseech you to use whatever relationships with which you are bestowed to return home at once my most senior staff member, be they, these relationships, with the police, the politicians, or with her abductors themselves. If any more harm, any lasting harm, comes to Sukeena,

I shall hold you personally responsible, John. Any resulting investigation will, by necessity, include you and your role in her initial removal from this household.

Your wife,

I signed it "Ellen Rimbauer," as I have found deliberate use of my formal name to be suggestive of a strong attitude on my part and quite a successful technique where negotiations with John are concerned. I licked the envelope, sealed it and wrote his name on the front: Mr. John Rimbauer, all informality gone.

Since that time I have turned to your pages as a means of escape, for I cannot bear the thought of my dear Sukeena in the condition in which she presently finds herself. About the only good any of this has done is to distract me from a mother's sorrow, however briefly. Sitting here just now, I have heard John's motorcar depart the property. My heart swells with hope that Sukeena is to be returned! But there is a second sound as well, which I shall now investigate. It comes from inside the walls, and sounds ever so much like the sawing of wood. Perhaps not inside the walls, exactly, but overhead instead. Guest chambers occupy the space directly above my own rooms, and above these, the attic. I shall return to your pages, but first I must find the source of these peculiar sounds, if for no other reason than to put my mind at rest that little April isn't still to be found here, having been mistakenly overlooked while having gotten herself injured. Hope clings to every branch. I quiver in the wind. I shall dress in pants and a sweater, and I shall explore Rose Red like never before. Damn them all!

4 A.M.

I have always taken your pages in confidence, but never so much as now, as the darkness of this place makes itself so plainly evident. My curiosity drove me to the floor above my own West Wing chambers in search of the mechanical noises that sounded to me like wood being sawed. To no great surprise, I found the chambers above my own unoccupied. However, in a keen search of the hallway there, I found a panel that when pressed upon with both hands sprang open far enough to admit a person. I slipped inside, studied the panel to make sure I knew I could reopen it, and deciding I could, pulled it shut. I entered a dark, narrow passage, no wider than my slim frame, and moved around a corner to where I found myself standing at a cloudy window—yes, a piece of glass, large and substantial—that looked in on the principal dressing room off the guest quarters' master bedroom. Only then did I realize this piece of glass was the dressing room's mirror, and that I was on the other side of it. I continued on down the narrow corridor past the next turn, finding a panel that moved out of the way. Climbing up a step clearly intended for same, it allowed me to insert my head into a wooden box and to find my eyes looking out the mouth of one of John's African game trophies—right at the guest bed itself! Farther down the corridor, another back side of a mirror, this time inappropriately looking in on the sink, toilet and bath. My husband's fantasies might very well include watching women dress and undress, might include watching the couples invited to stay the night as they are engaged in the most intimate courting rituals. But the idea of my husband, or any man, leering at a woman in the privacy of her toilet made me sick to my stomach. I had heard of such observation stations built into the staff quarters. Having never found one, I had not protested. But locating such a nefarious viewing platform as the mouth of a dead beast, and another allowing study of a woman's toilet habits—and both directed at our dear guests—filled me with anger.

Worse, this hall of delight did not stop there. I followed it more deeply into Rose's walls, turning left twice, a fraction of

light seeping in through holes I gather were drilled for this purpose. A right-hand turn and then, at my feet, a perfect square of white lines. Light. I knelt, tried to move the square panel there in the floor, and finally made it slide open exactly an inch. I put my head to it, lying on the floor as I imagined was intended.

I was looking down onto my own bed, the electric lamp by my pillow strong enough to turn the sheer suspended over my four-poster into a transparency. I could see clearly enough to read the Holy Bible in gold on the nightstand. I panicked as only a guilty person can. First in anger, then in guilt. Not everything in that bed had been innocent. Not every moment of tender loving in that bed had included my husband. Now I thought I understood his jealousy and anger toward Sukeena. Now I knew, his fantasies aside, he had witnessed me—us—there, and that no matter how it may have excited him, it had repulsed him as well, and he had taken action. For the faintest moment I even allowed myself to believe my husband had done something to little April, or (and I'd thought this earlier) had hired one of the staff to take her away briefly to allow suspicion to fall upon my maid, to satisfy the convenience of the police being in attendance. Perhaps more than one of the staff, perhaps his loyal core of servants—the children's young governesses had been acting strangely of late. Conspiracy worked hard to replace my own sense of debauchery and unfaithfulness, and I managed to turn my own misgiving into a strong resentment of my husband in no time.

I continued on. Shortly thereafter, the corridor did rise and climb via a set of steep stairs to a padded trapdoor that led directly into the attic. Here were kept many of the dozens and dozens of items collected while on our honeymoon and still not put to good use. Here were sewing stands, pottery and a second set of stairs that, when descended, led directly into the back of the lesser closets in my husband's primary changing room. This second set of stairs afforded him escape to his rooms if overheard or pursued, or a way to reach from his rooms into the attic, back down to the guest quarters and out into the hallway. I was guessing already that I had missed a secret door leading right into the guest bedroom—a way for John to enjoy the pleasures of our single women guests while escaping attention. A certain opera star came to mind. For a while, a year or so ago, she had lived with us while performing downtown. I sensed she had been performing in my house as well. (When I look at it this way, there is much for Rose Red to be angry about, Dear Diary—we have abused her repeatedly.)

I did not return immediately, for what took my breath away, what startled me to the point of swooning and nearly fainting, had nothing whatsoever to do with John's philandering, or even his secret passages. I'd come to grips with my husband's perverted shortcomings years ago. No, Dear Diary, not my husband! It was the fresh board, the steel carpenter's saw, the horses and the fresh pile of sawdust that caught my eye. A door that I did not remember. I inspected this work. The saw's blade felt warm to the touch! The sawdust smelled of fresh cedar. There, a framed door stood in the middle of the attic. Alone, and all by itself. A door to nowhere. Connected both top and bottom. For unexplainable reasons, I picked up the saw, inserted its warm teeth into the sawed slot, and put my hand to it. A moment later, the end piece of wood broke free and fell with a clatter, for I had neglected to hold it, or to catch it.

Someone had been up here working while I lay in my bed trying to pray for Sukeena's release to freedom. Someone had been building Rose Red. But who, Dear Diary? Who on our staff works this time of night? What carpenter saws in the dark?

And why did I see that board and that handsaw much more as an invitation? Far less mystery than mastery. I am to help build this house—the tower where my captured daughter is said to live and from where she will seek her freedom. A tower that has yet to be built.

I am to help build it. I know this with absolute certainty. To build it in secrecy. Perhaps Adam will help when he's home from school. He, too, will want to reach April as soon as possible.

Am I losing my mind? As quickly as I'm losing those I love?

I must schedule my day to make room for this endeavor. I must prepare to wear blisters on my hands—to smuggle lumber stolen from our other construction and into the attic late at night when no one else suspects. April, I fear, lives on the other side of that unbuilt door. April awaits her mother.

John has just now returned from his journey into town, and I could wait no longer. I ran—yes, ran!—down the Grand Stair to that very same spot where he had shoved me days earlier, and I pleaded with him for some news of my friend.

"Your friend?" he asked.

"Yes, John. She is my friend." I practically dragged him into the Parlor, the suit of armor our only eavesdropper. I secured the doors shut and beseeched him, "Dear husband, I beg you for news of my friend."

"You call me husband and yet do not allow me into your chambers, woman. What kind of husband is that?"

It had never crossed my mind that the man wanted into my chambers. Our child was missing—how could any other words escape his mouth? All these months of not so much as a kiss between us, I had assumed his transgressions with the women of the night had satisfied whatever urges a man like John Rimbauer has—substantial urges indeed. But now I saw before me another man altogether, pitiful, and I wondered (a deeper, darker thought) if some curse had not befallen my husband, some curse that is said to afflict some men, and that if, in his twisted, self-centered way, he had attributed that curse to Sukeena, and that this explained her abduction by the police and therefore, quite possibly, my missing daughter. Had John not dared to harm Sukeena himself, because of her substantial powers? Had he concocted the disappearance of our daughter as a means to rid himself of my maid with the help of the police? Or had he spent time in secret observation of my bedroom and the acts that have taken place there between me and my friend? Was jealousy his master now? Had I somehow risen to a level of power over him that to this moment I had been unaware of?

"I was unaware you had interest in my bedroom, John. I have not heard your knock upon my door for many months."

Or (I was thinking) had the act of man with woman become meaningless without the sense of love? Had the only curse upon my husband been a curse he had brought upon himself? Perhaps he was now incapable of the other kind of love and in need of the love he and I had once shared, however briefly. Perhaps April's disappearance had something to do with this—making John aware of external powers that he could not, in fact, control; powers he associated with Sukeena, and hence his lashing out at her. Perhaps this man was boy again, and in me sought a mother to whom he could turn.

It was everything I could do, Dear Diary, to remain composed under the weight of Sukeena's prolonged absence and the disappearance of my lovely daughter. For these were the only two subjects of my inquiry, and I found John's diversions annoying and entirely self-centered, which should not have surprised me one bit.

"I believe you've had other interests," he said. "You've been preoccupied with April and Sukeena."

And they were both gone. This fact did not escape me. I shuddered, head to toe. Had my husband conceived of this grand plan to remove my two loves and refocus my ardor upon himself? Had I misread him all these years—was he, in fact, more deeply in love with me than I'd ever understood? I prayed for composure, understanding fundamentally that these next few minutes were to determine the fate of my maid. In truth, I feared the fate of my child had already been decided, and that my husband had had nothing to do with it (no matter how my mind schemed!). My discovery in the attic, the voice in the wind telling me of the tower—it all made so much sense to me now: John was jealous, and so was Rose Red. I swallowed my pride and said, "My bedroom door is always open to you, dear husband. You will find me a most needing and willing partner, in this regard."

"Will I?"

"Oh, yes." I hated him for this. Me, picturing Sukeena being beaten, or worse, while my husband negotiated his visitation rights—and my obligations to his depravity. Always the businessman. John Rimbauer got what he wanted, and he played any card necessary to that end.

"I know you've been with her," he said. I lowered my head in shame. I could not look at him. Why, I wondered, did this man—this man in particular—possess the power to make me feel guilty? How could such an exaggeration be allowed? I nodded, acknowledging his accusations.

My lips quivered, my breath drew short. "Your needs are physical," I whispered dryly. "I need love, John."

"And you've found it?"

I said nothing. I felt afraid. So terribly afraid. Not of him, this weak excuse of a man. But afraid of losing both April and Sukeena—afraid of being driven to a place where my only friend might turn out to be this witch of a house, Rose Red herself. I could see myself driven to torment over her construction—my hands raw, my eyes filled with sawdust, my clothes dirty and dusty, as I worked furiously to build her bigger and stronger. I feared the future. I wished then—wished with all my heart—that I had been brave enough to jump those several nights earlier. Only death would offer silence. Sanctuary. I knew this absolutely.

I said, "I've found companionship. Solace. I'm at peace, John." I lied.

"I will taste this peace as well," he said, stepping up to me. He'd been drinking. Heavily, I thought. Another consideration entered me, flooded me with possibility: he was tormented himself. He'd not been sleeping. I knew this. Had been drinking too much of late. Perhaps his past sins had finally caught up to this man in the late stages of middle age. Perhaps he saw that the end was near—at least nearer than the beginning—and that he had isolated himself in a place where peace was only a word, not a form of existence, a concept, not a reality. Mistakenly (as always) he thought this peace could now be negotiated—bought, instead of earned. "You, and this woman," he said. He could rarely bring himself to say her name. "I will join you in your chambers."

The rumblings of a drunken man? I wondered. Or had he witnessed the affection, the kindness, the pure love that transpired between my maid and me and believed he could include himself in this exchange?

Shaking from fear, I stepped even closer, my voice now more like that wind I'd heard whispering in my ear. "Whatever you want, John. It's yours for the asking." I felt nauseous. I wasn't going to make the mistake Douglas Posey had made. I said, "I am here to serve you."

He took his hands and placed them on my shoulders. His fingers extended like antennae, they gently rained down my body, lingering over my breasts, my waist, and hugging the curve of my hips. He let his hands once again hang at his side. He looked pale, and quite frightened. Later, I would realize it was excitement at the thought of his proposal. His touch was eerily electric—I felt it like a poison running through my veins.

"I believe I can help her," he said.

He stormed from the room and back out the house. I heard his car sputtering toward the gates. I fell to my knees, and I retched.

Regardless of the price I had just paid, my Sukeena was coming home.

John has worked tirelessly to free Sukeena and at last has brought her home. To see her, my dear friend, in such a state as this brought me to tears and for a time threatened to return me to fever and the echo of my African illness, but to my credit I held these symptoms at bay, determined to be of help. Part of the long delay in my receiving her was John's delivering her to the hospital for the setting of bones and the mending of wounds. She is missing three front teeth and has a broken left wrist and a bandaged nose. In the privacy of her room, as Donna and I help her out of her bloodied and torn clothes and into a nightdress, we are painfully aware of the other atrocities that did befall her—atrocities that a woman readily recognizes and that need no detailed explanation here in these pages. Suffice it to say her black skin is deeply bruised from ribs to loin, from her breasts to the soles of her feet, and there is tearing and bleeding in places that make childbirth appear tame. I weep openly at the sight of what they've done to her, the uniformed men assigned to protect us. What cowards. They should all be made to hang for these crimes. Instead, they will return home to their wives, a bit weary, explaining away their fatigue as just another day on the beat.

For her part, Sukeena is sanguine as usual. She stops short of making jokes about her condition but manages to impress us with a wincing smile, half pain, half delight, at her return to those who care for her. Donna is eventually replaced by Carol, a nurse that John has hired specifically to care for my maid in her weeks of recovery. Carol changes dressings on Sukeena's wounds, applies ointments and feeds her medicines. Sukeena tolerates these efforts but bids me to prepare her own herbal treatments, which include the burning of ropelike grasses, teas and salves made from a variety of herbs she keeps in a rosewood chest in her changing room. I try to follow her instructions, requiring her to repeat them several times. I touch her all over, applying these African remedies, and reel when she winces in pain. There are clearly broken ribs and, I fear, the bruising of internal organs, for her abdomen is quite enlarged on her right side, and she is refusing all food.

Hours on end I pray for her, reading scripture aloud. She seems soothed by this, and we've talked about how Christian scripture can heal given devotion and faith behind the words. Morning comes, another day passes.

13 MARCH 1917—ROSE RED

There is little doubt that April (whose month approaches with great sorrow) is not coming home. John did not hide her in some pretense or scheme. She is gone, lost to the walls of this place. Her residence here ensures that I shall never leave this place, never leave my child, not for more than a luncheon or dinner in town. (I wonder if Rose intended this fate for me, thinking back to Sukeena's claims that the house was jealous of my devotion to my daughter, and knowing that a mother would never leave her child when distant hope is held that my April may someday walk right out of the walls that have apparently claimed her. If, indeed, there was method to this house's madness, it has won that battle: I am here to stay!)

Sukeena's recovery impresses me greatly, and I attribute that recovery in no small part to both her herbs and my prayer. Some of the bruising remains. Bandages have been removed from her nose, and other areas as well, and she is able to spend some time on her feet now and to tend to her toilet herself. Her wrist remains in plaster, her breathing shallow and quite evidently painful. She chants herself to sleep in that singing language of hers, almost like humming as it resonates inside her. I brush her hair and pat her head and rub her limbs when her legs go numb. She smiles and climbs to her feet and struggles around the room slightly bowlegged. I wince, unable to conceive of the awful things they did to her during her days in captivity.

A policeman, a detective, returned to our home, ostensibly to follow up on April's disappearance, and upon sight of him, I ordered him from our home. I shouted, quite undignified, until the man, paralyzed with fear, fled from this place, hat in hand. No policeman shall ever set foot in this house again. Not without proper paperwork and the order of a judge. I've had quite enough of the "protection" the police provide us. If they think they'll ever figure out Rose Red, they are fooling themselves. There is no earthly explanation for the events of this place. I have lived within these walls more than eight years now, day in and day out, I have consulted Madame Lu and Madame Stravinski, and I am wont to explain the goings-on. Young women disappearing. Men, dead of everything from suicide to murder. My daughter claimed. My husband now tortured with sexual inadequacy.

I shudder with this last thought, recalling my negotiations to win Sukeena's release, and dreading the day I must report to my maid the price we both must pay for her freedom. Dreading even more the moment of payment itself. When will my husband come to my chambers? When will that demand be met?

19 APRIL 1917—ROSE RED

A grim mood envelops us all as we mourn the loss of my dear daughter on this, her day. The staff feels this loss as painfully as John and I. (The house maids elected to forgo their white aprons today, leaving them in all black as they mourn.) For the most part the house is quiet and the only activities amount to the bare necessities to keep it operating. Construction, for the first day since Christmas, has been suspended. About the only occurrence of note was a shuddering growl heard by all sometime around 1 P.M. this afternoon. There was no mistaking the source: this house.

This same time of day—1 P.M.—has lately been the hour of my retiring after lunch for "rest." In fact, I have used these two hours to tend to my carpentry in the attic, making good headway on the stairs that are to lead to the Tower. Only Sukeena has noticed the splinters and callouses on my hands—and in typical fashion has thought better than to ask me their source. I wonder now, has this sound we all heard anything to do with my absence from the attic on this day? Is Rose Red so "alive" that she can even sense time and absence? If so, what is it she demands of me, and what am I to do to appease her?

I take a late tea at four o'clock in the Parlor, at first made weary by the unexpected arrival of Tina Coleman, but then made happier as I realized how badly I needed this distraction. Tina is very much aware of the significance of this day and comes to help me forget. (She even brings a flask of alcohol, and laces my tea with same!) As our discussion wanes, I note that she can't take her eyes off the large leather globe in the corner of the room, recalling perhaps the stories of one of our first disappearances here. Do I see temptation in her eyes? Does she too want to spin this globe and see if Rose Red will claim her? (She could try if she liked, but the truth is I had one of the staff place a screw into the globe to prevent its spinning many years ago. Each and every time Sukeena identifies what she believes to be a portal into this house, I order it closed or shuttered. The stall in the Carriage House, for instance, had been nailed shut following Daniel's brutal stomping.)

I must admit to a sense of melancholy and distress as the afternoon wore on. All the small talk in the world could not rid me of memories of my sweet little girl, and I fear the alcohol only served to increase my unease. Finally, too late, I'm afraid, Tina excused herself and took her leave, returning home by chauffeured motorcar.

I skipped dinner, filled with scones, and headed to my rooms to write here in your pages.

2 A.M.

Do I dare write openly and honestly of the events of this evening—the evening anniversary of the birth of my missing child? If I do not, I fear that I shall carry this with me to my detriment, for I experience such relief when applying my pen to your pages. But oh, Dear Diary, so private are these words, so frightening, that I scarcely dare repeat what has happened. Unable to sleep, unable, barely, to sit down, I have paced my chambers for the last hour debating whether to share here in your pages the events of the past several hours, and now, alas, I take to your pages like the sinful to the confessional.

It was shortly after eleven o'clock when I heard a knock on the outer door to my chambers. I had already let the staff go and so was made to answer this inquiry myself. Believing it to be Sukeena, who has found it difficult to sleep since her ordeal with the police, I approached in my nightgown, not bothering with a robe.

To my great surprise it was my husband. Further to my surprise was his apparent sobriety. I had not seen him since before tea, and had presumed him to be drinking quite heavily on this day.

"Ellen," he said, his voice barely a whisper, "the pain is too great." I admitted him and we embraced—hugged each other in a way we have not done in years. I cried. My husband remained stalwart, though was visibly shaken. As we hugged, his large hands held me from behind, rubbing me and pressing me to him, and I sensed immediately he had turned his grief into need—he wanted physical soothing.

He kissed my neck, my throat, and I confess I shuddered with apprehension. I, too, needed this expression of love, needed some escape from my grief. He stopped my heart with his next words. "Send for her."

I stammered, unable to draw a breath. There was no question to whom my husband referred. "John . . . ," I pleaded, but he pressed his finger to my lips and repeated himself, and I knew there was to be no arguing.

I approached the door, preparing to summon one of my staff. I turned to him again, one final attempt to win favor. "John, dear husband, I offer myself in whatever regard you do wish. You may dress, undress me. Position me any way you like, ask anything of me you so choose—but do not ask this. I have yet to inform her of our . . . negotiations. I dare not tell her this way."

Clearly, he considered my offer thoughtfully. He touched me—touched me as only a husband may touch a wife. Then he stopped abruptly and bid me to summon her. "Send for her," he repeated.

I knew better than to challenge him, especially in the face of his rescue, which may have saved Sukeena's life. "Very well," I said. "But leave my chambers for a time. Let me speak to her in private. Grant me this favor, my only request. Return in thirty minutes. You shall have what you wish."

Sukeena arrived quite promptly—never one to dismiss a summons from her mistress. I sat her down and spoke quite plainly of the arrangements I had made to secure her release from jail and torture. I informed her of my discovering of John's viewing hallway, and how I believed he watched every woman in this house from similar vantage points. I had no doubt whatsoever that he'd visited Sukeena in this regard for several years now.

"You ask me to do this thing for you, ma'am, you know I do."

"You loathe him, I know, sweet friend."

"He bad man, Miss. Not bad in soul, but bad in action. Bad for the children, bad for you, Miss Ellen."

"We must do this thing," I bid her. "We must grant him this whenever he asks, and he has asked for to-night to help rid him of the haunting that results from the loss of sweet April."

"You ask me do dis, I do dis."

I kissed her, kissed her on the lips long and tenderly. "I had hoped nothing might ever spoil our privacy, dear friend." Her eyes burned into mine and I felt her displeasure with me—perhaps she would rather have died in jail than take to bed with my husband. I didn't blame her for this.

"This one night, he never forget," she said. "Sukeena make sure of that."

"It's a night none of us shall forget," I said.

"Oh, no," she contradicted. "Me, ma'am? I forget this before I return to my own room." And she smiled.

When Sukeena smiled—missing teeth and all—the whole room grew brighter. She slipped out of her robe and nightdress and stood before me naked, a powerful and wildly attractive female form. "Take off the nightie, miss." She stepped forward and helped me out of my nightgown. "You say he coming," she said. "Then we give him an eyeful." With that, she took my hand and led me toward my bed.

EDITOR'S NOTE: AS ARBITER OF THESE ENTRIES, AFTER MUCH DISCUSSION WITH MY PUBLISHER, IT WAS DECIDED THAT THE SPECIFIC REFERENCES (1 APRIL 1917) WERE FAR TOO GRAPHIC AND DISTURBING TO BE PRINTED HERE, WHERE READERS MORE INTERESTED IN THE HISTORY OF ROSE RED SHOULD NOT BE MADE TO BE BURDENED WITH THE PERSONAL EXPLOITS (AND EXPLOITATION!) OF THE AUTHOR. WE HAVE, AS A CONCESSION, MADE THIS, AND (A FEW) OTHER EXCERPTS AVAILABLE ON THE WORLD WIDE WEB AT THE FOLLOWING ADDRESS: WWW.BEAUMONTUNIVERSITY.NET. USERS FAMILIAR WITH THE WEB WILL NOTE THERE IS NO "LINK" TO THESE EXCERPTS FROM ANY OF THE WEB-PUBLISHED PAGES. YOU MUST THEREFORE TYPE IN THE URL GIVEN HERE (EXACTLY AS IT IS WRITTEN) IN ORDER TO REACH THIS PRIVATE LIBRARY OF ELLEN'S MOST PERSONAL MOMENTS. A FURTHER WARNING: SOME OF THE CONTENT THEREIN IS EXPLICITLY SEXUAL, AND IS NOT INTENDED FOR PERSONS UNDER THE AGE OF EIGHTEEN.

IN POINT OF FACT, ELLEN RIMBAUER APPARENTLY BECAME OBSESSED WITH RECOUNTING HER NEARLY NIGHTLY BEDROOM ACTIVITIES OVER THE NEXT SEVERAL MONTHS, WRITING ALMOST EXCLUSIVELY ABOUT HER HUSBAND'S INCREASED ADDICTION TO THESE EVENTS AND THE ELABORATE ACTS HE CONCEIVED FOR BOTH HIS WIFE AND HIS WIFE'S BEST FRIEND AND SERVANT. THERE ARE VIRTUALLY NO ENTRIES OTHER THAN THESE (OFTEN REPUGNANT AND DEGRADING) UNTIL EARLY IN 1918, AN EDITORIAL TIME JUMP I READILY MAKE IN ORDER TO SPARE YOU, THE READER, THE SORDID DESCRIPTIONS OF THE DEBAUCHERY TO WHICH JOHN RIMBAUER STOOPED. THE ONLY ELEMENT YOU LOSE BECAUSE OF MY RED PENCIL IS THE GROWING FRUSTRATION ON THE PART OF ELLEN AND SUKEENA AT

BEING USED IN THIS WAY, TO HAVE WHAT WAS ONCE A PURE LOVE BETWEEN THEM CORRUPTED AND POISONED BY A MAN WHO COULD NO LONGER FIND ANY SATISFACTION IN LIFE. EVEN PHYSICAL PLEASURE NOW ROBBED HIM OF ANY VICTORY OVER THE SENSES. HE WAS CONSUMED IN GRIEF, HE FELT HIMSELF A FAILURE, AND THE DEEPER HE SANK, THE MORE BIZARRE HIS REQUESTS, THE MORE DESPERATE THE TWO WOMEN BECOME. (THERE IS EVEN AN ACCOUNT OF A LATE NIGHT SPENT IN THE BARN!) BY THE TIME WE JOIN BACK UP WITH ELLEN IN THE PAGES TO COME, THERE HAVE BEEN HINTS OF A CONSPIRACY FIRST FORMING, AND THEN GROWING, BETWEEN THE MISTRESS OF THE HOUSE AND HER MAID. ELLEN WILL NOT ALLOW THE SPECIFICS OF THIS CONSPIRACY TO REACH HER PAGES, FOR FEAR OF HER DIARY'S DISCOVERY, BUT IT IS QUITE EVIDENT THAT JOHN RIMBAUER IS THE TARGET AND THAT PLANS HAVE ALREADY FORMED TO SET INTO MOTION JOHN RIMBAUER'S DEMISE.

—JOYCE REARDON

9 MARCH 1918—ROSE RED

To look back at the entries herein, it is quite obvious to me how nothing has affected me quite so much as the late-night encounters with John and the disturbing nature of his demands upon the women of this house. The events of this day finally are cause for reflection on the larger nature of the problems with Rose Red and her apparent need of "fuel," both in terms of her physical expansion (her continued construction) and whatever spiritual needs she has.

To-day, she killed again.

The coroner will put the death of George Meader down as an allergic reaction to a bee sting. But that bee sting came inside the Health Room [Editor's note: Health Room = Ellen's term for the Solarium, post 1917] and that room did burst with color upon his death, the same way it exploded with color on the tragic night of April's disappearance and Sukeena's confrontation with the policeman there.

Meader, a railroad executive who has stayed the week with us, was a big drinker, and clearly a womanizer. He flirted with many of the staff and may have had relations with more than one. It was the attention he paid poor Sukeena that may have led to his untimely demise. More than once he cornered her. (For she tells me everything that happens in this house.) More than once he attempted to grope her. (Who knows if John had a part in any of this? I cannot see John sharing stories of our "alliance," our triad, but I put little past the man.) For her part, Sukeena finally arranged for George to meet her in the Health Room at the stroke of midnight.

George appeared, quite drunk, but on time. Alerted to Sukeena's plans, I kept watch of the Health Room from above, alert to any lights coming on in various hallways or the Kitchen.

If I saw any such activity, I was to switch the lights of my room repeatedly. Sukeena would be able to see my chamber's windows from inside the Health Room.

All went according to plan.

George showed up in the Health Room, and Sukeena immediately began dancing in a most fluid, provocative and suggestive manner. Even distanced as I was, I felt the power of that dance. No man could fail to respond to those hips, the loose-jointed nature of her body as it expressed itself. I could see George Meader reach for his collar (for the Health Room is considerably warmer than the rest of the house, even without Sukeena dancing) and attempt to unbutton it. He slipped off his coat—perhaps at Sukeena's instruction. Only moments after he had removed his coat, Sukeena sank to the floor, her legs crossed, and apparently set her mind to prayer, or whatever it is she does exactly. Barely seconds passed before I saw George Meader swat his arm—the bee had stung him, summoned, I remain convinced, by Sukeena's substantial meditative powers. Sukeena waited only briefly for George to sink to his knees. Then she slipped quietly into the garden, and through the Pool House returned by the south stairs to her rooms.

Meader died without so much as a sound. Upon his death, the first blooms of red roses appeared, vines wandering and growing and extending themselves before my eyes. Within minutes, I could no longer see inside the Health Room, overgrown as it was by the wandering vines.

Nothing was found of George Meader for several hours, except that coat he had removed. Only the next day, as the vines impossibly receded and returned to their previous state, was the body found. (The flesh was torn by thorns as if he'd been rolled in a bed of roses.)

John instructed the stable boys to cart the body downtown,

knowing I would refuse the police entrance into my home for anything but outright murder, and even then only with the proper documents.

Was it Rose or Sukeena who took George Meader from this world? Does it matter any longer? I feel half crazy with it all. (More than half, if you believe the staff.) I have nearly abandoned my own suspicions of the Indian burial ground, and yet Indian artifacts continue to surface in the house—and one, an earthen ceramic bowl shaped as a beehive, did find its way into the Health Room, as I recall!

Perhaps the mysteries of this place will never be solved. Perhaps some scientist will come along in future generations to explain what I, sadly, cannot. Who's to tell? One thing is for certain: I will continue to build Rose Red until the day I die—or until I myself am claimed—even with my own hands when necessary (as I continue to construct the Tower). I will continue to attempt to negotiate a longer life for myself that I might outlive my husband—this I pray for more than anything. That I might find my child still alive. (Adam is barely a part of my life, as John will not allow him to return to this place—I know my son only through letters, and these letters are less frequent each year.)

Another has died. I barely mourn the loss. Rose Red has her needs. Sukeena and I must protect ourselves. Arthritis has found my fingers, I am in excruciating pain, and I fear my entries here in your pages, Dear Diary, shall be fewer and farther between.

What more is to be said? I live in a world, condemned. Made into someone I am not by night, in my husband's desperate attempts to find satisfaction, reduced to prayer and silence by day. Sneaking off to build with my hands what this house demands of me. "The Tower," she whispers at night. My little April.

Soon, our reunion, as I have ordered the exterior of the Tower to be built, my stairway nearing completion. A year or two at most, I'm told, following on the heels of projects already planned. A golden cherub has been ordered, cast in Italy by artisans in Florence. This cherub will stand high atop Rose Red and lord over our property. Perhaps over Rose Red herself.

Plans are taking shape. My daughter is coming home.

EDITOR'S NOTE: ALTHOUGH THE SUBSEQUENT LACK OF DIARY ENTRIES IS ATTRIBUTED TO ELLEN RIMBAUER'S ARTHRITIS, THERE IS SOME EVIDENCE THAT THIS PERIOD PROVED TRAUMATIC TO HER AND THAT SHE SUFFERED AT LEAST ONE BREAKDOWN. WITH THE DOCTOR'S RECOMMENDATION SHE ATTEND "A CLINIC" (SEE 16 NOVEMBER 1921) IN SWITZERLAND, ELLEN RIMBAUER REFUSED TO LEAVE ROSE RED AND HER BELOVED SUKEENA. RECENTLY RECOVERED DOCUMENTS (THE DIARY OF TINA COLEMAN, FOR ONE) PROMOTE THE IDEA THAT JOHN WAS BEHIND ELLEN'S "ILLNESS," AND THAT SWITZERLAND WAS HIS ATTEMPT TO REMOVE HER FROM ROSE RED ONCE AND FOR ALL. THIS PLAN FAILED, REGARDLESS OF ITS SOURCE. ON 17 OCTOBER 1920, A SERIOUS FIRE CLAIMED AN ENTIRE WING OF ROSE RED. THE CAUSE OF THAT FIRE HAS NEVER BEEN NAMED. IT MUST BE CONSIDERED AS A POSSIBILITY THAT ELLEN SET THAT FIRE HERSELF IN PROTEST TO JOHN'S ATTEMPTS TO BE RID OF HER.

A STUDY OF THE CONTRACTOR'S NOTES AND PLANS SHOW NO WORK ON THE TOWER SCHEDULED FOR NEARLY TWENTY MONTHS. ANOTHER THEORY BEHIND THE FIRE AND ALL THEIR RELATIONSHIP PROBLEMS WAS THAT ELLEN FOUND OUT JOHN WAS PURPOSELY DELAYING WORK ON THE TOWER. REGARDLESS OF DISAGREEMENTS, CONSTRUCTION ON THE TOWER BEGAN IN EARNEST IN EARLY NOVEMBER 1920. TO THIS DAY, THREE IMPORTANT QUESTIONS REMAIN SURROUNDING THE PERIOD 1918–1920: (1) ELLEN'S MENTAL STATE; (2) THE "ACTIVITY" OF THE HOUSE (E.G., THERE ARE REPORTS OF NEARLY A DOZEN DISAPPEARANCES IN THIS TWENTY-FOUR-MONTH PERIOD); AND (3) JOHN'S GROWING FEAR OF HIS WIFE; HIS WIFE'S MAID, SUKEENA; AND THE HOUSE THAT TOGETHER THE RIMBAUERS CONTINUED TO BUILD, AND REMODEL, AT AN ALARMING PACE.

THERE ARE WRITINGS (THOUGH NO SUBSTANTIAL EVIDENCE) THAT SUGGEST IT WAS JOHN, NOT ELLEN, WHO HAD LOST TOUCH WITH REALITY, AND THAT DURING THIS TIME HE BECAME BADLY ADDICTED TO LAUDANUM, SPENDING DAYS AT A TIME IN THE OPIUM DENS SOUTH OF THE CITY AND AWAY FROM THE MONSTROSITY OF A HOUSE HE HAD COME TO FEAR.

—JOYCE REARDON

19 JUNE 1921—ROSE RED

Sparks. I see robins outside my window. Twiddle-dee, twiddle-dum, I smell smoke in the auditorium. Where have I been? I ask myself, looking back at your pages. Is it possible I have not written my thoughts down here, except once in a blue moon? I feel as if I write here every day, but perhaps that is just my imaginings. I have been overcome with fever quite regularly. In truth these fevers always seem to follow my nights spent in the company of my husband—a pleasant way to write down here what is not often pleasant at all. For several years now he has included Sukeena in our . . . participation. I'd rather not say. Twiddle-dee, twiddle-dum. Sparks. The servants are out testing explosives for our annual Fourth of July party. I watch from my window, singing songs I recall from my childhood. How can childhood seem so far away, a part of another person's life, surely not mine? Sparks. Boom, boom, boom. If once I held any innocence, it has burned away like the gunpowder in these displays I watch. No innocence in the bedroom. No innocence at the window (at least not the night I helped Sukeena wrap George Meader in thorny vines). No innocence inside my head, where I spend an increasing amount of time trying to foresee my husband's maneuvers to remove me from this place. I've hidden from him—up in the attic, still working on the stairs to the Tower—for days at a time. John wandering the house calling out, perhaps secretly hoping Rose has claimed me once and for all. Me, waiting. Waiting. Letting him wet his whistle on this notion, letting his heart beat with excitement at the possibility I'm gone forever. And then I waltz into the Breakfast Room, as if not away from him for more than a few minutes. I watch his face sag. I smile enormously and greet him with bright, rested eyes and good humor. Later, he stews. Angry. Alone. I like him that way: angry and alone. I want him to pay for all the innocence he has taken from me. From us.

I talk to Rose openly now. No longer afraid. I tell her I want to see my daughter. I offer myself to her walls. But she asks strange things of me. We have remodeled an upstairs hall to become the Perspective Hallway: it diminishes in the same fashion as train tracks, one end to the other. It's in honor of the late George Meader and his rail company, but this is a hall—and the deeper you enter it, the lower the ceiling, the tighter the walls. It is not unlike my life itself—the longer I have lived, the more confined I feel by my surroundings. (At thirty-four, I feel more like eighty years of age.) I have hidden doors off the Perspective Hallway, in the same manner my husband has hidden his viewing rooms throughout this palace. Some go nowhere. Others lead to mazes of hallways. (In one such secreted hallway I hung a great nude on the other side of glass, just to annoy my husband should he stray inside. Life imitates art, they say. Or is it the other way around?)

To-day marks the grand opening of the Tower. (Our friends, I hear tell, are referring to my endeavor as "the tower folly." Be that as it may, I'm quite proud of the addition.) It includes the stairs that lead from the attic to a single room of generous proportions offering a full, panoramic view of all of Rose's wings, our property and its forests, as well as the commanding sight of the city and Elliott Bay beyond. It is the most beautiful, most important addition to our grand home, and is certain to take its place as one of my favorite spots. Now that it is open—complete with the lovely Venetian glass window and the twenty-four-karat gold-plated Italian cherub that adorns the peak of its roof—I feel as if I have a retreat of sorts, a place to hide, a place to pray, a place to seek my missing daughter.

John has not been in favor of the Tower. (He fears I put too much faith in the Tower helping me to locate April, and I admit here that he is quite right about that—my faith, that is—but our beliefs differ so greatly that John also trusts that there is little or no hope of any such physical structure providing a conduit, a medium that might reconnect us with our missing April, a fallacy in him I strive to correct!)

My mind wanders so frequently now, led as I am in so many directions. My "wonderings" come with more frequency and last longer. I see the staff steer clear of me in the hallways, shaken by my pale face, no doubt, or my unsteady walk. They have never lost a child, as I have. They have never compromised their existence as I have, obeying my husband and tolerating untold embarrassments in order to remain in the house of my child's disappearance. (To leave John would certainly mean leaving Rose—and that is even more unthinkable now than it was before.) Sukeena and I have agreed to meet at midnight (providing John does not call for our services) and, with the completion of the Tower, attempt to summon sweet April. We will climb and listen for the winds that have instructed me for these past several years, my hands bloodied with my efforts as a carpenter. It seems to me I shall always be putting finishing touches on my attic stairway, which ascends, through three turns, to the Tower. It will never be perfect, will always require attention—but so does a child, of course. This Tower is my child, just as my child is this Tower. How could I ever neglect it for even a single day? But alas, I am late for my rendezvous with my maid.

Sukeena and I meet in the upstairs hallway, alongside the panel that I had discovered previously, and let ourselves in. I carry a battery-powered flashlight, heavy as it is, and lead the way along the now familiar route, past the guests' quarters, up and into the attic. We stand at the base of my stairs, where the early work of my carpentry is seen for what it is: crude and poorly done. Through the door, the bottom stair is crooked, as are the next three, those in lessening proportions. The wood is still raw and untreated, as I have much work yet to do and will not allow any of the workers to touch a thing here. We climb slowly, to cries and complaints of the poorly assembled stairs, and I shine the light on Sukeena as she lags behind. Even she appears frightened. I take this as a good sign and encourage her on. I certainly must look a bit ghostly myself, drained of color as I am of late, standing there in my sheer nightgown, the yellow light flashing around unsteadily as I wave the flashlight unintentionally in my right hand, directing her. Perhaps Sukeena is more afraid of me than this Tower. I shouldn't be surprised, everyone else seems to fear me and my condition.

Now, as we approach the second turn, I finally hear what it is that has frightened my dear friend, what she has heard that I did not—the creaking of the stairs no longer sounds like lumber rubbing on lumber, nails straining against nails—increasingly it sounds like a voice, a familiar voice, a child's voice. April! The higher we climb, the more the creaking goes to wind, the wind to voice: "Ma-ma . . ." it calls, and I hurry my ascent, climbing all the faster. Sukeena, protective perhaps, is nearly running to keep up with me. "Miss Ellen!" she calls, the condition of warning carried in her tone. It is as if she fears that the door at the very top of these stairs, a door that grows larger by the moment, will lead not to the panoramic view I anticipate but to some dark, foreboding place, where young April is kept hidden. And those who enter, along with it.

Alas, as I burst through the upper door and out into the brisk night chill (the Tower is not heated) I am bathed in colorful light. For a moment, I feel as if I'm in the "light of God," and I wonder if indeed Rose Red has not claimed me and is in the process of transporting me to wherever April lives. (I always think of April as alive, but in another place; my motherly ways will allow no other consideration.) Then I see Sukeena circling the Tower in front of me. It is the moon and the stained-glass window that have poured this light across me.

"April," I call out, the wind rushing up the stairs below and encompassing me: "Ma-ma, ma-ma." I feel dizzy. My child is so very close. I can smell her. Taste her sweet cheeks as I kiss away her tears. I fall to my knees, trembling. I am pointing. Sukeena misunderstands, believing I am pointing to her. Then, she slowly looks around behind her, in the same direction as my finger is aimed.

She, too, falls down onto her knees. She lowers her head and kisses the boards we kneel upon—the floor to the Tower. The Temple, I shall think of it from now on. I ordered that stained-glass window of the rose more than a decade earlier, while on my honeymoon with my husband, before the birth of Adam, before the birth of April. And yet here, backlit by the full moon as it is, the sound of my daughter's voice swirling through the rotunda, so clear, and crisp and young, this multicolored window does not depict a rose at all. The tones and patterns have shifted in this shimmering light, the moon playing tricks on the eyes—or so some would say.

Instead of a rose in that window, it is a face that Sukeena and I now see. As clear and as apparent as if I'd instructed the artisans to fashion it in this regard so many years ago. But how could they have? She wasn't born yet. For you see, Dear Diary, the image in that lovely window is not a rose at all, but a portrait. It is the face of my child, April. Just as she looked the day she disappeared. As the wind blows eerily in our ears, her lips move. And she talks to me.

16 NOVEMBER 1921

I return to your pages after too long an absence. John's proclivity toward moodiness has increased with each month. He seems tired so much of the time. He returns from the city late, late at night with odd smells on his clothing. (The closest I have come to experiencing these same odors was while visiting Madame Lu.) His husbandly appetites have subsided. He has not visited my chambers in nearly three months. I cannot speak of my fears on these pages, but I imagine the worst for poor John. While his fortune continued to grow, his partnership dissolved, a good friend had "an unfortunate accident" in his Health Room, his daughter disappeared and his home began building itself without him. (A protracted battle erupted between John and our contractor when the contractor accused my husband of shopping out work to a moonlighting crew, for a great deal of carpentry work is often accomplished overnight within the walls of Rose Red. No explanation has been given, but the contractor has been replaced by one who asks no such questions.)

In the midst of his "depression" (what the doctors are calling it) John has twice tried to force me to travel to Switzerland (once, this summer, and again, in late September) to attend a health clinic where he hoped I might find peace from my affliction with fever. Reunited with my daughter as I am in my late-night visits (wisely, I have told John nothing of this), I refuse to budge. Nothing can take me from Rose Red now. (Sukeena believes this was the intention of the house all along. Perhaps a bit jealous herself, my maid believes this rambling palace is somehow in love with me and wants me all to herself.)

The reason for this entry in your pages, the cause of my alarm, is that to-day John issued an ultimatum that I was not to visit the Tower any longer. He ordered it boarded up and padlocked. Although I long to understand his reasoning—does he sense a change in me?—I cannot, of course, allow him to make such impossible demands. I wonder if John himself did not stray up to that lofty place late one night and see the face, hear the voice himself? Perhaps it proved too much for him. Perhaps he snapped and has slid downhill ever since. Perhaps, only now, can he begin to come to grips with what happens in that magic place and strive to prevent me from experiencing it myself. I have never understood John Rimbauer, and I understand him even less now, but we have had a conversation about this demand of his, and for the first time in our marriage, I threatened my husband with his life.

I suggested that poison might find its way into his food, a mechanical failure might befall his motorcar, a dockside whore might run him through with a knife. The biggest threat of all, I saved for last. I offered to reinvite his recent houseguests—we've entertained a series of prominent bankers of late as John negotiates a pipeline deal—and to parade them down the back hallways that afford my husband the opportunity to regard their wives in a full state of undress and while taking their toilet. (I dare say the loans would dry up quite quickly!) After a brief consideration, John removed his ultimatum, but the look he gave me chilled me to the bone.

I fear what little peace still exists in this house is now destined as a part of our past.

9 JUNE 1922—ROSE RED

My husband has taken a turn for the worse. Violence surrounds him, follows him like a shadow. He eats alone, leaves the house early in the morning and sometimes stays away for days at a time. I'm told by those who should know that he has been seen gambling (quite heavily) in the Chinese district south of the city, that he has lost a considerable amount of money and that a certain intemperance has left him in need of regular visits to that community, sometimes several times a day.

To-night, he threatened our headwaiter with a carving knife, ostensibly because the beef was prepared too rare. (I don't see the problem—John is hardly eating at all any longer.) He then threw a tureen on the floor, shattering it, and causing the girls who work in the Dining Room to flee and not return. Our headwaiter quit—walked out. We will need to replace him to-morrow—that is, if news of John's temper has not reached everywhere in this city, which I fear has resulted in a protracted difficulty in Mr. Tammerman securing domestics of any quality. Rose Red has turned. She is in a season of decline. I attribute this to John's reduction of the construction budget—he has cut building by half. And whereas our fine home now accommodates over thirty-five thousand square feet of living space, can sleep forty-two and feed several hundred in grand style, she could have been more grand, more luxurious had John not started pinching his pennies.

To-night, Sukeena and I spoke of this at length—for even she now acknowledges that we have seen less of April during this time of slow growth. Rose Red must be allowed to expand. The faster the construction, the more visits from my daughter. My husband and I vary greatly in our opinions on this matter. I do not know if my maid suggested it, or if perhaps it was I, but a very clear need exists for the departure of John Rimbauer. He is in my way, in Sukeena's and the staff's way and is now in the way of the house herself.

Something must be done. I fear it is up to me to decide exactly what.

AFTERWORD

MY GREAT-GRANDMOTHER'S DIARY ENDED HERE, AND WERE IT NOT FOR THE WORK OF JOYCE REARDON'S RECENT EXPEDITION INTO ROSE RED, IT MIGHT HAVE ENDED HERE FOREVER. HOWEVER, I WAS A PART OF THAT EXPEDITION AND HAD THE GOOD FORTUNE TO DISCOVER IN THE ATTIC A SECOND INSTALLMENT TO THE DIARY, HIDDEN IN THE WALL OF THE TOWER, IRONICALLY, ON THE OTHER SIDE OF A FALSE DOOR INSTALLED BEHIND AN OLD DISCOLORED WATERCOLOR OF A RED ROSE HANGING ON THE WALL. (I BELIEVE GREAT-GRANDMA MAY HAVE PAINTED THAT WATERCOLOR HERSELF.)

THE ENTRIES THAT FOLLOW ARE DISTURBING TO SAY THE LEAST, BUT THEY DO CONFIRM SOME OF WHAT WAS DISCOVERED DURING THE REARDON EXPEDITION, THE INTENTION OF WHICH WAS TO PSYCHICALLY AWAKEN THE SLUMBERING BEAST OF ROSE RED. AS THE OLD SAGE HAS SAID, "BE CAREFUL WHAT YOU ASK FOR . . ." WE KNOW NOW, THROUGH THIS CONFIRMATION, THE CAUSE OF AT LEAST ONE FATALITY, AND PERHAPS IN THE YEARS TO FOLLOW WE SHALL UNCOVER MORE. MUCH OF THE LATE DIARY IS WRITTEN IN A "CODE," AN ENCRYPTION THAT HAS YET TO BE BROKEN. MY GREAT-GRANDMOTHER HAD EITHER UNSPOKEN TALENTS OR A CONNECTION TO A PLACE THAT FEW, IF ANY, OF US WILL EVER ACCESS. WHAT FOLLOWS ARE EXCERPTS FROM THE SECOND DIARY.

—STEVEN RIMBAUER

SEATTLE, WASHINGTON, SEPTEMBER 2000

(JOYCE REARDON'S FINAL EDITORIAL WAS RESPECTFULLY MOVED TO CONCLUDE THE DIARY.)

19 FEBRUARY 1923—ROSE RED

4 P.M.

Winter has proved especially vexing and tiresome. I put into your pages now what never must be revealed to any living person. I have, for this reason, made amendments to my last will and testament, ensuring your destruction, Dear Diary, should anything happen to me.

For the past several months, and more so, in recent weeks, Sukeena and I have conspired—yes, I choose my words carefully—on some way to do away with John Rimbauer. Try as I have to drive him from this home in recent months, my efforts have been to no avail, in part because my husband is no longer the man he once was. His trips to the Chinese sector are more a part of his life than anything here. He returns disoriented and confused, and he strikes out in terror at anyone in his way. He has become far more than a nuisance. Last week, when he violently took liberties with Julie, the fifteen-year-old-daughter of Mrs. Cruthers, our housemaid, I promised an end to it. This very evening, my maid and I shall deliver on our promise.

8 P.M.

I am told by Sukeena that the first part of our devious plan is now in place. She visited my husband in his upstairs office at teatime—a visit she had never made once in all her years in our service—and I'm told the conversation went something like this:

(To give you the benefit of imagination, Dear Diary, I should tell you that Sukeena's full black form when clothed loosely in white Egyptian cotton is so provocative that my husband banned her from this dress early on in her service. I should also add that during the days of John's visits to my chambers with my maid "in attendance," he never "knew" her, in the biblical sense. He watched. He leered. But he never knew her. As odd as this may sound—and it does so to me even here on your pages—I believe this omission of the act has been out of respect to me, and I also believe it has thrown him into internal turmoil that has, these many months, resulted in a string of self-destructive acts.)

"Evening, sir."

"Sukeena."

She says he was seated behind his great English partners desk, a fire burning in the fireplace, a brandy held in hand. His dark blue velvet and black satin smoking jacket. Charcoal gray trousers. Ascot. Cigar. The snifter of brandy.

"Is there anything you are needing, sir?" Sukeena is my maid, not his. Surely her approach—this arrival in his private chambers—must have struck him oddly.

"Such as?"

"Anything at all." I can just imagine her lilting tone, the shifting from one broad hip to the other, the way she does. When Sukeena moves, it is like a cheetah. John has always been slightly afraid of the big cats.

"Anything?"

"Anything, sir." She added, "Miss Ellen, she asleep, sir. Took some bourbon with milk not an hour ago."

I am prone to finding my sleep quickly when under the influence of spirits. No one is more aware of this than my husband.

He looked at her with a cocked head and curious eye.

"I be wondering, sir. About things. About you. About you and me, sir. A woman can't help but wonder."

"You've been wondering about . . . ?" Astonishment. I imagine the laudanum must dull my husband's good senses. (He has not shown any such senses in many months.) Lull him. Fool him. How else could others trick him into parting with his money so easily? This man who amassed a fortune only to squander it away. I wish, Dear Diary, I could summon even a modicum of sympathy for my dear John, but reason does not allow me such luxury.

Except for a brief period of courting, I have known him to be a selfish man. I served a purpose in his life—the same way a railroad tycoon can provide his oil transportation—I offered legitimacy of his offspring. He poisoned my womanhood with his dalliances, made me barren and robbed me of the one thing I could offer. He takes women like he takes meals—often and hungrily. He lavished no love upon his daughter and yet offered his son anything he desired, including a way out of this house. With his good looks and winning smile, he has cajoled many a businessman and every woman into surrendering whatever it is they hold dearest, all the while believing John Rimbauer was doing them a favor. The only thing I've ever see frighten him is this house—my dear Rose—and so it was to Rose I turned in my hour of need.

"I . . . I told you not to wear that clothing around this house, woman! It's not proper."

"I be having a problem sleeping, sir. Thinking about . . . Sukeena sorry if my dressing gown does not please you."

"Please me?"

"Yes, sir."

He rose slowly out of his chair, the fire crackling. "Please me?" he repeated.

"It's not something I ever speak to the Miss about. You can see that, sir."

"Indeed."

"Something I got-to know. A woman got-to know." She paused, then turned for the door. "Was thinking about da Tower, sir. Put a quilt in the Tower, I did. Heavy quilt. The one from Sveden. You know the one. Maybe Sukeena take her sleep in the Tower."

She left his study then, fully confident that behind the haze of the laudanum and the brandy, the cigar and that ruddy confidence of his, my husband would follow like a puppy to its mother. Sure enough, he did just that.

She walked luxuriously, strolling down the great wide halls of

Rose Red as if in a processional, my husband trailing a few yards behind. Down the hall, she turned into his own changing room, and this must certainly have shocked him. She walked straight into his closet, opened the secret panel at the back and entered the narrow hallway that led directly to the attic. By now he must have thought her possessed of black magic, for he never missed a step, ducking through his own clothing and following that path he had followed so many times before. Even then with lurid thoughts occupying him.

I see it in my mind's eye as a spectacle: Sukeena in front of him by a few steps, my husband's slightly drunken gait following a few paces behind. His heart racing with anticipation—this cherished prize that has remained out of reach all these years. In our African camp, I got to Sukeena before John did, as she was assigned to me as my handmaid. I can only imagine the frustration this caused in him now that I know what was always on my husband's mind. Now that I know it was there in that camp that he exposed himself to sinful disease. I have wondered many times what our lives might be like had I taken to God the way so many women do. Would we now be blessed? Why did I choose to pray to the dark side, make alliances with powers beyond my understanding? God, too, is beyond my understanding, so why not God? How much better this might have all turned out. Forgiveness instead of revenge, faith instead of accusation and hardship. (Perhaps now is the time. I hear it is never too late to turn to the Christ. Just think: all that I have imagined, all that I have suffered through, and yet still a chance for salvation!)

Up my twisting and complaining staircase did they come, Sukeena now leading my frightened husband by the hand. The winds began calling behind the creaking of that lumber, "Da . . . da. Da . . . da." My husband's blood ran cold; despite the brandy, his eyes grew large with fear. He stopped his ascent, nearly pulling Sukeena over, who had the lead.

"Come," she said.

"I can't. Do you hear that?"

"Hear only the wind, sir," she lied. "Mustn't be afraid of the wind."

"Is that all it is?"

"Oh, yes, sir. The Tower get all sort of the winds." She reminded him, "The quilt, sir. When we to lie down, the wind no longer make the sound." She tugged on his arm. "The master not afraid of a little wind?"

When one needs John to budge, one resorts to his playing against his own impressions of himself. This trick worked. He fluffed himself up, expanded his chest and took after my maid once again, slowing ascending the misshapen staircase leading to the Tower.

She threw the door open.

It had to be the right night. We knew that in our early stages of planning. First, a full moon—for these are the nights that April will visit. Second, that time of night when the moon sits just above the horizon, fully lighting the stained-glass window there. We knew what would be said. The stress of an infirm wife. His daughter disappearing like that. The gambling. The visits to Chinatown. The social pressures that wealth can bring.

Sukeena entered the Tower first. The voice was so clearly April's now. "Da . . . da . . . ," it said. John stepped in behind, and the door gently swung shut behind him. In the stained-glass window, the lovely rose changed before our eyes into a ghostly specter of my daughter's misshapen and withered arm. The wind asked, "These are your gifts to your children?" My husband stood as if his shoes had been nailed to the flooring. The hand in the window, my daughter's hand, plain as day, beckoned him, her finger waving him toward her. "Da . . . da. Come . . . Look . . ."

If all those years ago in Africa a person had told me that

someday the spirits would join me in the fulfillment of my wishes, I might have imagined pure love between husband and wife—worldly travel and long sumptuous meals that added not a pound to my frame. A family of six children. Songs by the fire in the evenings and a game of whist with friends after supper. I might never have imagined this.

John took one final step closer to the window. He looked to his feet: no quilt. He looked up and saw me hovering behind the door, for it had been me who had shut it, closing him in.

The power of two women can be formidable, especially when combined with the determination of years of struggle and anger that had steeped inside both Sukeena and me. She took an arm and yanked, spinning him. I charged with all my strength. But in the end it was neither Sukeena nor me. I only wish it were so. It was April—that enormous wind—that did the job for us. I threw my weight into John, certainly. Sukeena pulled with all her substantial strength. A look of shock and surprise—the hunter hunted—my husband lifted off his feet in an ungainly and weightless manner. There, he faced our daughter in the stained-glass window. April smiled and blinked and repeated one last time, "Da . . . da." (At that moment I wondered, had it been Sukeena's and my idea, or had it been April's all along?)

John Rimbauer planted his feet. He skidded across the wooden planks, and I swear I smelled burning wood as his heels dragged. He flew up and through the window, exploding it into a thousand pieces, and plunged down and off the slate roof from some fifty feet above the flagstone terrace. I recall him insisting upon the construction of that abysmal front terrace. I had never cared for it.

I like it a lot better now that it's rose red.

26 FEBRUARY 1923

My son came home to-day and together we buried his father. Hundreds attended, from women whose names I did not want to know, to the dockhands who thought of him as a personal friend, to the bankers, businessmen and public officials who have made their careers off him. I stood in all black, crying real tears, holding my son firmly by the shoulder—the first time I have seen him in nearly three years.

It is difficult to express in these pages the acute sense of loss, of grief that I am experiencing. Despite all the atrocious things John Rimbauer did to me, the pain he brought to my life, I admired him greatly, loved him at times and marveled at his success. Even with the gambling losses he leaves behind a dynasty, a king's fortune as it turns out.

Adam and I spent the later part of the afternoon walking the woods where he and his father hunted squirrels and rabbit. After some reminiscing and retelling of stories about his father, Adam finally brought up the subject he had avoided for years.

"Is it haunted?" he asked, looking not at me but at his own boots in the wet leaves.

"It's possessed," I answered honestly. "That's the best way I can put it."

"As in 'ghosts'?"

"Spirits."

We stopped on the trail, overlooking Lasky Pond.

"And April?"

Here was the discussion I had so longed to have with my son. I knew that John had colored his opinion. The newspaper, perhaps at John's bidding, had reported a day or two later that the ice on Lasky Pond was found broken, and that April might have fallen through. (I wonder, then, that we never found the body!) This became the generally accepted view: an accident on the pond; a bear who had gotten close to the city; a mountain lion. Anything but the truth.

"She's in the house, Adam."

"That's preposterous, Mother!" It was my husband's voice, though carried in my son's body, and the effect was disarming. How quickly they learn.

"Why do you think your father found ways all these years to keep you from returning to the house? You think he was afraid of the woods? This pond? He was afraid of the walls."

"Father was afraid of nothing."

"We're all afraid of something, dear. Your father was a great man. But he was afraid of the truth. He fired Douglas Posey to avoid facing the truth; he kept you from this house, your home. Never fear the truth, Adam. It's the only real passport you have to reach new levels of understanding. You may find it corny, but the truth can set you free."

"It is corny." He toed the fallen leaves, burrowing a wet hole into the forest floor and overturning a small, shiny rock.

"If you stay long enough, it may be possible for you to hear her voice."

"Mother . . ."

"What? I'm crazy? You can tell me, Adam. You tell me."

1 MARCH 1923

So it was that on a perfectly still night, three days later, my son and I climbed the creaking Tower steps toward that place where his father had met his death. Adam is a good-looking, strong boy of thirteen, with wide shoulders and thoughtful eyes. Despite his adolescent strength, he moved cautiously and nervously up those stairs, the wind rising in our ears. Wind, at first. Then the soft calling of his sister's voice.

As their mother I had forgotten how close these two had been—nearly inseparable, until Adam was shuttled off to boarding school. They had grown up nearly as twins—Adam helping his slightly incapacitated sister; April as foil for his games and test subject for his inventions.

My young boy, whom this school had developed prematurely into a young man, collapsed down onto the steps and wept openly, falling into his mother's arms, and knowing this was no trick. He was afraid, and I should have thought about his tender age and realized it was too soon for him. There would be plenty of time for all this. Why had I insisted on rushing it? Why had I felt nearly desperate to prove my sanity to my child? (Is such a thing provable anyway?)

As it was, mother and son eventually reached the Tower, sitting on its wooden floor. The open hole that had been the stained-glass window was now boarded up. Someday I will manage to replace that window. We huddled together, crying, laughing. Adam tried to talk back to that whispering voice, and though I did not understand the exchange, I would swear here on these pages that he spoke with his sister. I know for a fact that he returned to the Tower each and every night and spent hours up there.

He is back at school now. But he's writing me, nearly daily—this son who had been virtually absent from my life. I feel whole again. Woman. Mother. John's absence is more tolerable each passing day. Peace has returned to Rose Red. Adam and I are a family again.

Nothing so sweet.

19 FEBRUARY 1928

Dear God in Heaven! Give her back to me!

Sukeena has gone missing! Last seen in the Health Room! No sign of her anywhere, I wander this tomb's endless hallways wondering why everyone who becomes so close to me ends up stolen from my life. Robbed from me. I hate this house. Despise it! I will never invite Adam back again.

The staff is nearly sick with looking for my maid, so many hours—days now!—have we been at it. The house is impossibly large. Believe this or not, Dear Diary, we all have witnessed physical transformations. Hallways change structure and appearance behind your back. Rooms disappear! What is going on? How can it be? A physical structure, a building, and yet fluid as water. A chameleon. She no longer requires growing larger—she reinvents herself internally. Once a hallway, now a ballroom; once a basement, now a dungeon!

I ordered all Sukeena's plants uprooted from the Health Room (for upon her disappearance, it bloomed more richly than I have ever seen—every plant at once in full blossom!). I watched that task carried out—watched it with my own eyes from up in my chambers, recalling my past observation of other events down there as well. Seven workers took three hours to clear the room down to bare soil. By the time they reached the west end, the east had sprouted new plants. By the following morning, the plants were six feet tall—taller than they'd ever been, and in full bloom. That is Sukeena providing that bloom—her love, her energy, her powers.

We all—every one of us!—heard Rose Red laugh last night. Laugh at me. At us. It was the most frightening sound I've ever heard.

If there is a game to this, she has clearly won. They are all gone. My loved ones. I am alone. Alone in my thoughts, alone in my silence, alone in this house.

I shall fire the entire staff (before she gets another of them!).

I shall dwell in this place alone for a time. Let her suffer. Let her fail. Perhaps then we can strike a bargain, this house and me.

Perhaps then she'll allow me to visit Sukeena as I do April. My husband taught me well: everything is negotiable.

EDITOR'S NOTE: BOOKKEEPING RECORDS SUBSTANTIATE ELLEN RIMBAUER'S CLAIM OF FIRING THE THIRTY-FOUR STAFF MEMBERS FOR A PERIOD OF FOUR MONTHS. DURING THAT TIME IT IS BELIEVED SHE LIVED IN ROSE RED COMPLETELY ALONE AND WITHOUT A SINGLE VISITOR. WHATEVER HER MENTAL STATE GOING INTO THIS SOLITUDE, SHE CAME OUT THE WORSE FOR WEAR. OVER THE SUBSEQUENT TWO MONTHS, SHE REINSTATED A STAFF OF TWENTY. SHE THREW PARTIES. AT THE LAST, 1946'S ANNUAL INAUGURAL BALL, ONE OF THAT PERIOD'S GREATEST FILM ACTRESSES, DEANNA PETRIE, DISAPPEARED IN ROSE RED (THERE ARE UNCONFIRMED RUMORS THAT HER FRIENDSHIP WITH ELLEN WENT BEYOND THE NORM). THIS WAS THE LAST GREAT PARTY THROWN IN ROSE RED. THE STAFF WAS REDUCED TO FIFTEEN AT THE START OF THE U.S. INVOLVEMENT IN WORLD WAR II. BY 1950 ELLEN RIMBAUER HAD DISAPPEARED.

IN 1950, AS SHE WAS APPROACHING THE AGE OF SEVENTY, A NEARLY BLIND ELLEN RIMBAUER IS SAID TO HAVE ENTERED THE PERSPECTIVE HALLWAY NEVER TO RETURN. STAFF THERE CLAIM TO HAVE SINCE HEARD SAWING AND HAMMERING IN THE ATTIC.

AT THE TIME OF HER DEATH, ELLEN RIMBAUER, ONCE THE MOST BEAUTIFUL AND ENVIED WOMAN IN SEATTLE'S HIGH SOCIETY, WAS A WIZENED OLD LADY, FEVERISH, HALF BLIND AND SLIGHTLY MAD. IT IS SAID THAT FROM TIME TO TIME ROSE RED CAN BE HEARD LAUGHING OR CRYING—THAT THE SOUND CARRIES FOR MILES AND IS OFTEN MISTAKEN FOR EITHER A WILD ANIMAL OR A SHIP'S HORN.

• • •

SOON I SHALL VENTURE INSIDE ROSE RED, ARMED WITH SOPHISTICATED DETECTION EQUIPMENT; STEVEN RIMBAUER, A DESCENDANT OF ELLEN AND JOHN RIMBAUER; AND SOME OF THE MOST POWERFUL "PERCEPTIONISTS"—PSYCHICS—IN THIS PART OF THE COUNTRY. WE HOPE TO AWAKEN THE "SOUL" OF THIS ENORMOUS STRUCTURE, THE BEING THAT LIES WITHIN THE WALLS, AND TO OPEN COMMUNICATION WITH EITHER APRIL, SUKEENA, ELLEN OR ROSE RED HERSELF. IT IS THIS LAST OPTION THAT I FEAR MOST OF ALL. THIS DIARY CONFIRMS A FORMIDABLE PRESENCE. AS ALWAYS IN THE STUDY OF PSYCHIC PHENOMENA, ONE ACCEPTS A CERTAIN AMOUNT OF THE UNKNOWN, THE UNCHARTED. SPIN A GLOBE, OPEN A DOOR AND WHO KNOWS WHAT MAY HAPPEN? WE SHALL SEE. LIFE IS AN ADVENTURE. ROSE RED OFFERS THE RESEARCH OPPORTUNITY OF A LIFETIME. WHO, IN MY FIELD, WOULD TURN DOWN SUCH AN OPPORTUNITY? AND SO I GO FORWARD, UNCERTAIN AND YET EXCITED. WE CANNOT DISCOVER THE PSYCHIC BOUNDARIES THAT EXIST IF WE DON'T DARE LOOK FOR THEM. WHAT WE FIND IS OURS FOR A MOMENT, SCIENCE'S FOREVER. IT IS THAT MOMENT I CHERISH—THAT SINGULAR MOMENT WHEN WHATEVER IS OUT THERE IS MINE, AND MINE ALONE. IN THAT WINKING OF AN EYE, THE WORLD IS LIMITLESS, AND I ALONG WITH IT.

—JOYCE REARDON, P.P.A., M.D., PH.D.

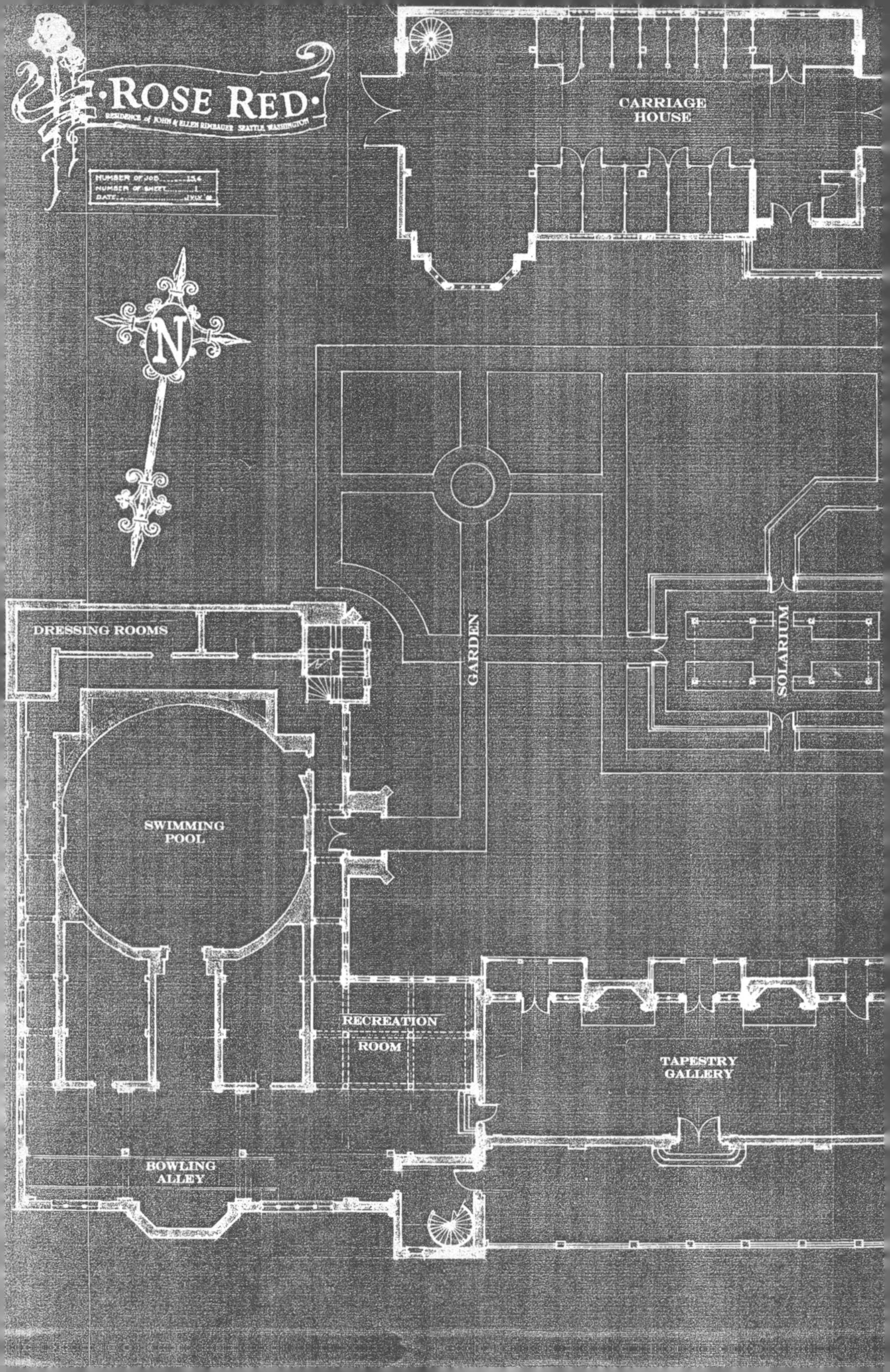
·ROSE RED·
RESIDENCE of JOHN & ELLEN RIMBAUER SEATTLE, WASHINGTON
NUMBER OF JOB 154
NUMBER OF SHEET 1
N
CARRIAGE HOUSE
DRESSING ROOMS
GARDEN
SOLARIUM
SWIMMING POOL
RECREATION ROOM
TAPESTRY GALLERY
BOWLING ALLEY